Threads

A Depression Era Tale

Charlotte Whitney

THREADS is a work of historical fiction. Aside from actual known people, places, and historical events, the names, characters, locales, and events are products of the author's imagination and are used fictitiously.

The typeface used in this book is Century Schoolbook.

DEDICATION

In memory of my Grandma and Grandpa B. who raised three daughters during the Great Depression. When I was younger I asked my grandma about those times, she replied with only one sentence: "We were very, very lucky—we only went hungry for one year."

A NOTE ON MID-MICHIGAN FARM DIALECT

It was not until I was in graduate school that I became aware of my own dialect that was acquired while growing up on a Michigan farm. A friend who was a linguist brought it to my attention and was both fascinated and irritated by my "quaint" speech. I mispronounced words, used unusual colloquialisms, and frequently was guilty of subject-verb disagreement, such as "he don't," and "she don't" which is still used in Midwest farm country.

In this book I have tried to replicate the authentic farm dialect to the extent that it doesn't distract from the story line. Most of the time I do not utilize common mispronunciations like "winner" for "winter" and "ruff" for "roof." However, I felt compelled to include the ubiquitous pronunciation of "crick" for "creek" because it holds a critical piece of the book's literary landscape. My mother was twelve years old in 1934. A few years back I asked her about her memories of playing down at the creek. She looked puzzled. "Creek," she replied. "We didn't play creek." I immediately understood her puzzlement and answered, "Playing down at the crick." She smiled and went on with some wonderful stories of the "crick."

Some common phrases that are still part of the farm vernacular include "down cellar," and "to home" which are most likely poor literal translations from German. Contractions commonly used are also still prevalent today, such as "gotta" for "got to," and "posta" for "supposed to."

Sparse language is also a characteristic of Michigan farm people. Notably a single word or phrase may be used in place of an entire sentence. Ma and Pa both use "yup" to indicate they are in agreement with one another. Its simplicity and terse sound reflects the conservation of words so common of their day.

All in all, finding the right dialect posed a challenge to this piece of writing. All authors want their work to flow. However, historical novelists also want to capture the authenticity of the period. This was the intention here, to keep the dialogue genuine, yet free of unnecessary disruptions to the reader.

Nellie
Wednesday, April 4, 1934
Afternoon

I finished sewing that red button on my Sunday dress. It kept coming off most every week so today I sewed it on so good that when I tugged and tugged, it jist wouldn't come off. I used lots of thread and once I'd done the needle part, I wound the thread around the back of the button six times before I made the knot. Since I turned seven, Ma told me that I have to sew on all the buttons that come off my clothes. I have to mend and hem, too. Anything to do with sewing that don't require the Treadle.

I'm in second grade so I git home two hours before my sister Irene who's in sixth grade, even though we go to the same one-room country school. My sister Flora gits home from high school even later, around five-thirty. I like the afternoon time I have all by myself. I can talk to Pa while he works, visit my favorite animals, and explore the meadows, woods, and crick.

After I'd showed Ma the button, I asked her if I could go down to the crick and play. Ma nodded yes, so I ran out of the house and took off down the lane before she could change her mind. Little did I know I would have preferred sewing on buttons or washing windows. Or scrubbing floors on my hands and knees or washing manure-crusted eggs. Anything but what I discovered.

Once I reached the first meadow, I found the cows and said hello but didn't stay and talk to them for long. All five cows had been grazing under a couple of wild cherry trees, one of their favorite places. They once told me they like it there cuz it's shady and the cherry blossoms smell good. I don't take a hankering to the spot myself cuz of all the cow pies underneath those trees.

The cows say that the manure helps the plants and trees to grow. They're right 'bout that.

Most of the time I go barefoot to the meadow cuz it feels good in warm weather. But I hate it when I don't look down and step into a cow pie. Then it squishes between my toes. You can walk on top of the older dried-up cow pies barefoot, no problem. They're a little rough across the top, but not nearly as bad as walking on gravel.

Next summer there will be big circles of green grass under the cherry trees marking each of this year's cow pies. Easy to understand why Pa spreads manure all over his crops before they come up. It's a stinky job but, boy, does that manure help the corn grow. And the wheat, rye, and alfalfa, all the crops.

Pig manure is a lot stinkier than the cow manure but you git used to it. Same with horse manure and chicken manure. I can tell the smell of each kind of manure with my eyes closed. Pa says he can tell the smell of each of our five cows' manures and of Ace and King, our two workhorses. I don't know if he's kidding or not. Pa seems to kid around with me a lot more than he does with Flora and Irene. Maybe cuz I'm the youngest of us girls.

The only thing worse than stepping in a fresh cow pie barefoot is stepping on a live frog. Last year I stepped on a frog when I was running to catch up with my sister Irene down at the crick. She's eleven, four years older than me. I started crying right away. Irene ran back to me, looked at the smashed frog and laughed. But the frog was dead and I had killed it. I hated myself for weeks, so now I always look down at the ground whenever I go to the crick. I've told the other frogs I'm sorry so many times. They seem to ignore me and I don't blame them. Who would wanna talk to a girl who killed your cousin?

I walked to the second meadow past the stone fence, the lilacs, the poison ivy tree, the rusty gate, the old bus, the log cabin ruins, then on to the stile. That corner's one of my favorite places to play, my favorite spot for 'magining things. I like to lie down and 'magine my outer space friend ZeeZee who sometimes uses the old bus to fly to outer space. Then there's my Indian friends Yellow Feather and Broken Wing. They're boys who used to live around here, down by Johnnycake Ridge. Sometimes I jist lay down on the ground and close my eyes and see who appears. It could be pirates or animals, anything.

But today I wanted to git to the crick, so I didn't stop and 'magine anything. I ran straight to the stile, crossed over it, and ran down the path through the woods that leads to Parson Creek. I was watching the ground and spied some horse manure. Horses don't ordinarily use this path. Well, not our horses anyway.

Could Gypsies be using the path? Pa says they'll be coming back again this year now that the weather's warming up. He says I should hide if I see them. It makes me mad. I consider this my special place, and I don't like other people coming here. And yes, I know that Pa don't even own the woods. Old Man Keller does. But he never comes over here. Nuthin' really for him to do here and it's way 'cross the crick from his farm.

There are a few mushroons and some wild sperrygas stalks off the path near the woods, but me and Irene usually find them first and pick them so no one else gits them. That's the rule. You always keep your mushroons and sperrygas secret. Town folks come looking along the side of the road each spring but us farmers git there first. Some of the mushroons are poison so we have Pa look them over, specially the little sponges that taste the best. My sister Flora calls them morels. She's sixteen and pretends she's all grown up and knows the proper name to everything.

I love those little sponge morels fried up in butter. Once Ma didn't have any butter churned up, so she fried them in lard. They warn't near as good. Butter makes jist about everything better, 'specially bread.

So here I was down in the woods looking at these horse droppings trying to figure out how old they were. Not fresh, but definitely not old and stale. Probably two or three days old since it hasn't rained in a week. I was puzzled 'bout how the horses got here. Did they come down Keller's lane or from the other side of the crick?

As I studied the horse droppings I noticed a mound of fresh dirt a few yards over. Wouldn't have even seen it if I had stayed on the path. It was about a yard long. Buried treasure I decided. The mound was 'bout the right size to bury a treasure chest, jist like in my *Pirate Book*. Maybe pirates had buried some gold and jewels right here in Old Man Keller's woods. Maybe in a metal box like Pa uses to bury his money or maybe in a wooden pirate chest with a big gold latch. So I stood there wondering if the treasure would belong to me cuz I found it or to Old Man Keller cuz it's his land. Well, I decided, maybe there'd be so much treasure that we could split it up.

It would be really fun to find lots of jewels so I could give Ma a diamond. She don't have one, but Mrs. Geist and Mrs. Vandenberg both have diamond rings. I'd give Flora a blue jewel and Irene a red one, their favorite colors. I'd keep all the rest and hopefully there would be a crown I could wear, too. I'd only wear it for special occasions, like Christmas and Easter, cuz it might be hard to wear when I'm running and playing in the haymow. I don't think I'd be able to wear it doing my chores cuz it might fall off. Nasty Ma-Hen would probably pick out the jewels when I'm in the chicken coop gathering eggs.

So I looked around for a big stick to use to dig up the treasure. No success. I could go back to the tool shed and bring back a shovel but I wanted to dig up the treasure right away. Besides, if I went up to the tool shed, Ma might see me and ask me to do some chores. You can't say, "no" to Ma. Or to Pa, for that matter.

The more I thought about the treasure, the more excited I got, so I kept looking for a stick. Finally I found a small dead tree not too far from the hollow ash, and I broke off a limb that was real strong. Then I ran up to the mound and started to push the dirt away, hoping for gold and beautiful jewels.

I probed and probed with the stick, finding nuthin' and gittin' kinda discouraged. Maybe someone dumped a stinky johnny and buried it in this rather large johnny hole. The woods is a long way from any outhouse and people use johnny holes when they don't have a privy. Of course, this one was so big it could hold three or four johnnies. It was jist 'bout then, when I was deciding to quit cuz I didn't wanna dig up some old pirate's johnny, when I saw it. A TINY BLUE-BLACK HAND. I jumped back and shrieked louder than I have ever yelled before.

I can't remember nuthin' after that 'cept that I was back in the field near the barn and Pa was holding me as I cried. I couldn't quit bawling and he held me tight.

Nighttime

Tonight I couldn't git that dead hand outa my mind. Ma gave us girls each a piece of bread for supper, but I couldn't eat. I wanted to pretend it never happened. Even though I wanted to go to sleep and forget about today, the heat register was still calling to me.

Jist 'bout every night I listen in on Ma and Pa from the heat register on our bedroom floor. It's right above where Ma and Pa sit in the parlor, right down from my side of the bed. Me and Irene share the bedroom and the bed. I sleep on the side of the bed near the heat register and she sleeps on the side near the window. She chose that side cuz she likes to look out the window when she wakes up to figure out the weather. Being older than me Irene gits to choose all kinds of things. But frankly I'm happy I can drop down to the register and spy on Ma and Pa without having to crawl over her.

I always wait until Irene is asleep cuz she's a tattletale. The heat register is an iron square with lots of holes that lets the warm air come up into our bedroom; otherwise the room ain't heated so it gits real cold in winter. Tonight I really wanted to listen. That dead hand had been haunting me ever since I found it. I was hoping it was jist a bad dream. Ma tells me that I 'magine too many things. She thinks I make up lots of stuff in my head, but I love all my 'maginary friends. I have reglar conversations with all of them.

Tonight Irene started snoring right away. She kinda snorts through her nose like a piglet for a little while and then goes into a steadier snore. I've gotten used to it, and usually I don't even hear it after I start listening in.

For a long time tonight Ma and Pa didn't talk. But I knew they were down there in the corner where Pa has his chair and Ma has hers. The kerosene lamp was lit and I could smell the smoke from Pa's pipe.

Ma was kinda crying, sobbing softly.

"If we hadn't buried our own baby down there at that pretty spot near the crick," Ma sobbed.

Pa didn't answer.

"Maybe this baby was born dead, like ours." Ma's voice again. "But you said it was a full baby, not just a half-baked sweetie like ours. Never knew if ours was a boy or girl."

"Sheriff said it was a boy," Pa replied in a low voice. "But real young, probably newborn."

"We can't let the girls talk about this," Ma insisted. "No one needs to know there's been foul play on our property."

"Twarn't our property," Pa reminded her. "And the Sheriff and his guys know—so do Hazel and Elmer."

"It might as well be our land," Ma answered. "People are gonna think we're in cahoots with whoever buried that poor thing."

"No, they won't," Pa responded.

"Who would bury a child there anyhow?"

Pa didn't answer at first, then he began. "I've been thinking about that. A stolen baby that died. A baby the parents don't want. Or the parents are too poor to give it a proper burial." Pa had a lot of possibilities.

"Well, we're gonna keep this to ourselves," Ma answered. "Won't no good come of talking 'bout this to all the neighbors. They'll think we done something to deserve this happening here."

"Dorothy, twarn't nothing that anyone in our family has done that caused this. Don't be so worried. It's okay if you don't talk about it, but we didn't make this happen. Our family isn't to blame. It's not Nellie's fault. It's not your fault. If Nellie hadn't been looking for pirate treasure, we'd never have known about this. That poor baby would've been someone's secret to eternity. But for better or worse, Nellie found it. That's just the way it is."

There was silence for a long while until I heard them both shuffling around gittin' ready to go to bed. Suddenly the kerosene lamp was turned out below. I silently crawled back in bed and pulled the covers from Irene's side of the bed and rolled up in them. I wanted to go to sleep real bad, but I couldn't stop thinking 'bout that poor baby.

Irene
Wednesday, April 4, 1934
Afternoon

Today I was thinking about asking Ma to teach me how to make potato salad. That would kinda guarantee that we'd have it for supper someday soon. I know it's sneaky, but I've had a hankering for potato salad all winter long. I'm so tired of eating boiled potatoes, bean soup, and old stale bread. So I'd decided to ask Ma as soon as I got home from school. Little did I know that potato salad would become small potatoes, so to speak.

It was four o'clock and I was walking home from school with my cousins Jake and Alvin. They're ten-year-old twins, a year younger than me, and they live on the farm right beyond ours, Unc Elmer's and Aunt Hazel's. Their older brothers, Dan and Dalton, go to high school with Flora. Dan drives their Model A to school and Dalton and Flora ride along. Jake, Alvin, and I always walk home together from Parson Creek School, our one-room country school. Nellie's just a second-grader so she goes to our same school, but she gets out two hours earlier at two o'clock and walks home by herself.

Me and my cousins have a spot where we race from the corner of Green Lake Road up to the wooden gate where Mr. Lutz drives his cattle across the road. Today we were racing with me in the lead when a car pulled up beside us. It was Pa driving with Unc Elmer sitting on the passenger side.

In the middle of the afternoon.

Something must be wrong.

My cousins and I jumped in the back seat. Pa had planned to clear the west field today so naturally I asked why he wasn't working.

"Your little sister found something down in the woods," Pa answered, "so we went to find Sheriff Devlon." I turned and looked through the small back window and saw the Sheriff's car following right behind us.

"What'd she find?" I asked.

"Don't know," he replied in a tone that I knew meant, *Don't ask no more questions.* Of course, as soon as we got home I got Nellie to spill the beans. She'd found a HAND. A little baby's hand. Down in the woods. I wanted to walk back there along with the Sheriff, Pa, and Unc Elmer, but Pa said no. Unc Elmer told Jake and Alvin to go home and do their chores, so they took off running down the road toward their farm.

All the grownups were unhappy. I don't know why they were taking Nellie seriously. She gets things mixed up all the time. Last week she told me there are boats inside the Town Hall. That's the building down Wheatfield Road where we go for potlucks and card parties. It's just a big open room. No water, no boats. When I asked Nellie why she thought there were boats in there, she said that Ma told her that people boat there.

"Boat there?" I questioned her.

"Yes, grownups go there to boat."

When I asked Ma about it later, she laughed and said, "Vote. We vote at the Town Hall."

Another example of Nellie's stupidity: Last year Nellie told me that Ma had jewels in her knitting basket, pearls like the treasure in her *Pirate Book*. But when Nellie looked for them she couldn't find them. She figured Ma had hidden them or put them in the metal box where Pa buries his money. So once again I had to set Nellie straight and explain that purl is opposite of knit, not a jewel. I have to explain a lot of things. I knew a whole lot more than Nellie when I was seven. She ain't near as smart as me. Thank goodness our teacher Miss Flatshaw knows how smart I am.

I'm thinking that with this "hand" situation Nellie has gotten everybody scared and even sent the Sheriff on a wild goose chase.

So I waited with Ma, Aunt Hazel, Nellie, and finally Flora, when she arrived home from high school. Still it was kinda fun. Aunt Hazel always thinks of interesting mind games.

When the Sheriff, Pa, and Unc Elmer came walking back, no one was talking. I think they were mad at Nellie cuz of all the time they had all wasted. Nellie don't get things straight. Pa spent the rest of the afternoon trying to make up for lost time clearing the west field. He worked way past suppertime, so Flora and I milked the cows. They had come up from the meadow on their own and were mooing like crazy, wanting to be milked. We put each of them in their own stanchion and milked them in the order that Pa always does, starting with Bessie, then Rosie, Clover, Cocoa, and ending with Moo-Moo.

Nighttime

"There wasn't a dead baby," I declared at supper. We only had a crust of bread with a little butter. Nothing hot. Nothing else. I wasn't happy about supper or any of this nonsense. Nellie with her "magination" had made up more fibs. Lies, really.

"Irene, you weren't there when they dug it up," my older sister Flora told me. "You must think you're the Sheriff." Flora has a tendency to side with Nellie, probably cuz Nellie's her pet, the baby.

"Don't anyone say no more." Ma jumped into the conversation. "We're not gonna have any dead baby talk tonight or any other time. Do you hear me? No more talk about this. It didn't happen. If I hear any more 'bout this you'll get a whoopin'. Flora, that means you, too. No dead baby talk or there'll be consequences. Not tonight or any other time. Now all three of you git on to bed. Pa will be coming in from the field soon and I want all of you upstairs."

"But I wanna read my *Bible Story Book* in the parlor," I protested.

"You're backtalking," Ma shouted at me. "Get to bed NOW."

Pa walked in right then, and all three of us girls jumped up and ran to our bedrooms.

Flora
Wednesday, April 4, 1934
Afternoon

When I got home from high school today, Jeepers, I knew immediately that something wasn't right. Aunt Hazel and Ma were sitting out by the milk house on a couple of turned-over pails, and Irene and Nellie were sitting on the ground close by. All of them were looking towards the lane that goes down to the two meadows and onto the woods and crick. The county sheriff's car sat empty near the silo. No one was talking.

Worried, I raced across the yard. Could Pa have gotten hurt? As I ran toward Ma I looked over at the west field and saw Ace and King hitched up to the wagon piled with brush. Rover was sleeping near the wagon.

It looked like Pa had finished about half of the field, but he was nowhere in sight. Pa never leaves the horses hitched up when he isn't working. When he comes up for noontime dinner he always puts them in the barnyard so they can rest, too. Naturally, I panicked.

When Ma saw me running over she jumped up and walked over to me, a strange look on her face.

"Is Pa all right?" I blurted out.

"Yes, yes," Ma answered. "He and Elmer are down in the woods with Sheriff Devlon." Nellie pushed me aside and threw her arms around Ma's legs.

"Nellie thinks there's a dead baby in the woods," Irene piped up, all knowingly. "The Sheriff's gone with them to look at it. Who in their right mind would bury a baby in that woods? Nellie musta gotten it all mixed up."

Irene always likes to have all the answers. She loves to "pontificate." That's a word I learned in my English class this year and it fits Irene to a "T." She loves to be the authority in all matters. I think she's a little jealous of Nellie, too.

"Irene, come sit by me," Aunt Hazel said. "We don't even know if there's anything down there, so let's not jump to conclusions. Let's talk about something fun. Tell me your favorite foods."

Aunt Hazel has a wonderful way of calming Irene. I think Aunt Hazel's talents were wasted when she had four boys and no girls. Also, she's simply beautiful. Even when she's tired and has her sandy-blonde hair brought back in a bun, she looks lovely with her round face and large green eyes. She has long eyelashes, too. She could easily be a movie star. Most of my growing up years I wished Aunt Hazel was my own mother. But now that I'm older I understand Ma better.

Ma's more of a brunette like Irene and me. Dark wavy hair, brown eyes and oval faces. Nice enough but not drop-dead gorgeous like Aunt Hazel. Nellie looks more like Pa's family with curly blonde hair and a round face and blue eyes. Ma says all three of us girls are pretty, but she also says that pretty don't mean much these days. Hard work is more important on the farm.

Ma seems demanding and harsh, but it's really to help us girls become good people and learn all the things you have to know in order to survive. The girls in town may know how to cook and sew and maybe even can fruits and vegetables, but they've never milked a cow, fixed a fence, or churned butter. I know how to feed the pigs, sheer sheep, and raise chickens. I've also helped Pa with fixing farm machinery and done about a million other chores, including butchering.

When Aunt Hazel invited Irene over to list her favorite foods, Irene jumped right up, ran over, and leaned against the pail Aunt Hazel was sitting on. Irene started rattling off all kinds of food: strawberry shortcake, corn on the cob, apple turnover, bacon, fried corn meal mush, and even ice cream. I happen to know Irene has only had ice cream once in her life. It was last summer at the Fourth of July church picnic when Reverend Blackman let everybody take a turn churning the ice cream maker. When it was done we each had one spoonful. It was so delicious, smooth and cold.

As Irene kept reciting her favorite foods, I realized how few of these we've had in the past two or three years. Bread, potatoes, and beans are what we eat—and we are farmers who supposedly have lots of food. Hah! During the summer, Ma puts up everything for the winter. We ourselves eat bruised fruits and vegetables that can't be put up, and we dry and can everything else. Back in the day Ma used to make a beef stew with an entire quart jar of beef, but now she makes five or six stews out of one jar with lots of extra potatoes, carrots, onions, and whatever leftovers we might have. You might get one little hunk of meat, but that's it. Ma sneaks a little extra meat for Pa from her own plate because he works so hard. She used to make homemade noodles with beef for church potlucks, but now she makes noodles and puts a little butter and cheese on it, and that's only if we have any cheese. Most of the time we don't.

Instead of butchering a beef steer for ourselves we split one with Aunt Hazel and Unc Elmer two years ago. Everybody decided to eat less meat. That way both of our families would have extra beef to sell. Of course beef prices dropped so bad that I heard Pa say he shoulda butchered one for us after all. But how was he to know?

Even with all our cutting back, we don't know from year to year if we'll be able to pay taxes and the mortgage. If we don't, we lose the farm. Lots of people have been losing their farms. Mainly younger farmers who have large loans. But Pa's still worried. He and Ma borrowed money from the bank to buy our farm from his parents. We have to pay the bank every summer when the mortgage is due. If we don't have the money, then we have to clear out and leave. Where would we go? I worry about that.

At least we've been spared the dust they have out west, but we haven't been spared the low crop prices. Ma and Pa used to do one project every summer after paying the mortgage and taxes. One year it was adding what we call "New Part" to the barn. One year it was a new roof for our house. Another year it was drilling a new well. We didn't have any choice that year, the old well having already gone dry. But over the past few years there haven't been any extra projects. All of Ma's egg peddling money goes into a metal box they've buried somewhere in the yard. We don't buy anything.

Irene and Nellie complain about the plainness of Ma's cooking. But they don't understand hard times. Irene and Nellie haven't heard stories about men jumping off buildings. Heck, they haven't even seen food lines. Nor have they seen the people's faces when Ma and I peddle eggs in town. People look longingly at the eggs, but you know they don't have a single penny in their pockets.

Irene and Nellie haven't seen much, just the train riders. But once those boys find out Ma is gonna give them each a bean sandwich, they are friendly enough and don't talk about how hungry they are. Irene and Nellie just don't understand what's going on. I've wanted to own a radio so we could hear President Roosevelt give his talks. But maybe it's for the best. Irene and Nellie are pretty much having a good time as kids should; they're ignorant of the outside world.

So us farmers who have these huge gardens and spend the entire summer putting up food don't have enough to eat. I know. I see Ma and me taking very little at supper. If there's any spare bread, Ma and I share a slice and wipe our plates clean with it. Pa works so hard in the fields, but he never asks for more. He knows there's nothing left in the pan.

Nellie and Irene both sneak food for Rover. As a pup, he used to survive on table scraps. But now there are no table scraps.

Every morsel is gone, so mainly he gets bones. Rover's a good dog and he deserves to eat, too. Sometimes he gets bread that has gone moldy or butter that's turned rancid. Not surprisingly Rover has grown scrawny over the past couple of years.

Suddenly I came out of my reverie about hard times when we saw Sheriff Devlon, Unc Elmer, and Pa walking up the lane toward us. Irene quit her list of favorite foods mid-sentence. All of us just stared. Pa was carrying his shovel, and Sheriff Devlon was carrying a burlap bag in his arms. It could very well have a baby in it. None of the men said anything. All three had stern, stoic faces.

We women folk all jumped up and waited. The Sheriff went directly to his car and put the gunnysack and its contents on the passenger seat, and he got in the driver's side and started up the car. Pa and Unc Elmer walked over to us as the Sheriff drove away.

"I'll tell you later," Pa said to Ma. He used a tone that meant, *Don't ask anything.* He looked over at Ace and King, still harnessed up to the wagon, walked over to them, patted them, and asked Irene and Nellie to bring the workhorses a couple of pails of water. After Ace and King drank, he took the team back to the west field and started clearing brush again.

Without a word Aunt Hazel and Unc Elmer walked down the driveway, turned right at the road and started walking back to their farm. Then Unc Elmer put his arm around Aunt Hazel; I had never seen him do that before.

Nellie
Thursday, April 5, 1934
Forenoon

When I woke up this morning the first thing I thought of was that baby. What a dark, scary place for a baby to be buried. So alone, away from everyone. Where were its parents? Babies need to be held and cuddled and kept warm. Even dead babies need to be buried in the churchyard with purty flowers, not off in the cold, dark backwoods.

I keep thinking 'bout the Preston's baby girl, such a sweet baby. I held her once when Mrs. Preston was sitting beside me on the davenport. The baby kept sleeping, then blew a little bubble and later I could feel her little fart that warn't stinky at all. All the time she jist kept sleeping. When she finally woke up and fussed, Mrs. Preston picked her up and jiggled her and talked baby talk to her so she quit fussing. That's how babies are posta be treated.

But thinking 'bout the Prestons made me sad, too. They lost their farm and had to move away to Mrs. Preston's parents' place in Indiana. Ma said we might never see them again. Ma and Mrs. Preston both cried when we said goodbye. Pa and Mr. Preston shook hands and Pa bit his lip. I'd only seen him do that once before, at my grandpa's funeral.

It's scary to think that we might lose our farm. None of my grandparents are alive so we'd have nowhere to go. The County Farm don't take whole families. Jist old men who are down and out. Also, that place stinks to high heaven. Last year at Christmas me and Ma took food over there and even the kitchen stunk of manure and old men. The lady who runs the kitchen thanked us heartily for the food. I think she was happy to have reglar people visit her.

Then my thoughts came back to that poor baby.

"So whatcha see in the woods yesterday?" Irene whispered to me as we walked to school. We'd had a cold, silent breakfast. No one had said a word, so it kinda startled me that Irene was asking 'bout the baby.

"A little black hand," I answered, trying not to cry. I sniffed a couple of times so my nose wouldn't run.

Irene scowled at me. "Well, buck up. It's not the Preston's baby, and that's the only baby we know. If it actually was a baby, and I'm not saying that it was, it was probably a Gypsy baby."

"We don't even know if the Gypsies are back," I answered. "And you heard Ma last night. We're not posta talk 'bout it."

The schoolhouse was in sight so we both started running, Irene taking the lead. Irene always tries to git to school early cuz Miss Flatshaw lets her ring the nine o'clock bell. She's Miss Flatshaw's pet and gits to do lotsa special stuff like trash burning, cleaning the blackboard, and sweeping the floor.

"We'll get to the bottom of this," Irene yelled back to me. "No one is gonna get away with burying a baby in the woods. And don't you tell Ma or Pa I talked about it."

Like I was gonna go blab 'bout it and git a whoopin'.

Afternoon

After school I tried and tried to git the baby off my mind. I started thinking 'bout Mr. Goldberg, the peddler. I wish he would stop by with his cart full of goods. I love looking at his stuff and hearing him tell stories 'bout traveling around the countryside. He has so many things in his cart, like pots and pans, sewing notions, and tonics. I like looking at his tiny toys, like itty bitty dolls, colored marbles, and tiny boxes with surprises in them.

Mr. Goldberg's family lives in a place named Toledo, a long way from here. He only gits home once a month cuz he makes his living driving his cart from farm to farm. He always talks 'bout missing his family. I wish he would come more often.

We live in Michigan on a farm in Fonsha Township between Marshall and Albion. I've never been to Albion, but Ma goes into Marshall on Fridays to peddle eggs. Guess people look forward to seeing her, jist like we do Mr. Goldberg. Me, I'm not so curious 'bout eggs, having to gather, wash, and sort them every day. But us farmers have lots of chores, even seven-year-olds like me.

So after I decided Mr. Goldberg warn't gonna show up today, I snuck out of the house and went down to the first meadow where Pa was fixin' fence. I talked to him a long while, mostly 'bout fixin' fences. He warn't gonna say a word 'bout the baby, so I moseyed over to the second meadow and found the cows and talked to them for a spell. They have a good life, eating and sleeping. I think of all the animals on the farm, I would like being a cow the best. Gophers come in a close second. I like how they scamper around and play games in the stone fences.

Me and the cows have reglar conversations. Most of the time they tell me they like warm, sunny days in the meadow eating clover. They ask me to bring them special treats like oats mixed with sugar and honey. Today I forgot to bring treats. Whenever I come to visit the cows, Moo-Moo comes over first and licks my hands to see if I brought her anything. Rover, our dog, is the same way. He always wants a treat and licks my hand to find one.

All five cows are used to me and never run away when I come to visit. I know how to treat them right. I always walk slowly towards them. They tell me where they plan to graze next and we talk 'bout the weather. When the wind picks up and dark clouds come in, they know a storm is coming and they tell me to head back to the barn with them. Usually Bessie leads the parade back to the barn, then Rosie, Clover and Cocoa. Moo-Moo is always the last of the five, maybe cuz she's the youngest. I kinda like that cuz I'm the youngest in my family, too.

After talking to the cows I decided to play in the old cabin ruins. It's at the back corner of the second meadow. There's lotsa interesting things there. There's an old broken-down bus that belonged to my Uncle Lester who got it for free from a friend. He planned to use it to drive Up North but it kept breaking down, and he finally gave it to Pa when he and Aunt Caroline moved to Iowa. Near the bus is the poison ivy tree, a rusty gate, and, of course, my favorite, the old cabin ruins. After that is the stile to the woods.

I love the cabin ruins and the crick. You have to run through the woods to git to the crick. But after yesterday I jist wanna stay away from the woods, so I won't be seeing the crick for a good long while.

The cabin ruins are kinda magical. Sometimes in good weather I lie down there and shut my eyes. That's when I see things from olden times. I make up stories 'bout the Indians who used to live here and the runaway slaves on their way to Canada. ZeeZee from outer space is one of my most special 'maginary friends. Maybe he's from the future; I don't know. I used to talk to him in a 'maginary language but now he talks to me in English. I love his stories 'bout flying away in the old bus.

Today the stories came to me fast and furious. But they weren't the kind I wanted. I saw a man digging a baby grave, but no baby was in sight. Then I saw two men on horseback fighting over a baby. Another was 'bout an Indian shooting an arrow towards the cabin. Another was 'bout ZeeZee trying to bring a baby back to life.

I couldn't tolerate no more baby stories today, so I got up and walked back down the lane and climbed a tree I'd never climbed before. It was an old walnut that hadn't leafed out yet. Walnuts are always the last to git leaves in the spring and the first to lose them in the fall so they're naked a lot of the year. When I got to the top I figured I could wave to Pa. But Pa warn't fixin' fence no more. Guess he'd gone up to the barn. I moved around on the limb and looked back toward the cabin ruins and the woods. There was someone climbing over the stile from the woods toward my magic corner of the meadow. A large man. He kept looking 'round like he was trying to find someone. Maybe he'd heard me telling my stories at the cabin ruins cuz I usually speak them out loud. I hoped he wouldn't look up high. I lay flat along the branch and tried to become invisible. I closed my eyes and wished and wished. Finally I lifted up my head, hoping he was gone, but instead he was underneath looking up at me.

There he stood, a large ugly man wearing a dirty brown hunting jacket. He held a knife and slid it from hand to hand. "You say anything 'bout seeing me, little girl, and you'll be disappearing," he growled. "If you know what's good for you, you'll stay outa the woods. There's lots of bad stuff back there. Bad things for little kids. Otherwise you choose your torture." He laughed out loud, an ugly, low-pitched chuckle.

This scared me to death but it made me mad, too. After all the bad stuff I went through yesterday and now here was a real live person threatening me. I wanted him gone. I decided to toughen up.

"Jist try to git me," I yelled down at him. I figured he couldn't climb all the way up to the top of the walnut tree. Most grown-ups have trouble tree climbing unless they're real skinny like Unc Elmer. I sat up and looked him in the eye. "You git out of my Pa's field right now. You're trempassing."

With that I sat there, stuck out my tongue and stared at him. Then I yelled again, "Git out of my Pa's field. You're trempassing. Git out."

I was glad when he turned around and walked back down the lane, over the stile, and into the woods. When I couldn't see him no more, I hustled down the tree and ran in the opposite direction up the lane and back to the barn to tell Pa.

Nighttime

After Irene fell asleep I crept down from the bed and started listening in on Ma and Pa.

Pa spoke first. "Nellie had bad daydreams today. She was down at the cabin ruins where she always makes up her stories and talks to her imaginary friends. Today she had dead baby daydreams and she imagined an evil man threatening to kill her."

Ma gasped. "Oh, what if it wasn't made up? What if it was someone real?"

"Unlikely," Pa answered. "First, she didn't convince me he wasn't just one of her daydreams; she wasn't sure herself. And second, Nellie defied him. She stuck out her tongue and told him to come git her. So he turned around and left."

"Well, it does sounds more like a tall tale than a real person," Ma answered.

This upset me. That ugly man was a real person, not one of my 'maginary friends. It's true that I like to 'magine stories down there in the second meadow. But he was no frigment. He was real and ugly and mean. And yesterday that baby's hand was real, not a frigment.

Flora
Thursday, April 5, 1934
Forenoon

"Don't you go telling no one 'bout that dead baby at school today,"
Ma was looking me straight in the eye as I sat eating a dry piece
of slightly burned toast for breakfast. I longed for strawberry jam.
We haven't had a jar since last fall.

"Don't you be telling Jean or Henry or anybody else," she continued. "No one must know, you understand?"

"No I don't understand," I answered her. "Why should we lie
about it? We're good, honest people. We don't lie."

"I'm not telling you to lie," she answered. "Just don't bring it
up. It's bad luck to talk about such things."

"But what if Henry asks me? Maybe he heard about it."

"Then just change the subject," Ma replied. "You don't need to
be spreading gossip. We got enough problems raising crops; let's
not create more bad stuff."

"Ma, is this another one of your crazy, superstitious notions?"

Ma's face scrunched up and she took in a big breath. Then she
backed away and shoved a piece of wood in the cook stove. She
turned around. "You sassing like you was five-years-old, and you,
almost a grown woman. You know better than to sass your Ma.
Now go off to school and do as you're told."

I got my lunch pail and went out to the road to wait for
my ride with my cousins, even though I was way early. I just
wanted to get away from Ma when she was in such a mood.
Most of the time she's the nicest, sweetest person in the world,
just like her sister Aunt Caroline. But today she wasn't making
any sense.

Pa told me that Ma's ma, my Grandma Corley, died when Ma was ten and that Ma didn't have a mother to guide her during the rest of her growing up years. So sometimes Ma has strange notions about stuff, like the number thirteen. Pa says to ignore it. It's just her way.

Ma raised her younger sister, my Aunt Caroline who was six years younger than her. Last year after Aunt Caroline broke both her legs and most of her ribs in a buggy accident when the horse got spooked, I went to Iowa to help out. Aunt Caroline was laid up almost a year, so I did all the cooking, housekeeping, sewing, and taking care of my two little cousins, Roy and Daniel, for her and Uncle Lester.

During that year Aunt Caroline told me so many stories of Ma being kind and wonderful while taking care of her as a child. In the early weeks after her accident Aunt Caroline would wake up confused when I was bathing and dressing her and she'd think I was Ma and she was a little girl again. As she got better and better that didn't happen, but she was so grateful and told me over and over how kind and gentle I am, just like Ma.

Afternoon

So now I'm in a dilemma about whether to tell Henry about the baby. I want to tell him, but I don't want to defy Ma. I think the thing to do is not say anything until he asks me. But, golly gee, I sure would like to have something new to talk to Henry about. We eat lunch together every day and we run out of topics all the time. It's so rare that he brings up something himself.

I've been hoping that Henry will ask me out. I see him every day at school and every Sunday at church. He seems to like me. I just don't know what to do that will make him want to go on a date. It makes me feel bad that I just have to wait until he's ready. But what if he's never ready?

Henry's just a few months older than me. I'll be seventeen in two weeks. A while ago I overheard Pa telling Ma that I am too young to start "courting." All of my friends use the word "dating," so naturally I use that word. I like using cool, hip words. I hope Pa changes his mind when Henry finally decides to ask me out. If he asks me out.

Overall I'm feeling real blue. I'm getting the feeling that we're on the brink of losing the farm and there's nothing I can do to help Ma and Pa prevent this. Of course I'll be working hard in the garden this summer, but the test will be if we get enough rain to grow the crops and I have no control over this. I don't seem to have control over anything in my life.

Last year I was helping out Aunt Caroline and with so many chores: taking care of her, watching over the boys, cooking, washing, mending, cleaning and a million other things. I had an important job, and I knew I had to be there for their whole family. Aunt Caroline told me over and over that she couldn't have done it without me. While it was a lot of hard work, I did have a sense of purpose that I no longer feel.

And again, there's Henry and all that frustration. Maybe that's why I keep thinking about that little baby Nellie found. It would be a kind, Christian act to figure out this puzzle and to bring to justice anyone responsible for burying an innocent baby in that dark, gloomy woods. That'll be my purpose for now.

Irene
Thursday, April 5, 1934
Forenoon

Dang, both Flora and Nellie have gotten me to believing there actually was a baby buried in the woods. Nellie always tells stories that are make believe, but Flora was quizzing Nellie so seriously this morning that I just couldn't help but think she fell for the story, hook, line, and sinker. Ma and Pa were off doing their chores, and Flora asked Nellie what else she had seen besides the hand. When Nellie shook her head, Flora then asked Nellie if it was a girl or boy.

"Boy," Nellie replied.

One more ridiculous thing from Nellie. If all she saw was the hand, how could she possibly know it was a boy? Nellie is about as stupid as any seven-year-old can be. I never made such ridiculous claims at her age. Pirates, Indians, outer space friends, and now a dead baby. Maybe our teacher, Miss Flatshaw, can knock some sense into her. Miss Flatshaw is a real smart teacher and she don't believe in imaginary stuff. She's good at explaining stuff like why bread raises up and where the crick water goes.

Miss Flatshaw is our teacher at Parson Creek School. Weird thing about its name, the school is nowhere near Parson Creek. The crick is at least two miles away and you have to go down our lane past the bluebird houses and lilac bushes, through two meadows, and then down the path through woods to get to it. Or you can go down to Fonsha Road, but that's the long way.

Anyway, our school has eight grades plus kindergarten, and this year there are sixteen students, all told. Two other kids are in my grade, sixth grade, and my two cousins, the twins, are in fifth grade this year. May Hendrick is the only eighth-grader. She's already fourteen cuz she flunked fifth grade. Her younger sister JoEllen is in fourth grade.

We're best friends, Miss Flatshaw, and me. Most days we eat our lunches together, and she tells me lots of secrets. I knew the Preston's farm had gone under long before Ma and Pa did. I also happen to know that May Hendrick's father is a drunk, and that Camp Meeting has started up again after being gone since last fall. It's a church-type place, only outdoors with benches and campfires.

Miss Flatshaw says I'm the smartest kid in school. She told me not to tell that to anybody. I sure do get worn down with everybody's secrets, but I do like knowing that I'm the smartest kid. Being the middle of three girls I get overlooked. Flora is the oldest and gets lots of attention cuz she went to Iowa for a year. Nellie is the baby and everybody thinks she's cute cuz she's got curly blonde hair and is always telling silly stories.

Nellie never gets in trouble for her tall tales and naughty adventures. If I had climbed to the top of the haymow last year to look at the carnival, I woulda gotten a whoopin'. But not Nellie. Last summer Nellie did just that, and Pa only scolded her, nothing more. I actually found Nellie that day when she was staring out a little window at the top of the barn. It was a nice view of the carnival; we both watched the Ferris wheel for a long time before I coaxed Nellie to come down. But did I ever get any credit for finding her? Nope.

Nighttime

After supper Flora leaned over to me and whispered to meet her and Nellie behind the granary after kitchen cleanup and NOT to tell Ma and Pa. I'm never gonna do it, I thought. This was risking a bad whoopin'. But my curiosity got the better of me and when I got out to the granary I found Flora and Nellie nestled together like two little bunnies. They quickly drew me in and it felt so good.

"We're gonna find out about that baby boy," Flora whispered. "Ma wants us to pretend that it never happened. But it did. And I for one don't want to ignore the truth."

"Well, I'm a good girl; I do what my parents say," I snapped back at her. "Besides, we don't even know if it was a boy. None of us saw it."

"I overheard Pa say that it was a boy," Nellie said sniffling. She is such a crybaby. But now I understood why she knew. Nellie spies on people all the time.

Flora looked a me sternly. "I learned a lot from Aunt Caroline and Uncle Lester last year. And one thing is that you don't ignore the truth. We all talked about how we would make do if Aunt Caroline never walked again. And how they would all make do after I returned home. They had plans in place. They didn't pretend that Aunt Caroline's accident didn't happen."

I looked at her and shook my head.

"So Irene, maybe some rules can be broken," Flora continued.

I lay there stunned. Flora had changed so much in a year.

"Okay," I answered weakly, not totally convinced, but partially.

"Let's figure out whose baby it could possibly be," Flora insisted. "Burying a baby in the woods is a horrible thing to do. Who do we know that was in a family way this winter?"

"No one," I insisted.

"Maybe a Gypsy or pirate baby," Nellie added. "I saw an evil man down by the cabin ruins today. Maybe he stole the baby and murdered it."

Flora drew a big breath. "No pirates around here. Have the Gypsies come back from their winter camps? We need to find out." She paused for a minute. "Who was the man?"

"Well, a big nasty guy underneath a walnut tree," Nellie answered. "He's real mean and likes to scare kids. I stuck my tongue out at him and he skedaddled."

"But he was under the walnut tree, nowhere near the baby grave?" I asked her, trying to prove that her "man" was just a daydream.

"Did you tell Ma and Pa about him?" Flora asked Nellie, ignoring my question.

"I told Pa."

"What did the man look like?" Flora continued.

"He was huge and had a hunting knife," Nellie responded. "But Ma and Pa thought I 'magined him."

So do I. Frankly, I was angry about hearing another one of Nellie's fantasies. She needs to be more level-headed, like me.

"Come on, let's forget your imaginary stories. Let's put on our thinking caps," I said. That's one of Miss Flatshaw's favorite sayings.

"Who would bury a baby in the woods?" I asked. "Good, decent people bury their folks in the church cemetery. Maybe robbers and hoodlums, but not church-going people."

"Could be it's an Indian baby or a baby from outer space that's been living in the old bus," Nellie suggested. I knew right then that Nellie was gonna be no help at all.

Then Nellie piped up again. "It's gotta belong to someone real evil who would bury it without a gravestone in the dark, scary woods. Maybe a bank robber. Does that John Dillger have a baby? Or Bonnie and Clyde? I bet it was their baby."

Flora kept sighing. She clearly didn't like any of Nellie's suggestions any more than I did.

"Let's talk more about the evil man," Flora suggested. Flora actually believed Nellie! How could she? Nellie was always making up stories.

Flora, looked at Nellie, ignoring me. "Maybe he was down in the woods looking for the grave. Did he say anything about the baby?"

Nellie shook her head. "But he told me to keep outa the woods or he would torture me. Does torture mean kill?"

Flora shook her head and looked at me. "Irene, have you ever seen an ugly man down in the meadow or woods?" she asked.

"No, never," I responded firmly.

"Ma's voice could be heard in the distance. "Girls, girls, where are you?"

Flora raised her finger to shush me and Nellie. "We're out looking for wild strawberries," she yelled back.

"Well, come back right now, it's getting dark."

All three of us got up instantly and started running, but before we got to the house, Flora whispered, "Let's start a club and report what we find. Whoever did this needs to be caught."

"Okay," me and Nellie both whispered back.

"We'll try to meet every night and figure it out," Flora responded.

Actually this sounds fun. Our own Sisters' Club.

Later on I stayed in the kitchen reading my *Bible Story Book* after Flora and Nellie went to bed. I wanted to overhear any conversations between Ma and Pa. There weren't any at first.

Finally Ma said, "Hazel told me two girls have gone missing from Spring Lake. I don't think they ran away from home, but I don't even know their ages. I wonder if they were sisters."

"Hopefully the missing girls will show up at some relative's house."

"Yup."

"But then you never know what goes on inside a house. If those girls were hurt at home, maybe they did run away," Ma said.

"Yup."

"Scary business," said Ma. "On top of everything else we have to worry about this."

Then there was silence and I fell asleep at the kitchen table until Ma woke me up and told me to go up to bed.

Nellie
Friday, April 6, 1934
Afternoon

After Flora got home from school, the three of us met back of the granary again, our second Sisters' Club meeting. It was sprinkling rain and I was feelin' right miserable.

"Let's not meet. I'm wet and cold and wanna go back to the house," I said. "Besides I didn't find out nuthin'. I got no reports."

"If we're going to be a club, we need to get new information before every meeting," Flora answered.

"What did you find out, Irene?" Flora asked, ignoring my request to go back to the house.

"I overheard Fritz Geist say that the Gypsies came back about three weeks ago."

"And was there an expectant mother or a lady with a new baby?" Flora asked her.

"Well, I couldn't quite ask Fritz since he don't talk to me. I think he don't like me because I'm smarter than him and get better grades. I don't much like him either."

Flora groaned. "Well, did you find out anything else about the Gypsies?" Flora asked.

Irene shook her head.

"This isn't helpful," Flora responded.

"I'll ask Fritz," I offered. "He talks to me cuz I help his little brother Jimmy with lots of things, like taking off his coat, and gittin' him into the swing and opening his lunch pail for him."

Jimmy was born funny. Pa says he's *retarded*. He's a sweet little boy and he laughs so hard when I push him in the swing. I like helping him out. Miss Flatshaw helps him a lot, too. Once

31

she told me that he'll never be able to read and write, but he deserves to laugh, play, and have fun. I think she's right.

"Okay, you talk to Fritz about the Gypsies," Flora said to me.
"Ask him exactly what he saw the day they rode into town. Was
there a woman in a family way? Or was there a woman with a
newborn baby? Or a woman looking sad? "

"Well, I do have some news," Flora proclaimed. "I heard at
school that there are two girls missing from Spring Lake. No one
knows where they are."

"I heard the same thing," Irene piped up.

"Who told you that?" I asked.

"None of your beeswax," Irene snapped at me.

"Irene, you need to be nicer to your little sister if we are going
to solve this mystery," Flora scolded her.

"Well, I overhead Ma and Pa talking, if you must know," Irene
squawked.

"Hmm," responded Flora. She scowled. "Missing girls and a
dead baby. Could they be connected? Could the girls have run
away together if one of them was in a family way? We need to
find out when they went missing. I'll see if I can find out."

"Irene, do you have any other reports? With all the secrets
Miss Flatshaw tells you—you must know lots more."

Irene shook her head.

"Find out all you can from Miss Flatshaw about the Gypsies
and the missing girls. Maybe she knows more than we do."

It was raining harder and I was soaked. "Let's git outa here,"
I urged.

Irene and I jumped up.

"Wait," Flora demanded. "People must be talking about this.
This is much bigger news than when Old Man Keller killed that
bear."

"What?" I said, alarmed. My favorite bears, Ma Bear and Pa
Bear, live down in the thicket near the swampy pond. I go down
and talk to them now and then. Real nice bears. They live in the

briars in the middle of a blackberry patch. Sweet, kind animals, not like the mean bears in fairy tales.

"You didn't hear?" Irene piped up, all knowingly. "Everyone in the county knows that Old Man Keller shot a big black bear. He had all the grown-ups go look at it cuz bears jist don't live this far south in Michigan. It made me mad cuz Jake and Alvin got to go see it and I didn't."

I froze at the thought of Ma Bear being all alone down in the thicket without Pa Bear. I hoped the dead bear was some other bear, another one that had snuck down from northern Michigan. My mind was racing so fast and crazy that I didn't hear what else Flora and Irene had to say. All of a sudden we were running back to the house as it rained harder and harder.

Nighttime

At suppertime Ma and Pa talked to us 'bout the two missing girls.

"Two girls went missing from Spring Lake," Ma began. Their parents must be wild with worry. "Never ever go off with a stranger, and always tell us if you see someone strange near the school or anywhere on the road." Ma had given us this speech before.

"When did those girls go missing?" Flora asked. "And how old are they?"

Both Ma and Pa shook their heads?

"Why does it matter?" Ma asked.

"Just asking," Flora responded.

"Don't you use this as an excuse to talk about that dead baby," Ma exclaimed. She seemed to be reading my mind. She would really be mad if she found out about our Sisters' Club.

Flora
Saturday, April 7, 1934
Forenoon

A heavy cloud has been hanging over our family for the past few days. No one's talking about that baby in the woods, but everyone's thinking about it. I know because both my sisters and I are trying to figure it out. But no one has news. Nellie whimpers and Irene complains.

Ma and Pa haven't said a word. Every night at supper we all just sit there saying nothing. Even Ma and Pa don't ask us questions about school like they usually do. Dark silence.

But today is Saturday and, Dagnabbit, I'm going on my first date with Henry, and I'm gonna have a good time. A very good time. Period.

Henry's family goes to our church, the Parson Creek Church, just down the road about a mile from our house in the opposite direction of the country school. So I see him all the time at high school and after church. But it took Henry long enough to ask me out; I've been back from Iowa since Christmas. I'm hoping tonight's date is the first of many more.

Henry's picking me up at 6:30 so I'm sitting at the Treadle remaking one of Ma's dresses to fit me. I really wanted a store-bought dress, but Ma says we don't have enough money to buy any new fabric, let alone a ready-made dress. So Ma gave me her blue calico dress to remake for myself. I ripped apart the bodice and took in the darts to make it smaller. I'm thinner and smaller bosomed than Ma and about two inches taller. I'm happy that I have her pretty dark brown hair that's all wavy. It's in style right now and I like to be in style.

I'm going to remake Ma's dress to look modern and hip, adding a flouncy collar like I saw in my friend Jean's *McCalls* magazine, and I'm gathering it tighter since I have a smaller waist than Ma. I sure hope Henry don't remember Ma's old dress. She hasn't worn it to church for a while, so I think I'm okay.

Henry and his family usually sit in the pew in front of us at church. Last Sunday I watched the Fitch family come in and turn the corner in front of us. As he rounded the corner, Henry smiled at me. Did my heart flutter! I know that Ma and Pa say that my girlfriend Jean and I are boy crazy, and maybe Jean is. But right now Henry is the only boy I like. He's rather quiet and I spent most of last night trying to think of what to talk about on our date tonight. Any topic that's not about the baby incident, that is.

When I heard Pa's comment about me being too young to start courting a few weeks ago, I was sitting in the outhouse doing my business, and they were walking down the path to the garden, probably to look it over and plan this year's layout. I quietly put my ear to the open slat in order to hear the rest of their conversation.

Ma responded that she married Pa when she was just seventeen.

"Just a few days shy of eighteen," Pa responded. Then somberly he asked, "Are you trying to get her married off to have one less mouth to feed? You know the girls help a lot around the farm, especially in the garden."

"No, no, no," Ma replied. "I just couldn't abide her getting in a family way. My sister Caroline went through such hell before she married Lester. Everyone was counting the weeks."

I already knew Ma's opinions about girls getting in a family way. She was sympathetic with her sister, but no one else. She considered other girls who had to get married cheap and loose.

"Well, Flora and Henry are both good kids," Pa answered. "They know how to behave." I couldn't hear any more of the conversation since they were almost to the garden, but I was glad to hear Pa's comments.

I have to get the dress finished this afternoon before Henry picks me up. The good news is that I'm going to keep it the same length so I won't have to hem it up. I sure hope he takes me to the movies. Everybody has been talking about *King Kong* and I happen to know the movie starts at seven o'clock. It's going to be a swell night.

Nighttime

Ma gave me a talking to this afternoon just after I finished the dress. I am not to let Henry touch me anywhere. A first date is too soon to hold hands, kiss, or even snuggle up in the movie. Boy am I disappointed. I had the evening all planned out. Henry would come and pick me up, and we would drive into town and go to the Bijou to see *King Kong*. I'd snuggle up during the scary parts and we'd leave holding hands. After he brought me home, I would ask him into the kitchen for cookies, since people don't have money to buy ice cream or root beer in town any more. That's okay. Ma made some molasses cookies when she saw that I was working on the dress all day long. Ma is kind and generous that way.

During the "talking to" Ma told me that I'm a good girl who isn't cheap or gets in a family way before getting married. She has high expectations for me and I need to remember them. Like I hadn't heard all this before.

But, gosh, was I surprised about how the date turned out. Henry was more nervous than me when he picked me up. It seemed to start fine, though, and he was very polite with Ma and Pa. Henry drove his parents' old Model A that is just like our car. He told me I looked nice, and I thanked him. Guess working on that dress all day was paying off. But instead of driving into town to see the movie, he headed out Green Lake Road. When I asked him where we were going, he only replied, "You'll see."

I was getting nervous not knowing what was going on, but in a way it was exciting. However, when Henry turned onto Lovers Lane, I yelped.

"We are NOT going down that road. Let me out right now." I could see Ma's face right in front of mine.

Henry paused and turned the car into one of many pull-offs on the road.

"Right now," I demanded with more conviction than I really felt.

"Okay, okay," he answered. "Just trying to start the evening with a little fun."

"This is NOT first-date fun," I replied. "Take me home."

Henry's face turned ashen. He had turned around and we were going down Green Lake Road. "Let's just go downtown and sit in the park," he said. I thought he might have tears in his eyes.

"Okay," I answered. I wanted to mention that the movie started at seven o'clock, but I held back. He had never actually told me we were going to the movie. I thought so because that's what you do on a date. You go to a movie or a dance and there wasn't going to be a dance at the Red Barn tonight. I'd asked Jean about that cuz she loves dances and goes to a lot of them.

We pulled up to the edge of the city park and Henry led me to a park bench.

"I'd wanted to go to the movie tonight," he blurted out. "But I don't have any money. Our family is facing hard times. Every penny has to be saved for the mortgage and taxes." I could see the anguish in his face.

He was holding back tears. "My father didn't want me to take the car because of the cost of gas, but he knows your family, so he agreed."

"It's okay," I replied, because I'm always nice, no matter what. I looked around and people still seemed to be sneaking looks at us. I wanted to get up and leave. But where could we go?

"Hey," I said to Henry, deciding to ignore the stares directed at us. "Cheer up. It's not your fault the country's in such a mess. I hear that President Roosevelt is going to change things around and get us out of it."

Sitting on the park bench, Henry and I talked for quite a while. It's easy to talk to Henry now that I understand his situation. I wanted to tell Henry about the baby incident, but I decided not to say anything unless he brought it up. It's a small town, and news travels fast so I imagine most everyone in the county will know about it sooner or later.

"Hey," I said. "What are you going to do after you graduate next year?"

"I love farming," he answered. "I'm gonna help out my pa and save up some money until I can get my own farm." I already knew this.

Of course, I was thinking that what I want to do more than anything else is to become a farm wife. But I wasn't saying anything about that on our first date.

I remembered the molasses cookies at home and we drove back and ate them at the kitchen table and played a couple of card games with my little sisters. Henry was very gracious and let them win. I never said a word about missing *King Kong*.

Nellie
Saturday, April 7, 1934
Afternoon

Flora spent all today gittin' ready for her date with Henry. I was hoping to meet with my sisters in back of the granary again and maybe talk 'bout pirates or Gypsies. I'd jist as soon give the poor baby a rest. I'd rather do our Sisters' Club with other topics, like figuring out how to make the old bus work. I've been wanting to do that for quite a spell. My 'maginary friend ZeeZee says he flies the bus back and forth into outer space. But ZeeZee hasn't appeared in a while.

I've been so worried 'bout the Bears. I sure hope Old Man Keller didn't kill Pa Bear. I tried to talk Irene into going with me to find the Bears, but she had already made plans with Jake and Alvin to turn Unc Elmer's empty corncrib into a pretend jail. I wanted to tag along but Irene said no. Only big kids are allowed to work on the jailhouse. Then later she said that maybe they'd let me play Cops and Robbers or Cowboys and Indians with them. I knew what she was thinking. She wanted to throw me into jail. But I'll figure out a way to outsmart her. Maybe I'll loosen up a board or two in the corncrib floor when they're not around and make a tunnel. I think it might be more fun to climb up to the top and git out through that hole in the roof that Unc Elmer keeps talking 'bout fixin.' Then I'd climb down on the outside of the corncrib. That jailhouse ain't gonna keep me locked up.

Finally, after Irene left, I decided to go find Ma and Pa Bear myself. I've seen where they make their beds right down in the middle of the thicket near the swampy pond. It's not too far from the south branch of the crick and you don't have to go through the meadows or woods to git there. I wouldn't be going against Ma or Pa's orders. But you have to be real careful in the thicket cuz there are lots and lots of briars there. I'm not sure how the bears keep from gittin' scratched, but they do.

I have to admit I was scared going off by myself after seeing that evil man. But the bears live on the other side of the barn to the west. I jist wanted to make sure that Pa Bear was okay. Pa used to say that bears only live Up North and that Ma and Pa Bear are 'maginary. But they're real. I know.

So I was gittin' a little scared when I pulled myself under the west fence by the lilacs. It was a tighter squeeze than last fall. I guess I've grown since the last time I came here. But I wiggled and wiggled and managed to git under it. Then I got up and looked around. There was the swampy pond and the little trail that goes around it. So I started walking around the pond on my way to the Bears' thicket.

Even though I was nowhere near the meadow or woods I was still feelin' kinda scared, so I decided to sing a song. I sang "The Bear Came over the Mountain," until I saw the turn-off to the thicket. Ma Bear was standing near her sleeping place.

"Oh, no," I cried, seeing her all alone and sad. "Pa Bear is gone?" I asked. She walked around in a circle, looking sad. I knew that this meant *Yes*.

I wished I'd brought her some honey. I did find some sugar wrapped in a handkerchief in my pocket that I had intended to give to Moo-Moo. So I pulled it out and poured it on a flat rock on the ground. Ma Bear licked it up and I could smell her musty odor. Then she looked up at me and I knew she was crying inside. It's amazing how much animals can be like people. She certainly is my saddest animal friend.

I walked back to the house all heavy-hearted. Life ain't much fun these days.

Irene
Saturday, April 7, 1934
Nighttime

I'm good at keeping secrets and I can be very quiet, too. Sometimes people forget that I'm around. Tonight Ma and Pa were in the kitchen playing canasta with Aunt Hazel and Unc Elmer. Flora was on her first date, Nellie was upstairs, and I was in the parlor reading my *Bible Story Book*. My favorite story is when Lot's wife looked back and turned into a pillar of salt. Why didn't she just do what she was told? That woulda never happened to me. Not in a million years. I do what I'm told. Always.

Nellie's favorite story is "Noah's Ark." She loves animals. She's friends with all the barn cats, especially Three Foots. She spends lots of time with our dog Rover and she likes to talk to the cows, and even wild animals. Frankly, she'd be better off spending more time with people. Then she might be more sensible. All that time with animals makes her kinda odd. Miss Flatshaw thinks so, too. She told me so just a few days ago.

Flora told me that her favorite *Bible* story is "Moses Parting the Waters" cuz she likes miracles. Pa likes the "Christmas Story." Ma says she likes the "Loaves and Fishes" cuz so many people don't have enough to eat these days.

I don't understand why these hungry people don't grow bigger gardens. Then they'd have more to eat. Maybe they don't like potatoes. We have boiled potatoes for dinner and supper most every day. Sometimes for Sunday dinner we have mashed potatoes. We used to have scalloped potatoes and ham, but we haven't had that for a couple of years cuz we had to sell all our hogs instead of butchering one.

Anyway, I was being very quiet tonight while the adults played cards. I really needed to pee, but I was warm and comfy in the parlor and I didn't wanna put on my coat and overshoes to go out to the privy. I'd try to wait until bedtime. So the grown-ups were laughing and Pa and Unc Elmer were sipping whiskey and I started listening in.

"Never wanted to see a man lose his land, but the way Jones treated his horses, he kinda deserved it," Unc was saying. "That and starting his own religion, he was a bit cuckoo. He didn't have much of a farm anyhow, just forty acres. Wonder if he'll find enough followers to keep his church going." Unc paused. "He claims God gave him a new set of commandments. Maybe they contained *Treat your animals poorly*."

"Elmer, watch what you say!" Aunt Hazel scolded him. "Maybe he truly has a calling. Besides these are terrible times, and we all may end up losing our land. Look at the poor Prestons. They are right good people—they didn't deserve to lose their farm. If we don't get rain this summer, we may be standing in food lines next year."

"Or the AAA will do us in if the weather don't," Unc Elmer added.

"What's the AAA?" Ma asked.

"President Roosevelt's new-fangled idea that he thinks will save the farmers. Agricultural Adjustment Act, or something like that. We don't raise crops and we butcher our animals. Just slaughter them and bury them. Don't make no sense at all," Unc replied.

Pa, who hadn't said a word, chimed in. "Maybe it will help. Supply and demand, you know, and the govmint is gonna pay the farmers to do it, subsidies they call it. Hope it will help. Roosevelt seems to be getting the CCC going pretty well, anyway. I heard the Greenwood kid signed up a couple of weeks ago and is already working on a bridge in Kalamazoo County."

"And what's the CCC?" Ma asked. She hadn't heard of any of these new things using letters for names. Neither had I.

"A govmint agency that hires young men to work on special projects, planting trees, making parks, and building bridges and dams," Pa replied. "It's supposed to help us get out of this depression by creating more jobs for folks."

"I wish they'd build some bridges here in Calhoun County," Unc added. "We could use another one across Parson Creek. I have to go purt near five miles to get to my back forty across the crick. Same with Old Man Keller gittin' to his woods that's on our side of the crick."

"Don't know how it works," Pa admitted. "I've always stayed out of politics 'cept for voting. You need to know the right people. We'll probably have to build a bridge across the crick ourselves if we really want one. Until then just use a pair of high galoshes."

Then there was some whispering. I think they were whispering about the two missing girls.

"Just hate hearing about it," Ma said. "That and Nellie talking about an evil man down in the meadow," she went on. "As if we didn't have enough to worry about, just putting food on the table and keeping a roof overhead."

The grown-ups started shuffling the cards and played the next hand without saying another word. When I couldn't wait to pee any longer, I stood up and walked to the kitchen door, grabbing my coat from the hook.

Ma looked up. "Were you in the parlor?" she asked sharply.

"Oh, I fell asleep reading my *Bible Story Book*," I answered her. "After I go to the privy I'm gonna wake up Nellie and wait up for Flora to come home. I hope she and Henry will play cards with us."

I know the falling asleep part was a lie, but I think it was one that didn't hurt anyone. Besides, I didn't want to get tanned for listening to the grown-ups. If I'm gonna get tanned, I want it to really count. I want to overhear something really juicy.

Nellie
Sunday, April 8, 1934
Forenoon

Last week Reverend Blackman's mother died. So he and Mrs. Blackman and their two girls went to Canada for the funeral, and somebody else preached at our church. It was Brother Johnson, a scary rivalist preacher. He reminds me of the evil man who scared me when I was high up in the walnut tree: big, fat, ugly.

"This morning in church he was preaching, yelling, and telling everyone how we are all gonna go to hell. I was 'fraid he was gonna come down from the pulpit and pull me out of the pew and make an example of what a bad girl I am. After all, I listen to grownups' secrets and I play with lots of 'maginary friends. And I found that buried baby. That has to be a real big sin.

I was so glad that fat Mrs. Vandenberg was sitting in front of me so I could hide behind her. I didn't want that preacher looking at me with his accusing eyes. Every time Mrs. Vandenberg moved, and she moved a lot, I moved at the same time to stay hidden from Brother Johnson. Pa seemed to be amused by it, but I have no idea why.

Rivalist preachers are jist scary, I guess. Ma says that Brother Johnson don't have a reglar church; he preaches in a tent. She thinks he has rattlesnakes and other vipers down in that tent cuz she's heard rumors 'bout it. He sure yells at the congregation a lot. I can't wait for Reverend Blackman to be back. He's our reglar preacher and talks 'bout nice things, like helping out neighbors and creating heaven on earth. I don't know how to do that, but I'm only seven, after all.

Ma was particularly peeved that Brother Johnson passed the collection plate three times. "Once is enough," I heard her say to Pa on the way home. "How can he expect people to cough up more money in these bad times? He don't know how much food we give to the Blackmans all winter long. And Sunday dinner every two or three months. That's better than money in the plate," she added. "But no, Brother Johnson made everyone feel guilty that they can't throw in another penny. The shame."

Pa didn't say anything. He was probably jist as embarrassed as I was when the second and third time the plate was passed and he put nuthin' in it. I guess rivalist preachers don't know how pressed we farmers are for money. Probably Mrs. Vandenberg was fidgety cuz she was embarrassed, too. I think we'll all be glad when the Blackmans come back from Canada.

You can't believe how happy I was that Ma and Pa didn't stir an inch when Brother Johnson called people to the altar to confess their sins. The last thing I wanted to do was go up to that altar and have the rivalist preacher look at me with his creepy eyes and declare what a sinner I am. Maybe he knew 'bout the dead baby and wanted God to punish me. I'd rather take a whoopin' from Pa any day than go up to that altar.

Irene
Sunday, April 8, 1934
Forenoon

Brother Johnson preached at our church this morning. He's from the Camp Meeting down near Fonsha and is what you call a revivalist. He preaches hellfire and brimstone and the bad things awaiting sinners in hell. Miss Flatshaw explained it all to me, cuz she loves going to Camp Meetings and went all last summer.

Today after Brother Johnson preached, he tried to get everyone to come to the altar and confess, but no one did. He was shouting and hollering about heaven and hell, real loud. I wanted to go up to the altar and confess the few sins I have, but Ma put her hand on my leg and frowned at me. I knew immediately from the look on Ma's face that I was not to move out of my seat, so I sat frozen like a stone. Gosh darn, it's a trial always having to be good.

I rather liked Brother Johnson's sermon cuz I want all those bad people to understand they're not getting away with anything. They'll get their comeuppance sooner or later. I wish May Hendrick went to our church since she needs a little preaching to. She always has lice and bad BO. Ma says the Hendricks don't bathe on Saturday night. Once I asked Ma how she knew that. She said it was obvious. May has scarlet fever right now so it ain't gonna happen anyway. She's been outa school for quite a while.

Flora
Monday, April 9, 1934
Nighttime

Sometimes I overhear conversations that I'm not supposed to, but it's not often that I deliberately try to listen in on Ma and Pa. I'm not sneaky like Irene who's eleven and pretends to be asleep in the kitchen and listens in on Ma and Pa's private conversations. Then there's Nellie who's seven and just seems to disappear a lot. She hides in lots of different places. I've seen her a couple of times way up in the peach tree by the tool shed listening to the conversation below. Both of my sisters eavesdrop on any adults who are around. Me, I prefer Mrs. Vandenberg, who treats me like an adult and gives it to me honestly. Why eavesdrop when you can be treated like a grown-up?

Nellie found the buried baby last Wednesday and nobody's talking. I have to admit it makes me want to listen in on the quiet conversations in the parlor every evening, the way my sisters do. Also, babies have been on my mind every day for one reason or another.

On Saturday afternoon, before my date with Henry, Ma confided in me that she lost a baby once. It was when I was three years old before Irene was born. She said that it was the hardest thing to lose a child, even a baby that was several months from being born. Ma told me she was so happy that she already had me, a healthy little girl. Otherwise she might have worried that she couldn't ever have a live, full-term baby. When I asked Ma if the baby was buried up at the church cemetery, she said no. They buried it in a "special place down by the crick." But she didn't say anything else, probably because us girls have always gone to the crick to play.

So babies were still on my mind tonight when I was out in the kitchen finishing up my homework by the light from the west window. Ma and Pa had been talking about the usual: money and the lack of it.

"Mrs. Wainwright told me in no uncertain terms that she don't need help with her housework," Ma commented and sighed.

"Well, you just keep asking the widowers," Pa responded. "They're more likely to figure out they need someone to do cooking and housework. Mrs. Wainwright and other widows are used to doing all of it, even when they get older. But the widowers, they might say yes."

Long pause. I think Ma was thinking she had already asked every widower in town if he needed help. No one had hired her. They all said they were doing okay. She'd told me this every time she came back from town.

Frankly I think our new Sisters' Club is the only thing that's keeping me going. I feel so helpless regarding so many things—saving our farm, getting Henry to ask me out again, wanting just ordinary things like pretty clothes and going to dances and movies. If we solve this mystery I will have done something good this year.

Irene
Monday, April 9, 1934
Afternoon

After Flora came home from school today she whispered for me and Nellie to meet her up in her bedroom since Pa was up from the fields early today and would likely find us in our usual spot behind the granary. I liked the idea of meeting in Flora's room for the Sisters' Club better anyway. No rain and no mosquitoes. It's just that we have to whisper so Ma don't hear us.

"I think we should have a secret sign when we wanna meet," I said as soon as we all got up on Flora's bed. "How about a finger in the ear followed by blinking both eyes?"

"Or making a rooster sound," Nellie said, pursing her lips and crowing loudly.

"That would take all the secret out of it," I scolded her. Nellie is such a baby.

"I think the pinky finger in the ear is okay," Flora answered. "If we do anything else Ma and Pa are gonna figure out that something's up."

"So what did you both learn today?" Flora changed the subject.

Nellie was eager to talk. "Fritz told me that he and his dad were in town when the Gypsies arrived about three weeks ago. It was a Saturday since he wasn't in school. All the Gypsies drove their horses and wagons down through Main St. He didn't see any Gypsy ladies who were in a family way and he said there warn't any newborn babies either. But they had a bunch of kids, maybe six or seven."

"Where are they camped?" Flora asked.

"Down in that empty field near the Fairgrounds," Nellie answered.

Flora was frowning. "It would be easy enough for an expecting lady or one with a new baby to stay hidden in one of their wagons when they rode into town. I wonder if Fritz got all his facts straight. You two need to talk to the Gypsy children and find out all you can about their families. The kids are more likely to spill the beans about a baby than adults."

"How um I ever gonna get to the Gypsy camp?" Nellie asked. "Besides Ma and Pa always say to stay away from Gypsies. You know that. And they speak Gypsy, not English."

Flora looked at Irene. "Why don't you tell Miss Flatshaw you want to write a report on Gypsies and ask her about the Gypsy camp. Maybe she can take you and Nellie to the camp and talk to the kids."

"What are Ma and Pa gonna think about that?" I asked.

Flora shrugged. "It would be a school assignment and you'd have a grown-up with you."

I think Flora wasn't being very practical about this. She's really different after being in Iowa last year; she used to be a lot like me, never stepping out of line or crossing Ma or Pa.

Nellie
Tuesday, April 10, 1934
Afternoon

Today was real nice and sunny. Flora and Irene were still both in school so Ma let me go outside by myself. First I watched Pa fixing his hay rake, and then I told Pa I wanted to go into the woods and see what little plants were peeking up through the ground. My favorites are the Umbrella Plants that Flora calls May Apples. That's a silly name cuz they bloom in April and they're nuthin' like apples. Just nice little green umbrella leaves with white blossoms.

"Can you go with me?" I asked him. "I'm a little scared to go back there.

"Well, sweetie, I have to get this rake fixed. We'll be needing it for haying season. Maybe one of your sisters could go with you later when they're home from school. The Sheriff's been back twice to look over that grave, but nothing's come of it."

The Sheriff had asked me more questions, too. But he still didn't have any answers 'bout the baby. I think the Sheriff believes me, but he smiles if I suggest the baby was a pirate or Indian baby. He laughed when I mentioned that my friend ZeeZee might have brought the baby from outer space.

Pa was talking again. "I know you want to go play at the crick, but now isn't the right time, Nellie."

"Okay, maybe I'll jist go visit the cows for now," I told Pa. I could see they were up by the cherry trees in the first meadow. Cows are so nice. They happily let Pa milk them so we can sell the milk, cream, and butter. Mr. Hughes comes around every day with his wagon and picks up the milk cans. Ma filters the milk and keeps some for us and makes butter, too. She knows how to make cheese, but she usually don't make it cuz it takes too much time and we need to sell the milk and cream.

Pa keeps a close watch on the cows in the spring months during tornado season cuz they always know when a tornado is coming. A tornado ripped off the roof of Mr. Lutz's barn last year. Pa and a few other neighbors helped him git it back on. Funny thing, Pa said, there warn't much damage. The tornado lifted up the roof and placed it on the field south of Mr. Lutz's barn, real nice and gentle, like God was doing it with His hands. That roof sure looked strange jist sittin' there in the field with only a couple of shingles blown off.

So I left Pa and ran to the first meadow where the cows were grazing. All five of them were under the cherry trees near the stone fence. They always are happy to see me, Moo-Moo 'specially, and I try to remember to keep sugar in my pocket for her.

I need to figure out what cow treats I can take to them next time. Ma don't want me using any more honey, but I wanna take a little of that to Ma Bear. She's such a kind animal and is so lonely. The cows love to eat anything sweet. Pa sometimes gives Ace and King, our workhorses, some sugar. He also gives the cows molasses for a treat, pouring it over their feed in the winter, but that stuff's all wet and sticky like Ma's pancake syrup. I couldn't carry it down to the meadow. Well, actually I could carry it down in a cup, but I wouldn't have any feed or oats to pour it over.

The cows didn't have much to say today, only that they like the spring sunshine and gentle rain showers. I know the cows like the rain more than me. If it's a light drizzle they'll stand right out there in the field and let the sprinkles run down their backs.

I said goodbye to all five cows and started running through the second meadow. I love all the stuff down there at the end: the poison ivy tree, the cabin ruins, the old bus, the rusty gate, and the stile that goes over the fence to the woods. All my 'maginary friends live in the old cabin ruins.

Irene and I planted the daffodil bulbs along the fence row last fall, so they'll be all yellow in a week or two. That'll make a nice surprise bouquet for Ma since she don't come down to the second meadow much. I 'spect she's forgotten that we planted them.

Being gun-shy 'bout the woods, I decided to climb a large oak tree right near the path through the woods. The oak is all leaved out, so I'd be well hidden, unlike that bare walnut where the ugly man found me. After I got near the top I heard a noise some distance away so I decided to cozy up to the trunk on one of the big branches. After waiting a couple of minutes I heard the noise again: voices. They were speaking a weird language. I kept my eyes open figuring I'd soon see these people. Then they came. Three men were riding horses down Old Man Keller's lane.

Two were old men with gray hair and one was a boy 'bout twelve or thirteen. Probably they were headed to the crick cuz they came from the lane that starts at Keller Road. Frankly, I was relieved to see that it warn't that man who spotted me when I was up in the walnut tree. But why are all these things happening in the woods? The woods are posta be quiet and purty.

Old Man Keller owns the woods. But these men didn't look like friends of Old Man Keller. Meaning they didn't look like farmers. They were wearing strange-looking clothes, old-colored flouncy shirts, and tight black pants, not overalls. I wanted to know what they were doing. Since the Gypsies are back, I'd have to guess that's what they were. Pa had warned all of us not to let Gypsy horses drink from our horse tank. But Pa warn't real clear on how to figure out if a person is a Gypsy. And what 'bout letting the horses drink from the crick? Is that okay? Could Gypsy horses make the crick water bad?

I was sure that they were gonna look up and see me in the oak tree cuz I was right above, but these men seemed to be arguing in their strange language, kinda barking at each other.

Or maybe they were from the Camp Meeting and speaking in Tongues. Never having gone to Camp Meeting I don't know what Tongues sounds like. I listened hard to these men but I couldn't figure out one word.

Last month at a church potluck Mrs. Geist taught me and Irene some German. "Ick" means "I" and "bin" means "am" and "krank" means "sick." So if you say, *Ick bin krank*, it means "I am sick." Her husband Mr. Geist knows a lot of German. Mrs. Geist said she knows French too, cuz her people are from a place named Applesauce. Well, it's not quite Applesauce, but something that sounds like it. She also taught me *Je suis malade* which means "I am sick" in French.

The horses didn't look too good either. All three of them had seen better days or maybe they were sick from bad horse-tank water. I kept listenin' for the words *krank* and *malade* but I never heard them. When they passed under my hiding tree I held my breath. They kept on riding, never looking up at me, turning at the rusty gate and following the path to the crick.

Well, if the baby belonged to these guys, they sure didn't seem to be lookin' for the grave. They seemed more intent on arguing with each other and gittin' their old sick horses down to the crick. I counted to a hunert, climbed down the oak, and walked over to the cabin ruins. Finding my usual flat place by the fireplace I lay down and closed my eyes. Where was ZeeZee? And all of my other 'maginary friends? No one showed up to talk to me today.

Nighttime

During supper I told the whole family 'bout the three men I saw riding their horses down the lane. Everyone looked up and quit eating when I started talking.

"Thank goodness they didn't see you," Ma said. "You're positive they didn't see you?"

"Did they go anywhere near where . . . .?" Irene suddenly quit talking, realizing she was gonna mention the baby grave.

"Sounds like Gypsies all right." Pa took over the conversation. I think he was trying to help out Irene so that Ma wouldn't light into her.

Flora slowly stuck her little finger in her ear like she was cleaning it out. Our signal. I nodded at her and later I saw Irene stick her finger in her ear, too.

After the supper cleanup and nighttime chores were done, Irene and I went up to Flora's bedroom where she was doing her homework. We all huddled together on her bed.

"Sounds like they were Gypsies," Flora whispered to both of us. "Nellie, how old were those men?"

"The two old ones were lots older than Pa. And the young one looked to be younger than Dan and Dalton, maybe thirteen. No beards but long hair. They all had brown skin."

"Hardly the age to be fathers of newborn babies," Flora sighed. "Were they talking about trying to find the grave? Did they have any flowers to put on the grave?"

"No, no, no," I answered. "They were talking either Gypsy or Tongues. And they were arguing with each other. No flowers. No crying 'bout a baby. They didn't even look down at the ground. When they got near the grave they started riding faster. I think they wanted to git their sick horses to the crick fast."

Flora sighed, clearly mad at me for not finding out enough. "Well, what have you found out from Miss Flatshaw?" she asked Irene.

Ma had braided Irene's thick dark hair and she looked different.

"Miss Flatshaw said it might be hard to write a report about Gypsies cuz they don't like to talk to outsiders. Even if we went over to their camp, they wouldn't talk in English. She said we'd best leave them alone. Specially with those two girls gone missing in Spring Lake. She said maybe the Gypsies took the girls."

Irene shrugged. "I tried to talk Miss Flatshaw into taking me and Nellie to their camp anyway, and just see what they'd say. But Miss Flatshaw wouldn't hear of it. She said I should write a report on the Amish people in Pa's family, back in Pennsylvania. She said Pa would be a lot easier to talk to."

Flora sighed and shook her head.

"Well, it's a good idea," Irene went on. "Miss Flatshaw told me about the runaway slaves that came right through these farms on their way to Canada. She said the Amish people helped lots and lots of slaves get to freedom. It would be so fun to find out if our great-grandparents hid the slaves."

Flora looked mad. This warn't goin' the way she wanted. But I was interested in the runaway slaves, too. Once we get this baby mystery solved, I'm gonna help Irene with a report on the Underground Railroad. But right now Flora wants us to find out 'bout the Gypsies.

Irene
Wednesday, April 11, 1934
Afternoon

At noon hour, if me and Nellie don't walk home to eat dinner with Ma and Pa, I get my dinner pail and join Miss Flatshaw at her desk. If the weather is warm at noontime, like today, the two of us go outside and sit on the schoolhouse steps. Today Miss Flatshaw struggled, panting, as she heaved herself down on the top step.

Miss Flatshaw was very quiet, maybe cuz the weather was so weird. We could hear the noon whistle in town and that never happens. Never. Then we heard the 12:30 train, a sure sign of a storm coming. Miss Flatshaw says when there's a storm coming the kids get restless and feisty and you can hear things from ten miles away, like trains, and sometimes, cars. She said it has to do with electricity in the air before a storm.

I didn't quite understand about the electricity. I thought it was in wires, not in the air. But Miss Flatshaw explained to me that Thomas Edison didn't invent electricity, he just figured out how to get it into the wires so people could use it. I like that about Miss Flatshaw. She explains complicated things so that kids can understand. I'd already asked for the third time about taking me to the Gypsy camp, but she told me very nicely that she wasn't gonna change her mind. No more beatin' a dead horse.

Miss Flatshaw was right about kids getting feisty. Sure enough there were three fights in the schoolyard that she had to break up, including my cousins, Jake and Alvin. Finally, Miss Flatshaw rang the one o'clock bell. She rang it herself, and it was only a quarter of one. I know cuz we have a big round clock on the wall right next to the picture of George Washington. No one but her is allowed to touch the clock, not even me. She winds it up every morning before anyone arrives.

So even though it wasn't one o'clock Miss Flatshaw said the best thing to do was to get the kids inside so they wouldn't hit each other anymore. We went in and Miss Flatshaw played the piano while we sang songs as loud as we could. Then we played Upset the Fruit Cart, even though it's usually an outdoor game. During the fruit cart game I was an apple and so was my cousin Jake, who is a year younger than me. I was irritated cuz the apples never got called. The oranges got called three times, and lots of other fruits got called once or twice, but Jake and I had to sit still until someone said, "Upset the Fruit Cart" when everybody switches seats. I used to like that game, but no more.

Later around three o'clock, after Nellie had gone home, a strange thing happened. Miss Flatshaw was working with the three fourth-graders on arithmetic. They were all sitting on the bench facing Miss Flatshaw's desk. I was at my desk deciding what to do next. I could look at my spelling words again, but I'd memorized them down pat. Next, I don't know why, but I looked out the window and saw that it was incredibly dark. Miss Flatshaw seemed to notice it, too. She left the fourth-graders and walked over to a window and peered out.

"Close all the windows; it looks like a bad storm is coming," she said.

The air felt prickly and I noticed all the flies had gathered on the east wall just waiting to be swatted. I got the flyswatter from the nail on the wall near Miss Flatshaw's desk and killed five at once with my first swat. The rest of the kids laughed and urged me on. The next swat brought down only two cuz the flies were getting smarter, yet they still just kept buzzing near the wall. I'm not sure why the east wall and not any other walls. I need to ask Miss Flatshaw why.

"Everybody take your seats," Miss Flatshaw announced.

I always do what I'm told, so I sprang to my seat in a flash. Speaking of flash, there was a huge flash of lightning followed immediately by the loudest crack of thunder I'd ever heard. Then another, then another. I looked at Miss Flatshaw and her face turned white. That's when I noticed it.

Miss Flatshaw was sitting at her desk and a ball of fire was rolling along the floor towards her. It was about a foot in diameter, about the size of a chamber pot. It buzzed along the wooden floor with a hissing, crackling sound. Miss Flatshaw lifted her feet way up high so it wouldn't roll into them. Then it rolled under her chair to the back wall and disappeared. It left a burnt metal smell, kinda like the smell after the Jacksons' tool shed burned up with the plow and cultivator inside.

Later I found out that not everyone saw the burning ball; it was so fast, a few seconds at most. But Evelyn Hall, Dennis Hollenback, and Fritz Geist saw it too. If they hadn't, I woulda thought my eyes were playing tricks. Most of the other kids went to the windows to see if any trees were down. By then it was raining pitchforks and hammer handles, and you couldn't see nothing outside.

Miss Flatshaw continued to sit at her desk looking terrified.

"What was that fireball thing?" I asked her. She shook her head.

"God is punishing me," she whispered.

Nighttime

Tonight when I sat in the parlor reading my *Bible Story Book*, I kept thinking about why God would be punishing Miss Flatshaw. She's a lot like me. She does everything right. She's smart and a good teacher, and she agrees with me all the time. I think God must like her a lot.

Instead God should be punishing that awful bank robber John Dillinger. Or the bankers who got all Pa's money when the bank failed. Or the stingy people in town who don't buy Ma's eggs. That's who should be punished.

Nellie
Thursday, April 12, 1934
Afternoon

I love talking to my 'maginary friend ZeeZee. ZeeZee is from outer space and he sometimes flies around in our old bus taking it to far-off stars. In order to talk to ZeeZee I have to go down to the second meadow and lie down near the cabin ruins and the old bus. Then if I shut my eyes real tight ZeeZee jist may appear. Not always, cuz sometimes he's off on adventures.

The thing to remember 'bout ZeeZee is that he's still a kid but he's thousands of years old. His people take forever to grow up. ZeeZee likes to play with me and he's always telling stories of how he helps out people on other stars. He likes to find bad people and take them away so they don't hurt good people. Also, he don't like it when people don't have enough to eat so he takes his food machine with him and uses it to make food for them. The machine uses sunshine and water to make food. Kinda like our garden but without the soil.

ZeeZee is 'bout the nicest kid I know. He's kind and gentle with all the animals and he can speak lotsa animal languages. He does it by adjusting a little wheel he wears around his neck. I've watched him go from talking turtle to wolf to dog in a single minute.

Since I hadn't seen ZeeZee for a long time, I wanted to talk to him 'bout his latest adventures. I ran home from school real fast today and found Ma on the back stoop churning some butter.

"I'm gonna go to the second meadow to visit my 'maginary friends," I said. She looked at me and hesitated. I think she was gonna say no, but then she smiled at me and told me to take a gunnysack to lay on, so my coat wouldn't git all muddy like last time. Then she told me to have a good time but stay away from the woods. Like I wanna to see Gypsies again or find another dead baby. No Siree Bob.

So I skipped my way down to the second meadow, saying a quick hello to the cows who were standing in their usual place under the cherry trees. As I got close to the magical corner I noticed that a lot of grass had been smushed down in front of the door to the bus. It wouldn't have come from ZeeZee who is tiny and light on his feet. He can jump ten feet easy. So I ran over and peeked in the door. Instead of how it usually looks, all dirty with holes in the floor, I saw that there were boards over the floor and some blankets and gunnysacks on the seats toward the back. Maybe ZeeZee was making it more comfortable for when he travels.

I shut the door and walked over to the old fireplace ruins. That's usually where I lie down and talk to ZeeZee. But sometimes I see pirates, runaway slaves, and Indians, too. ZeeZee is my favorite but I do like my Indian friends, Yellow Feather and Broken Wing. They're boys who show me how to grind corn, string beads, and make arrows. They used to live down the crick a piece.

So today I took the gunnysack I had brought along to lie on, the ground being kinda cold and muddy. I carefully laid it down pretending there was a rip-roaring-hot fire in the remains of that fireplace. I warmed up right way when I closed my eyes and waited for ZeeZee to come.

Finally, he danced in front of my eyes. "Let's fly up to the oak tree and look at your part of the world," ZeeZee suggested. It's one of my favorite pretend things to do with him. He takes me by the hand and we fly right up to the top branch. I explain everything I see to him. For instance, he'd never heard of a smokehouse, where you put bacon and hams to cure. Neither did he know 'bout the ice house where Pa keeps ice until we use it in the kitchen icebox.

Today we looked down and ZeeZee started talking. "You and your sisters need to be careful, Nellie. There are dangerous things going on down there. I'm not around here much anymore so you need to take care of yourself."

With that I opened my eyes, still lying on the ground near the chimney ruins. Dang, even ZeeZee's no fun no more.

Flora
Thursday, April 12, 1934
Forenoon

That poor baby is on my mind a lot, even though Irene and Nellie have been getting nowhere with Gypsy information. I just wish I could talk to Henry about it. But Ma has made it clear many times that I'm not to say a word. I feel guilty enough about the Sisters' Club.

Well, I want to help Ma and Pa pay the mortgage and taxes. I want Henry to ask me out on a date every Saturday night. I want to have nice clothes and make-up. But none of this is happening. I understand how Aunt Caroline felt after the accident, flat on that bed, wanting to do stuff that she just couldn't do. I feel paralyzed too.

Henry and I have been seeing each other at school every day since our one and only date, but golly gee, he keeps apologizing that he don't have any money to take me out. I always tell him that's not a problem and that I don't have any money either. This isn't quite true because I have almost two dollars saved from egg money. Ma gave it to me a long time ago when she made lots of money peddling eggs. But I'm keeping it for a rainy day—or to help Ma and Pa with the taxes and mortgage. If I thought Henry would use it to take me to a movie or dance I'd give it to him. But he's too proud for that.

I was going to suggest that we go to the Camp Meeting down near Fonsha, but I'm so glad I didn't after I heard Brother Johnson preach. I was considering the Camp Meeting for a second date only because it would be a nice long ride and we could talk, both coming and going. And it would be free. But Brother Johnson clearly thinks his preaching is worth a lot of money: three collection plates' worth.

Camp Meeting keeps coming up in conversations. A couple of girls at my high school were talking about how, on a lark, they had gone to Camp Meeting. They were laughing and talking about rattlesnakes and how a man had been bitten by one. They said everyone got up and talked in Tongues and danced around in a frenzy yelling at the top of their lungs. I guess the girls just played along in order to blend in. I'm so glad that Henry and I didn't go there. Henry's a nice farm boy, not one to try weird things like that.

So Henry and I haven't had another date, but we do eat lunch together every day at school. We talk about our classes, our families, and the other students. I try to surprise him with a new topic of conversation every day, but that gets hard because each day is pretty much the same. Henry seems okay with eating lunch and not saying much.

Since I'm hoping to be Mrs. Fitch someday, I always try to talk to Henry's parents after church. I think it's important they get to know me. Also, I want Ma and Pa to get to know him. I've invited Henry over for Sunday dinner twice, but both times he declined. I'm not sure why. He just says he can't come. Too shy, I suspect.

A couple of times I've mentioned to him how I enjoyed talking to him on the park bench on that first and only date, hoping he would ask me to do that again. But if it weren't for the lunches I would be afraid that he's not interested at all. It's so darn confusing, this dating stuff.

Ma says to be patient about my future. She likes our President and his wife Eleanor and thinks he'll get the country out of the mess we're in. I'm afraid she may be wrong. Most of the farmers are worried because the President's solution for farmers is to slaughter their animals and not grow crops, getting a small subsidy for that. That just don't make sense to Henry or me. I know because I brought it up as a topic of conversation at lunch last Thursday.

Nighttime

I was so anxious to finish supper in order to hear what my sisters had found out about the baby. Nellie was chomping at the bit to tell us what she had heard from Fritz Geist and signaled with a quick finger in her ear. I saw it and nodded and later caught Irene's attention by putting my finger in my ear.

"Dang, if Fritz didn't tell me all he knew," Nellie said excitedly after we'd all landed on my bed after evening chores. I think she was happy about getting information that Irene couldn't. There's always some competition between my sisters.

"Well, what did he know?" Irene demanded.

"There's three families camped down by the Fairgrounds," Nellie answered. "And 'bout seven or eight kids, and the littlest ones all can walk and talk."

"Any stories about a new baby that died?" I asked.

"No, about three weeks ago when they rode their wagons in a caravan through town, Fritz saw them all. He was with his pa in town picking up some supplies. He stood by the street and looked at them as they drove by with their caravan of horses and wagons. No babies and no ladies in a family way. Fritz was certain of that."

"I wonder how he could be certain," I mused. Maybe Fritz, like Irene, likes to have all the answers whether or not he gets the facts straight.

"Any sad looking ladies?" I asked.

"No, but I think he saw the same three men who rode their horses down through the woods to the crick while I was in the oak tree. They were on their sick-looking horses along side the wagons with the others.

Irene
Thursday, April 12, 1934
Afternoon

One of my chores is to make bean sandwiches for the train riders who knock on the door and ask Ma for a bite to eat. The train riders are young men—boys, Ma says, usually around Flora's age, sixteen or seventeen. They can't find jobs so they ride on trains for fun and adventure. They come mostly from towns and cities cuz boys who live on farms need to stay home and work in the fields and help their fathers.

When the knock comes and Ma's not here we don't go to the door, so they leave without a sandwich. Ma always answers the knock, even if we don't have any beans in the crock. If we're outa beans she asks me to make sugar sandwiches for them. I love sugar sandwiches with fresh bread and lots of butter and sugar, so goo-ood. But Ma says bean sandwiches are more filling and will stick in their stomachs longer than sugar sandwiches.

Once I asked Ma why we give away sandwiches when we usually go to bed hungry. Supper is always tiny. Sometimes only a slice of bread.

"It's the Christian thing to do," she answered. "We have three small meals a day, but usually these boys have gone without food for two or three days. If they were my boys I'd want a farm family to give them a sandwich."

Last night I was reading my *Bible Story Book* in the parlor. I had the idea that I might overhear Ma and Pa with their secret conversations. It don't always work. Our Sisters' Club is trying to figure out more about the buried baby, and I wonder if Ma and Pa know anything more they're not telling.

Suddenly I heard Ma's voice. "Our girls are pretty, and with those Spring Lake girls gone missing," she said quietly to Pa. "Those train riders may have evil intentions. And how do they know to come here for a sandwich, even though the tracks are ten miles away in town? There are plenty of places to ask for a sandwich closer to the tracks." Ma was singing a different tune.

"I hear they make maps of the farms that give out food," Pa replied. "Also, there's a sign on Earl Lutz's gate with a cross and an arrow to our farm. Earl thinks the train riders put it there. Guess that means we're Christian folks and will help them out if we can. Besides nobody in town can give out food unless they have a half-acre garden like us. And no one in town has that much land."

"But I don't like strange men hanging around here," Ma said. "With the dead baby and those girls gone missing, it scares me to have strangers around. The train riders go out to the well and eat their sandwiches under the windmill," Ma continued. "I don't think I want them there."

"Then, tell them to fill up their cups with water and go over to the churchyard and eat," Pa replied.

"Well, yes, that's a good idea," Ma answered. "I want to keep giving those boys sandwiches," she said quietly. "I 'spect they're mostly good boys looking for work. They're always polite. But I still worry."

Their conversation was timely cuz today, right after we'd had our noonday dinner, two train riders showed up. Pa had gone out to do more plowing for the afternoon, and the two men came to the door and asked Ma for somethin' to eat. As usual she sent me to fetch two bean sandwiches. Ma told them to go fill up their cups at the well and she'd bring them the sandwiches. She didn't let me walk out to the windmill with her, like I had done in the past. So I snuck upstairs and peered out my little bedroom window that opens to the kitchen roof where you can see the windmill and the whole backyard. The window's on my side of the bed so I can sit and watch. There they were, the two of them, looking hungrily at the sandwiches.

Even though the window was closed I could hear Ma say, "You boys need to take your sandwiches and eat them at the church-yard down the road a piece. You'll see a farm on the right and then over a couple of hills is the church." She pointed east to-ward Unc Elmer's place and the church. "No one will bother you there. Just don't relieve yourselves in the churchyard and you'll be fine."

"Thank you, Ma'am," one of them said. "We'll be going right away. Neither of us has had food for two days, so we're pretty much ready to git to that churchyard."

"So how come you came to our farm?" Ma asked them as they picked up their cups and sandwiches.

"We heard that you was good Christian people," the other re-plied. "So are we. All we want is work and a paycheck."

"Well, keep it on the down-low," Ma answered. "There's a limit to the number of sandwiches we can hand out."

Both men nodded and repeated their "Thank-you Ma'ams."

I wondered if they would walk all the way to the church. If I hadn't eaten in two days, I'd be gobbling down that sandwich the moment I was outa Ma's sight.

Nellie
Saturday, April 14, 1934
Afternoon

After helping Aunt Hazel with beating her rugs this morning I wanted to play with Irene, Jake, and Alvin rounding up bank robbers for the corncrib jailhouse. But all three said I was too little to play. Usually my twin cousins are nicer to me than Irene. But today they ran off with Irene and I ran back home to eat dinner with Ma and Pa.

I was still feelin' bad for Ma Bear so I decided to take some honey and molasses to cheer her up. I'm still scared of the woods, but Ma Bear's den is west, not east. You can git there from the woods, but it takes a long time. My way is shorter.

I didn't take much honey cuz Ma has said over and over again that cuz the Wilsons lost their farm we won't have any more honey. Mr. Wilson had those honeybee boxes in his back yard and he always gave us lots and lots of jars of honey. We used to give them lots of apples and pears from our back orchard, so I guess it all evened out.

But, dang it, Ma Bear seemed so sad the last time I saw her. So I set out down the west lane toward the south fields, totally avoiding going anywhere near the east lane that goes to the first and second meadows, woods, and crick. I scooted under the fence near the lilacs and followed the path around the pond to the blackberry thicket, and saw her den underneath an overhanging boulder. Ma Bear warn't around, but I poured the honey and molasses on the flat stone near her sleeping spot, a nice worn round spot in the grass.

Then I hummed a song I knew she liked. It's a song without words—a sweet little song that reminds me of honey and molasses. Sure enough, in 'bout ten minutes, Ma Bear ambled over and sniffed the syrupy stuff on the stone. Then she started lapping it with her tongue. She jist had to have that sweet stuff.

Finally, after she had licked and licked that stone clean, she slowly walked back and lay down and looked at me. I knew that if she could smile, she would be smiling. I could tell she was still so very sad, but at least she had a little sweetness today.

Flora
Saturday, April 14, 1934
Forenoon

Today is my birthday and a Saturday. So cool! I slept in until there was so much noise downstairs I couldn't sleep another wink. Wondering what all the ruckus was about, I decided to get dressed and go downstairs. Unc Elmer and the younger two of my four cousins, Jake and Alvin, were in the kitchen with Pa.

"Happy Birthday," they all shouted out at once.

"Seventeen, I can't believe it," said Pa.

I felt giddy. Most times birthdays go unnoticed, except by the birthday person, so this was a nice surprise. "We brought you some biscuits for your breakfast," Jake announced. "Ma made extra ones jist for you."

"There's some strawberry jam, there too," Alvin added.

My mouth began to water just thinking about Aunt Hazel's biscuits and strawberry jam.

"Go ahead and eat them now," Pa said.

So I pulled a chair up to the table and started eating ever so slowly. I wanted this meal to last a long, long time. It's so rare to get three warm fluffy biscuits with jam. Most of the time we drink lots and lots of water with our meals and trick our stomachs into thinking that we're full after a really small meal.

"Where's everybody?" I asked.

"Ma and the girls went up to help Hazel with the housecleaning since they're having the Farm Bureau meeting at their place tonight."

"Oh, I'll go over and help, too," I offered automatically. Us girls have been raised to help out wherever and whenever. Growing up on a farm means there's always family or neighbors needing help. Specially these days when everybody's hard up.

"Well, Ma wants you to bake the bread instead," Pa answered. "I've already hauled a couple of pails of water," he said, pointing to the pails at the end of the table. "You won't have to carry water on your birthday." He smiled at me and I felt so happy.

Pa then added, "Irene and Nellie picked up and washed the eggs, so all that's left is the bread making."

I nodded. Heavenly. A quiet birthday with not much to do other than make six loaves of bread and watch them bake. I walked over to the large stone crock where Ma keeps the flour. There was just enough flour for six loaves, not a speck more. Just like Ma, I can eyeball the flour and tell whether there's enough.

"I'll be using all the flour," I told Pa.

"That's okay. I'm taking some wheat to the mill on Monday," he replied.

My little cousins had already gone outside to play, and Unc Elmer and Pa just kept sitting at the table talking about corn and wheat crops and whether there'd be enough rain this summer. I'd heard these conversations over and over during my childhood, and somehow the boring familiarity is comforting. I have to say I don't much like hearing stories about who's lost their farm or why President Roosevelt's programs and those farm subsidies aren't going to help the farmers.

I got busy making the bread, not really listening to their conversation. I think they also forgot that I was at the other end of the kitchen kneading the bread dough, rocking back and forth until it turned into that wonderful spongy, smooth ball. I love sprinkling flour on the breadboard so the dough won't stick and then the flour becomes part of the dough.

Rocking back and forth kneading the bread is so pleasant. I kept daydreaming about what I would do with my unexpected free time today. Play the piano for sure. Maybe walk over to

Jean's house. Think about some topics of conversation for my lunchtimes with Henry.

I was so caught up in my daydreams that I was startled when I heard Unc Elmer's voice. "Yesterday I noticed that a garden hoe and some gunnysacks have gone missing. I 'spect the Gypsies are back."

That's old news, I thought. But I just kept quiet, listening to them talk.

"Gotta be real careful," Unc went on. "The Gypsies sneak into barns at night and take stuff. If Rover barks be sure and get out to the barn fast—and take your shotgun to scare them off.

"I didn't pay attention," Unc Elmer continued. "Daisy was barking a lot on Wednesday night. I just figured it was a coon or something. The thieves musta been out in the tool shed and got the stuff, but Daisy scared them off before they could take much of anything else."

Pa looked at me and saw that I was listening. "You warn your sisters about this," Pa said. "We all need to be on the look out."

Nighttime

Another Saturday night at home and my seventeenth birthday, to boot. As much as I've hinted to Henry that we can go on dates that don't cost any money, he hasn't taken the bait. So it's one more dateless Saturday night for me. I just don't understand why Henry didn't figure out something special for a birthday night out. I'd talked about turning seventeen enough times this week. Maybe he just don't like me as much as I like him.

Ma says to be patient and he'll come around. After all, I see him every day at school, and he's with his family every Sunday at church. Well, I guess I'm just not that patient. I want to be asked out to movies and dances. I want to dress up and wear rouge and lipstick. My friend Jean has shown me how to wave my hair and look hip. But unless I have somewhere to go, no one will see it.

So tonight I sat in the kitchen and played rummy with Irene and Nellie while Ma and Pa went up to the Farm Bureau meeting. I figured I'd stay up until they came home. I was hoping Ma and Pa would bring me a bit of Aunt Hazel's bread pudding.

Finally, long after Irene and Nellie had gone to bed and I was just sitting around in the kitchen finishing my homework and re-reading an old magazine that Jean had given me months ago, I heard them in the driveway.

"Birthday girl, here's some bread pudding for you," Ma sang out as she walked in the kitchen.

"Oh, thank you," I answered.

Ma sat down and joined me while I savored the sweet dessert.

"I know you're disappointed that you didn't do anything special tonight," she commented.

I nodded, not wanting to talk about it. It would be so easy to burst out in tears.

"Well, Flora, just you wait. Your time's a comin'. It may be with Henry or it may be with someone else. You're a beautiful, smart, hard-working young lady with a lovely disposition. You don't ever have to worry about not finding somebody. You've got lots of time. You may not think so tonight, but I guarantee there's no reason to be feeling sorry for yourself. Go to bed now, and you can get yourself real pretty for church tomorrow."

Irene
Monday, April 16, 1934
Forenoon

May Hendrick was back at school today after having scarlet fever for over three months. "You need a new sweater," she said to me before school started, poking her finger into one of the holes near my right elbow. She's so annoying. As if her clothes are in better shape than mine. "Don't you know how to darn?" she said. It wasn't even a question, just a nasty comment.

"Well, don't you know how to bathe?" I answered. "I betcha it's been a month since you've seen a wash tub. Also, you need to lose weight. You must hog all the food from your little sister and brother."

"Fix your sweater," she answered, ignoring my comments. "The sweater's threadbare and you don't even care."

Actually, she's right; it is worn out. So what? It's my favorite sweater and I'm gonna wear it. It's red and has little flowers that I embroidered on it last year. I wear it every day except in the summer.

May Hendrick should talk. Last year she had lice and I never said a word. She didn't tell me, of course. I found out when Ma made me wash my head. It took almost two hours cuz I had to heat the water over the stove first. I wasn't gonna wash my head in that cold cistern water the way Ma does; cistern water is real, real cold mosta the year. After the head washing, Ma combed and combed, looking at every strand. Ma hates lice. She made me promise never to tell May that I knew she had lice, so I didn't. I always keep my promises, but a lot of people don't. Why can't everyone be good like me?

Last year when May had her monthlies I could smell it every month. I told Flora about it and she said that May didn't change her rags enough, cuz you can't smell it otherwise. That was probably the case cuz I even saw some blood stains on the back of her dresses. This year I didn't smell her, so I guess she was being more careful. But today I just couldn't help but make the bathing comment.

My sister Flora takes real good care of herself when she has her monthlies. She washes out the rags every night and puts them on the clothesline herself, even when the weather is terrible. She usually does it on the way to the privy. You'd never know Flora is having her monthlies and she don't want anyone to know. I'm gonna be just like Flora, nice and neat and clean.

Our family never skips Saturday night baths. Ma sees to that. She gets out the washtub and heats the water on the cook stove and then brings out the lard soap. It's all set up in the kitchen right next to the cookstove so it's cozy warm. Nellie is first, then me, then Flora, then Ma, then Pa. Pa jokes about how he comes out of the bath dirtier than when he started. Ma just rolls her eyes each time he tells that same joke. Besides, she always adds a lot more hot water for him. It just don't stay hot through five baths.

Speaking of jokes and baths, one Saturday last summer we all were taking our baths early cuz we were gonna go to the Geists' for a barn dance. Barn dances are always before hay season. You can't have a barn dance after haying cuz the haymow is filled with hay. Anyway, just as Pa was getting in the washtub, Aunt Hazel burst into the kitchen with a big bowl of raspberries. Was she surprised to find Pa bare naked! Even though he is her brother she was so embarrassed that now she always knocks on the door, even if she has already seen Pa in the yard.

So anyway, this morning May Hendrick was making fun of my sweater. I don't care if the elbows are worn and the sleeves too short. May is always finding fault. As if she has nice clothes. Just like me, she wears hand-me-downs, mainly from her mother cuz she don't have any older sisters.

May's family don't own a farm. The Hendricks are the only kids at school who aren't farm kids. They rent a tiny house on the corner of the Blankenship farm. I was there once. They have two rooms: a kitchen for cooking and eating and the other for sleeping. They ain't got no parlor or dining room, but they do have a cellar where May says her father sleeps after he's been drinking. I don't play with May much cuz she's three years older than me, even though she's only two grades ahead of me. Too many differences between us, Ma says. Ma don't much like the Hendricks. Maybe cuz of the lice.

Afternoon

At supper I told everybody that May Hendrick was back in school. Flora looked up, and I could tell she was surprised. Guess she didn't know about May.

"She had scarlet fever," I said. "The kind of scarlet fever you can't catch," I added.

"What?" Flora asked.

"The kind you can't catch," I repeated. "Another kind of scarlet fever."

"Yeah," Nellie chimed in. "She was out of school a long time. I wonder if she'll flunk eighth grade, like she did fifth."

"She got fat, too," I added. "She musta laid in bed and ate and ate the whole time she was sick."

Ma and Pa seem startled. I saw them looking at each other but not saying anything.

Ma finally spoke up, "Irene, be kind. That's not a nice thing to say about someone who's been sick."

"Well, today she kept telling me my sweater had holes in it," I replied.

"That's cuz it does," Nellie responded.

"Well, she wasn't nice about the holes. She was making fun of me."

"Now girls," Ma began again. "Let's have no more talk about May Hendrick."

Flora quietly put her little finger in her ear, like she was itching it. Later, when we were cleaning up from supper, both Nellie and I signaled back to Flora. Soon we were up in her room.

Nighttime

I felt so good, being the sister with the information this time. And it was so comfy on Flora's bed snuggling up close to my two sisters. Since I was the sister who had news, I decided to start out.

"Well, May was gone over three months, but before that she was getting fat. Miss Flatshaw would walk her out to the privy both in the morning and afternoon in addition to recess," I announced.

"Did she have her monthlies?" Flora asked me.

Nellie looked confused and whispered, "This has nuthin' to do with a baby. Absolutely nuthin'. Girls get their monthlies when they turn thirteen and they get taller, too. Why not May?"

"Well, we have another suspect," Flora announced in a reglar, non-whispering voice, ignoring Nellie: "May Hendrick."

"No, no," Nellie whispered back rather loudly. "May ain't married. No husband. No baby."

Flora immediately said to Nellie, "You're right. We should keep trying to find out more about the Gypsies. Has anyone told you more stories about them?"

Nellie shook her head.

"Let's keep looking for a married Gypsy lady who had a baby," Flora said. "Sisters' Club is dismissed."

Nellie and I ran back downstairs to the kitchen where Nellie started reading her *Pirate Book*. I pretended to look for my book but ran right back up to Flora's room.

"Did May throw up a lot?" Flora asked me when I came back.

"Only for a few weeks when she had the flu," I answered.

Flora shot me a serious look. "She came to school with the flu?"

"Well, yes, but she wasn't so sick. Besides she said she didn't wanna flunk eighth grade. She wants to go to high school next year."

"See what you can find out from Miss Flatshaw and I'll ask Jean, if she's heard any rumors about May," Flora answered. "Also, ask May's little sister JoEllen about her. It might all fit together. If she was expecting, and her baby was born dead, she could have buried it in the woods. Easy peasy. Case solved."

"Well, no more easy peasy for her," I shot back. "That's not how good Christian people bury babies. They go to church and confess, and they make sure the baby has a proper burial. No ifs, ands, or buts about it."

Nellie
Tuesday, April 17, 1934
Afternoon

The weather's been so gray and cold and everybody's mood is sour. I keep wondering where we'll go if we lose the farm. Pa says not to worry, that we'll have a good summer harvest. But how does he know? Losing the farm is on everybody's mind.

Maybe we could move in with Aunt Hazel and Unc Elmer, but what if they lost their farm, too? Besides, even if they don't lose their farm, they already use all of their bedrooms. Where would we sleep? Sleeping in their barn might be okay in the summer but in the winter it would be mighty cold. Even Daisy gits to sleep in their kitchen on cold winter nights. Same with Rover at our house.

Me, I jist wanna go down to the crick and git away from all the worries, but I hate the thought of going through the woods to git there. The crick's always been a special place to play. But now even going down to the cabin ruins is kinda scary. Still, I've been missing my 'maginary friend, ZeeZee and that's the only place he comes to see me.

So right after school today I decided to go down to the second meadow and see if ZeeZee would come say hello. I went straight to my usual spot near the cabin ruins by the fireplace, lay down, shut my eyes and waited a while.

I heard ZeeZee's voice. "Hey, Nellie."

I kept my eyes shut but I could see him. He was wearing his little pajama outfit that covers him head to foot. It's kinda a gold-silver color that reflects rainbow colors, a fabric like none I've ever seen. He always wears it, never anything else. It don't have any buttons either. So nice—never having to sew on a button.

"ZeeZee," I answered. "I'm so happy to see you. Can we fly up to the top of the oak tree together?" This is my favorite thing to do with ZeeZee. So we flew up to the top branch where we could look out over the whole world. Once we were up there he told me 'bout flying the bus off to some stars and catching some bank robbers there. After he caught them he dropped them from the sky right down in front of the jail.

I jist love my 'maginary time with ZeeZee.

Irene
Tuesday, April 17, 1934
Afternoon

Since Nellie don't know about how ladies get in a family way, it was my burden to find out anything I could about May. Why beat around the bush? So at lunch time when Miss Flatshaw and I were eating our sandwiches, I asked her outright.

"Did May really have a baby instead of scarlet fever? Cuz I know there's no such thing as a scarlet fever you can't catch."

Miss Flatshaw looked at me with her annoyed face. Her eyes looked into mine and she pursed her lips and stuck out her neck. She said nothing.

I felt like I had to give a reason for my asking. "Well, people do leave to go places but they don't lie about it. My sister Flora went all the way to Iowa last year after my Aunt Caroline was in a buggy accident and broke a lot of bones. Ma and Pa sent here there to help Uncle Lester and their boys. She took care of Aunt Caroline, too."

Miss Flatbush cleared her throat. "Well, I can't be saying anything about one of my students, but it is true that scarlet fever is a terrible disease and you can catch it from other people—always. But I'm not telling you anymore about May."

"Why?" I asked, wanting her to talk more. But Miss Flatshaw didn't say a word, so I continued.

"She got fat before she left school," I added, hoping Miss Flatshaw would take the bait.

Instead Miss Flatshaw snapped back at me, "You're Miss High and Mighty, making judgments about people who have put on a few pounds. Do you talk about me behind my back?"

I winced. "No, of course not. You're my best friend. I don't care what people weigh, but May is strange."

"Well, Irene, I'm not saying another word."

I so wanted Miss Flatshaw to name May's sickness out loud. But she didn't.

Later on I asked May's sister JoEllen about May's illness.

"Scarlet fever," she answered.

"But how come you can't catch it?"

She shrugged. I think she believed the scarlet fever story.

Nighttime

Tonight I went to Flora's bedroom without Nellie. I was bursting to spill the beans, but Flora beat me to it.

"Jean told me today that she heard from a friend that May Hendrick had left town. That's all I know, but don't tell Nellie. It could upset her. Ma would have our hides if Nellie knew."

"I won't tell Nellie," I answered.

"So here's what I think," Flora went on. "May had a wild evening out. Then to cover it all up she told everyone she had scarlet fever and when the baby was born dead she buried it down in the woods. What do you think?"

I nodded. "I 'spect you're right. Miss Flatshaw let the cat out of the bag that May didn't really have scarlet fever. But she wouldn't say any more than that."

"I wonder why Miss Flatshaw didn't tell you," Flora said. "She usually tells you everything."

"She sure wasn't gonna say anything about May this morning," I repeated.

"Well, I imagine we'll be hearing more about May through the grapevine," Flora added. "Let's just sit tight for a few days, keeping our eyes and ears open."

"May's not very smart," I added. "She can hardly read and do arithmetic. Miss Flatshaw's been passing her each year out of the kindness of her heart." I paused. "Oops, I wasn't posta tell anyone that. Keep that a secret."

Flora
Thursday, April 19, 1934
Afternoon

Golly gee, did I ever have a good time with Jean after school to-day, so different from the gloomy mood at my house. Because I eat lunch with Henry every day now, I haven't seen much of Jean and I miss our good times together. This morning Ma made me promise again not to talk to Jean about the baby incident. That's okay. I just want to laugh with my friend.

Jean and I walked from high school to her house. It's a little more than halfway to our farm. When I got there Jean showed me her new magazines and then we listened to some songs on the radio. She begged me to play them on the piano, and I plunked them out. They were all romantic songs about love: *Did You Ever See a Dream Walking*; *Night and Day*; and *Stormy Weather*. She knew most of the words and taught them to me. We sang so loud that we both started laughing.

Then she pulled me into her bedroom and started whispering.

"Now that you're seeing Henry all the time, tell me how it is. Do you kiss? Do you do anything else?"

I just shrugged and replied, "Nothing. Nothing. Nothing. We only see each other at lunchtime. That's it. No kisses, ever. And it's not because of me. I want to kiss, but the only time I see him is at lunch. We only had that one date and you already know about that."

Jean frowned. "I wanted to find out how babies are made," she whispered. I could tell she was nervous and embarrassed.

"I can tell you what happens without actually doing it." I laughed. "I've lived on a farm my whole life. You just see things and figure it out."

"Well, I haven't," Jean whispered, a little defensively. "We just grow fruit and vegetables here. You know that."

"Okay," I answered. "Let's shut your door in case your mother walks by."

Jean jumped up and shut her bedroom door in a split second.

Then I started whispering to her. I told her about boys' bodies. She'd taken care of her four-year-old cousin Dale many times since he was born, so she knew a little about that. Then I went on to talk about cows, pigs, sheep, and even horses.

Jean was astonished. "You mean when those horses jump on each other for a piggy back ride they're actually DOING IT?" she exclaimed.

I nodded yes.

"Well, how about people?" she then asked.

"They do it in bed," I answered. "But nobody talks about it. When Nellie asked Ma about it a few weeks ago, Ma just hemmed and hawed until Nellie finally went outside to play with Rover. It's treated like a big mystery."

"But how did you find out about the in-bed stuff?" Jean quizzed me.

"Listening to Ma and Aunt Hazel talking. They used to ignore me when I was little and took my nap, so lots of times I would close my eyes and listen to them before I actually fell asleep. Ma said she didn't want any more kids, but Pa always wanted to snuggle up in bed. Aunt Hazel said she couldn't say 'No' to Unc Elmer and my twin cousins are the result. It took me a while to put two and two together."

Then Jean and I just started giggling until we couldn't stop. We were laughing out loud so much that Jean's mother knocked on the door, opened it, and asked, "What's the joke?"

Jean paused for a couple of seconds. Then she said to her mother, "Flora told me a joke about Opperknockitty, the piano tuner."

"Oh, that's an old one," Mrs. Spinatti replied with a smile. "Opperknockitty tunes but once."

Jean and I burst out laughing again, relieved that we had pulled that off. A few minutes later Mrs. Spinatti brought us some oatmeal cookies.

"It's so nice to hear laughter. There's so little these days," Mrs. Spinatti said, handing Jean the plate of six cookies. Still giggling, we ate all the cookies. I can't remember when I've had three cookies all at once. It's so rare to have even one. It was heavenly to be seeing Jean again. I didn't realize how much I miss her. We used to play together every day at our country school.

Nighttime

Ma talked to me after I got back from Jean's today. She seemed happy to hear that I had such a good time, but she also quizzed me if I had said anything to Jean about the baby.

"Of course not," I answered. "You already told me not to say a word."

Jeepers, did I feel guilty about all the Sisters' Club meetings. But we deserve to know. Nellie was so upset the day she found the dead baby.

Next, Ma went into a tirade about my sisters. "Flora, you've gotta be responsible for your sisters. You're my oldest and you know that in these bad times there are so many more threats out there than when you were their ages. Keep an eye out for them. Irene thinks she's knows everything and, Nellie, she don't understand what the world's like. You gotta be a big sister and make sure they don't get hurt."

I think Ma had rehearsed this conversation. I'd heard it from her before, but never so directly. At age ten Ma took care of Aunt Caroline who was only four, so I understand how she thinks I'm plenty old enough to watch over my sisters. Still, it's not a job I want.

Ma went on. "Also, Irene seems to backtalk a lot, and Nellie is always in her own little world talking to animals and making up crazy stories. They both could use some guidance from you."

"But I'm in school most of the day," I answered her. "How am I gonna watch out for them when we're at different schools?"

"You can pay more attention after school and in the evening," Ma replied. "Make a point of talking to them at suppertime. Tell them to always be careful when they're alone. Point out if Irene is getting sassy or if Nellie is daydreaming too much."

"Okay," I sighed, thinking that this was gonna be impossible. How was I gonna change the personalities of my sisters? Like I have nothing better to do than be another parent. I wanna spend my time playing the piano and figuring out my next conversation with Henry.

At suppertime I announced to both my sisters to meet in my bedroom right after evening chores. Ma beamed. I'm sure she thought I was taking her seriously. Nellie and Irene both looked up and smiled, too. Guess they thought we were going to have a Sisters' Club meeting.

When they got up to my bedroom and piled on the bed, I asked Nellie and Irene what new information they had. "I've been thinking about May and wondering if that no good father of hers had his way with her," I said. Nellie looked confused. "Never mind," I told her.

But Irene was slowly nodding her head in the background. "May's whole family sleeps in that one room," Irene said. "I'll ask JoEllen about it."

"Miss Flatshaw said there was a rumor that the Spring Lake Girls ran away cuz they were bad," Nellie chimed in. "Bad girls might bury a baby in the woods," she continued. "Where do you think they are now? I wonder if they went to California or some place like that."

We all left the meeting with more questions than answers.

Irene
Tuesday, April 24, 1934
Forenoon

Finding that baby was the beginning of a lot of bad luck for a lot of people. Miss Flatshaw told me another secret: the Hollenbacks are losing their farm so Dennis won't be back next fall. She don't know where they're gonna go. I felt bad cuz I thought Dennis might become my boyfriend next year. He don't talk to me now, but you know how quickly things change.

Flora has such fun having a boyfriend. She spends a lot of time getting ready for high school every day cuz she eats lunch with Henry. Ma even gave her some rouge to wear on her cheeks. I would like to wear rouge and get all dolled up just like Flora. I wonder if Fritz Geist might become my boyfriend. But Fritz don't talk to me either, and Miss Flatshaw said it's Fritz who farts those stinky silent ones in the afternoon. She knows cuz he's the only one who eats onion sandwiches every day. So my prospects for a boyfriend ain't looking so good. Maybe there will be a new boy at the Hollenback farm next year.

But bad luck was hanging heavy over our neck of the woods and wouldn't go away. The day after I heard about the Hollenback farm, Jimmy Geist fell into their cistern and drowned. Poor little Jimmy, he just didn't know any better. Ma looked so sad the night Pa told us about it. I guess he let us girls hear the news so we'd steer clear of our cistern. Like I'm ever gonna go near that thing. Ma has warned and warned us about falling in. And I do what I'm told. Amen.

The next day Ma made noodles and gravy for the Geists and took it over to them. Ma and Pa didn't let us girls go to the funeral cuz it was during school time, but I saw the fresh grave when we went to church last Sunday. It was so tiny. Mrs. Geist cried all through the church service. I could see Ma holding back tears. Nellie, too.

Then more bad luck. Yesterday a fox got into our chicken yard and killed all the young chicks. The older laying hens were roosting in the chicken coop so they were spared. Ma was crying when Pa got back from the fields and she told him the bad news. Pa just shook his head and proceeded to clean up all the dead chicks. I'm glad he didn't ask me to do it. I love watching Ma dress roosters for Sunday dinners, but these were baby chicks, only a few weeks old, most of them still had some of that yellow fuzz. I just didn't want to get near them and their soft little broken bodies.

Preparing the rooster for Sunday dinner starts on Saturday afternoon when Pa chooses an old rooster and gets the ax and chops off its head on the stump near the driveway. It's a stump from an old hickory tree that used to be a huge tree when Pa was a little kid. Once the rooster's head is chopped off, he takes it to the middle of the driveway and throws it towards the milk house. The rooster then dances around the driveway in all kinds of crazy directions.

This used to be fun to watch. I loved watching it gyrate around the driveway until it finally fell down dead. However, last Saturday afternoon the headless rooster flew right towards me. I started running and it followed me so I decided to run in circles and I changed directions three or four times. But the headless rooster kept following me. Finally after circling and circling I ran inside the milk house and slammed the door. There's still a bloody mark on the door where that rooster hit. Pa thought it was funny, but, believe me, from now on I'll keep my distance from those headless roosters.

There are so many different smells with each stage of preparing a rooster for Sunday dinner. Flora always gags at the singeing and the dressing. But me and Nellie watch every single stage. My favorite part is when Ma cleans out the gizzard. There's usually corn and other stuff in there so you can see what the rooster's been eating. I also like it when she pulls out the heart and liver. She puts all of them aside and cooks them separately for Pa.

The loss of the chicks means loss of money this year cuz Ma won't be able to peddle near as many eggs. Ma said we'll have to cut way back on our spending. When I asked what things are there to cut back on, she slapped me and said to quit sassing her. I shut up fast. But frankly she don't spend any money at all. Just sugar, salt, and a few other items like molasses and baking powder. Ma don't buy coffee no more, but I can't stand coffee anyway.

Two days after the fox killed the chicks, Pa said that we wouldn't be having rooster for Sunday dinner no more. With no chicks to raise, and the loss of egg money, we'd be selling the rest of the roosters, 'cept for the two youngest ones. I wanted to cry. That's my favorite Sunday meal.

"I'll go with Elmer and the boys and hunt rabbit, coon, and squirrel," he told Ma. I wasn't happy to hear that. Squirrels just don't have much meat, and it's all greasy and bony. I can't stand coon; it tastes horrible. Rabbit is okay but not nearly as tasty as rooster, and it's rubbery. No, there's nothing better than rooster for Sunday dinner.

Every now and then I think Pa regrets not having boys, but Unc Elmer and my four boy cousins help us a lot, especially during haying and threshing. Ma makes sure that us girls help out Aunt Hazel in her house. We're always going up there to help with the baking, mending, and house cleaning. Ma says she loves having girls, and she couldn't bear having to send a son off to war.

After the Great War and all the horrible things about it, I doubt there will be any more wars. Ma's Uncle Ernest died in the Great War. Ma loved him and talks about him a lot, even though she won't talk about her brother Fred who died from lockjaw when he was twelve.

I asked Ma about the baby buried in the woods, right after she'd been talking about Uncle Ernest, but she turned stone silent and wouldn't talk about it. "Just hush up," she said. "No one's gonna talk about it, and for heaven's sake, don't tell Miss Flatshaw." For some reason Ma don't like Miss Flatshaw the way I do. Maybe it troubles Ma that Miss Flatshaw tells me secrets.

Nellie
Tuesday, May 1, 1934
Forenoon

Today is May Day, the day you make little bouquets and secretly leave them on people's doorsteps. It's posta make people happy and our family certainly needs some happiness. After I got home from school I made ones for Ma, Irene, Flora, and Aunt Hazel. Even though it was sprinkling outside I went out in the front yard and picked violets and lily of the valley. Then I looked and looked until I found four dandelions, so I could put one in the middle of each bouquet. Last year the lilacs were way early and I used those cuz they smell so good. I love lilac bouquets.

Ma knew what I was doing so she gave me some little cups with water so the flowers wouldn't wilt. Actually dandelions don't last long, even when they're in water, but they have such a nice yellow color and look so purty right in the center of the bouquet. So I put Ma's on the kitchen table, Flora's on her bedroom dresser and Irene's right outside our bedroom on the little landing. Ma let me go up to Aunt Hazel's by myself, but she said to run both coming and going and not to talk to any strangers.

Last year Aunt Hazel gave the vase back to me the following week filled with horehound candies. The first candy tasted kinda strange, but I got used to it and I really liked the second one and the third. I gave one each to Ma, Pa, Flora, and Irene, and there was still another one left for me. I think Aunt Hazel had counted them out carefully. She's the best aunt ever.

I did make the mistake of calling the candies, hore-candy. I thought Pa was gonna whip me, right then and there, but Ma came to the rescue, telling Pa that I didn't even know that word.

I was confused cuz I thought I had the right name for them. Ma told me again the name for them is horehound. So I won't ever call them hore-candy again. Still I wonder what hore-candy is. I asked Irene and she didn't know. Maybe she'll ask Miss Flatshaw for me. I 'spect it's a swear word.

I've learned a lot of swear words from our neighbor, Mr. Lutz, who swears at his cows jist 'bout every day and I've memorized all the bad words he uses. I have no idea why he gits so mad at his cows. They seem to be nice cows. Our cows really like to come up the lane to git milked every afternoon. Nobody has to use bad words to git our cows rounded up and ready to milk. All you have to do is say, "Here bossy, come bossy, here bossy," and they come. Sometimes I yell, "Here bossy, bossy, bossy," and they come, too. Pa taught me that.

You say, "Here sooie, sooie, sooie" to call the pigs and "Here chick, chick, chick" to call the chickens. Chickens come a lot faster if you throw some cracked corn on the ground when you call them. Rover comes if you say, "Rover, come." The cats don't seem to come 'cept if you show them you have some food, and mosta the time we don't give them anything. They're posta catch mice to eat. I still have a lot to learn 'bout all the animals, but they do a good job of telling me what they want. Food is at the top of the list, jist like for people. If someone holding a cherry pie in front of me would call, "Here Nellie, Nellie, Nellie," I'd sure as shoot come running.

When I arrived at Aunt Hazel's back porch to deliver the May Day flowers, Unc Elmer was working on fixin' some chicken wire near their chicken coop. He said to hide if I see any Gypsies when walking home. I asked how I would know if they were Gypsies. He said they'd be riding skinny sick-looking horses and talking a strange language. Well, that settles that.

Flora
Tuesday, May 1, 1934
Afternoon

When I got home from school today I immediately went upstairs to see if Nellie had made me a May Day bouquet, and there it was on the dresser, the dandelion in the center all wilted. It warmed my heart. Life has been so goll-darned gloomy these past few weeks. I so appreciated that little bouquet.

Nighttime

I gave the Sisters' Club signal at supper tonight even though I didn't have anything new to report, but I was hoping my sisters did.

"JoEllen don't know anything about May," Irene said. "She really seems to believe May had scarlet fever and went away to get well."

"Where'd she go?" I asked.

"Detroit."

"Why Detroit?"

"Her Aunt Rose lives there."

"Hmm," I thought. I betcha her Aunt Rose knows more about this. How could we talk to her? I could send a letter, but I doubt if she'd answer it, particularly if she was covering up for May. And then there's the matter of getting an envelope and a stamp.

"What have you two found out about the Gypsies and the Spring Lake girls?" I asked, changing the subject.

"The Gypsies keep to themselves," Irene answered. I wrote a report on the Gypsies cuz I kept telling Miss Flatshaw that I wanted to.

"They get married very young and usually their parents chose who they are going to marry. It's all very crazy. There's rumors that they steal children and have strange rituals at night around campfires. Miss Flatshaw said there are stories that they kill babies as a sacrifice."

"Like in the Bible?" Nellie asked.

Irene nodded her head. "It made me wonder if the baby was murdered and then buried. Kinda a weird religious thing?"

I shuddered. "What else did you find out?"

"They call themselves Roma and they take stuff they need, but they don't think of it as stealing, but really it is. They don't take more than they need."

"Kinda like my Indian friends," Nellie chimed in. Both Irene and I ignored her.

"Where do the Gypsies bury people?" I asked.

"Usually where they camp. They want their families to be near them. They cry and make a lot of noise when someone dies. According to Fritz the Gypsies camped in town aren't in mourning. Nobody died."

Irene
Tuesday, May 1, 1934
Nighttime

I didn't even see the bouquet until I went up to bed. Nellie thinks she's so special cuz she made me a May Day bouquet. It was all wilted and the dandelion had fallen apart. She shoulda known better than to include dandelions. When I came up to bed and found it on the landing, she yelled out, "Surprise, Happy May Day." Well, number one, it wasn't a surprise. Ma had reminded me to thank her for it, and number two, she didn't put enough water in the cup.

So I had to pretend to be surprised and happy about an old, wilted bouquet. Nellie laughed and laughed when I came through the door carrying it. I guess the May Day treat was really for her and not me. I never made May Day baskets myself even though Ma encouraged me. It just seemed like a waste of time.

Well, Miss Flatshaw and I are getting along okay again. For a few days she was stand-offish cuz of my asking about May. So I went home each day for lunch and Nellie did too. But now Miss Flatshaw and I are eating our lunches together every day as usual. I like things being back to normal.

Irene
Monday, May 7, 1934
Afternoon

I can't believe the secret Miss Flatshaw told me today. At noon we went into the woodshed where we were all alone and she made me promise that I wouldn't tell a soul. I can't tell no one, not even my parents, not my sisters, no one. The woodshed was a brand-new place for secret-sharing. Miss Flatshaw and I tell each other secrets all the time, but we usually whisper at her desk or on the schoolhouse steps. After I agreed to not to tell anyone, she made me promise twice more. So I did. I'm good at promise-keeping and I didn't think much about it. Not until she spoke.

"Irene, there are some horrible rumors going around about your sister Flora," she said in her deep secret whisper that is so familiar. But her words were not. "Rumor has it that a baby was found buried back on your farm and people are talking about Flora in an unkind way. They think Flora got herself in a family way when she was in Iowa last year."

I gasped. "No, No, No," I exclaimed way too loud. I jumped up ready to leave the woodshed, but I stopped myself. "Who said that?" I asked her in my reglar voice. I wanted to make sure I heard right. "Who said it and what did they mean?"

"Well..." Miss Flatshaw puffed herself up pulling her head back, pursing her lips, and looking me straight in the eyes, "They think Flora has been up to no good. It's as simple as that." She then drew her lips up into a big smile across her face just like she was sharing some fine thing about my sister. "I can't tell you anymore," she concluded. "But your sister should behave better. She certainly hasn't been acting like a good Christian girl."

"No, you got it all wrong," I shouted at her. "Why are you saying that about Flora? It's a lie." I figured any kids playing outside
the woodshed could hear me, but I didn't care.

"Well, your sister was gone almost a year. So how do you really know it's not true? You need to be warned that your own
behavior will be judged by your sister's," she added. "People have
been calling her *Jezebel* behind her back."

I couldn't believe what I was hearing. I left the woodshed
stunned. Miss Flatshaw headed for the schoolhouse and I walked
over and sat under the big boxelder tree in a state of shock. My
mind raced. Could Miss Flatshaw be right? Flora sometimes
makes me mad, but she's a real good girl. She's like Ma in that
she takes her religion seriously. No way was that baby Flora's.
But what am I to do? I promised Miss Flatshaw three times to
keep her secret. I have kept every single one of our secrets, always. This is gonna be a rough one for me.

Flora
Wednesday, May 9, 1934
Afternoon

Something's been puzzling me. There's been a lot of whispering going on at school. At lunch while we were eating our sandwiches I asked Henry if he noticed it, but he said he didn't. He said whispering just isn't important to him and not to pay attention to it. But, I still wonder.

Then after school, Jean came over to my locker and told me that we had to talk.

"Okay, let's talk," I answered.

"No, not here," she said, looking around the hall where all the students were putting on their coats. "We need to go somewhere private."

"What?"

"We need to go somewhere private," she repeated.

"Well, where?" I answered. I was annoyed. "I need to meet up with Dan and Dalton in about five minutes for my ride home."

"Well, let's go tell them you're walking home today," she answered. So we went out to the gravel lot and found them. Then Jean and I started walking out Green Lake Road toward her farm. It's about two miles from our farm on the same road.

"Someone's out to hurt you," Jean finally spoke up.

"Hurt me?"

"Yes, spreading lies and awful rumors."

"What do you mean?" I questioned her.

"Well, I'm gonna be blunt and tell you everything I know," she answered. "And I want you to know that I don't believe a word of it." She paused before continuing. "There's a rumor going 'round that a buried baby was found in one of your back fields and that it was your baby, Flora." She looked at me straight in the eye.

I was so shocked I couldn't say a word. I looked at Jean again to see if she was joking. Her face looked so serious.

"Who hates you so much that they would ruin your reputation?" she asked

I simply shook my head in disbelief. "Who hates you that much?" she repeated.

"No one," I answered. "No one hates me. I haven't hurt anyone. Why would anyone do this to me?"

"Well, they have, and people are talking."

We kept walking and I kept shaking my head. I couldn't believe this was happening. Had Ma and Pa found out? A ruined reputation is the worst thing that can happen to a girl and Ma has been careful to let me know that over and over and over again.

I shook my head, not knowing what to say. Ma had told me not to mention the baby to anyone, but my whole life was on the line. We walked in silence for about ten minutes as I kept shaking my head in disbelief. My whole body was trembling. I dropped my books twice and Jean took them from me and carried them along with her own.

"Okay," I answered, sucking in a deep breath. "I'm gonna tell you everything I know even though I promised Ma I wouldn't tell a soul." I inhaled deeply. Once again I was going against Ma and Pa and I felt terrible. But, gosh darn it, Jean deserved to know.

I proceeded to tell Jean the whole story, starting with Nellie, then moving on to Pa, Unc Elmer and Sheriff Devlon and then to Ma's prohibition of any of us girls talking about it.

Jean seemed visibly relieved to hear the story. "But why did your mother forbid you to tell anyone?" she asked.

I shrugged. "She's superstitious. She wanted the whole thing to go away. Just like it never happened. It was such a horrible day for all of us, 'specially Nellie. Nellie was so upset."

"Who was upset?" Jean asked. "Nellie or your mother?"

"Nellie." I stopped talking. "Yeah, Ma was real upset too."

Jean stopped walking and looked at me straight eye to eye. "We gotta stop the rumors cold. The only thing I can think of is that someone is jealous of you and wants Henry as a boyfriend."

"But no one seems to be flirting with Henry," I answered. "No one at school or at church."

"Well, you gotta tell your Ma," she said. "These rumors are awful and gotta be stopped. They're saying you got in a family way last year when you were in Iowa."

I groaned. "All I did there was housework and chores. I was so busy cooking, cleaning, sewing, and taking care of Aunt Caroline and the boys that I never went out. Most Sundays I didn't even go to church. On Sundays I was so tired that I'd sit by Aunt Caroline's bed and read the Bible to her while Uncle Lester took the boys to church. I never had one date."

Jean hugged me and told me she believed me. "Henry and his family are sure to find out soon," she said. "We've gotta stop the rumors right away."

We had arrived at her farm. I was still shaking as I said good-bye and walked the rest of the way home.

Nighttime

Telling Ma about the rumors wasn't easy. It was right after supper and Pa and my sisters had gone out to do the nighttime chores. I simply started talking and told her all at once. When I finished, she started crying and hugged me like a little child. Her body shuddered.

"This has always been my fear and now it's true, even though it isn't," she sobbed.

"What should I do?" I pleaded. I was sobbing now, too.

"I'll tell Pa," she answered. "And Reverend Blackman. He'll have some answers."

I went to bed sobbing. Maybe I cried all night long, I'm not sure. In the morning I woke up from a fitful sleep and Ma was in my bedroom telling me to stay home from school. As if that was gonna help anything. Staying home made me look guilty. What was Ma thinking?

Irene
Thursday, May 10, 1934
Nighttime

Well, the beans are spilled and I don't have to keep Miss Flatshaw's secret anymore. Tonight after supper Ma and Pa told us all to stay at the table cuz we all needed to talk something over. Then Flora started crying and so did Ma.

"Someone's been telling awful rumors that the dead baby was Flora's and that she buried it back in the woods," Pa said in a flat voice. "The worst thing that can happen to a girl is to have her reputation lost. You lose your reputation and no decent man will marry you."

Flora's and Ma's sobs grew louder and louder. Nellie scrunched up her face in confusion but didn't say anything. Nellie's really dumb but I think she figured out she needed to be quiet and let Pa talk. Me, I just sat there and waited. I wasn't gonna admit I'd heard any of this before. I'd promised Miss Flatshaw three times and she's my best friend.

"So we went to Reverend Blackman today to get his advice," Pa continued. "Reverend Blackman was shocked, just like us. At first he just shook his head. Then he asked Flora lots of questions like what she did at Aunt Caroline's last year and if she was alone with any boys while she was there. She wasn't. She was way too busy doing Aunt Caroline's work to have any free time. No way could she have gotten in a family way. She didn't come home from Iowa with a baby. But only our family knew that."

Pa looked like he was real mad. No one said anything.

"Well, what did Henry say?" I finally asked, trying to get this over and done. I wanted to have a Sisters' Club meeting tonight.

"That don't matter," Pa answered. "We think he don't even know about the rumors. Reverend Blackman's going to talk to him and his family."

Nellie had gotten up, walked over to Flora, and wrapped her arms around her. Flora's body shook as Nellie hugged her.

"Reverend Blackman told us to just carry on as usual. He says that Flora is a good girl and that people will soon forget the ugly rumors," Pa added.

I happen to have my doubts about that. People love ugly rumors. I have to admit that I've been hoping the baby was May Hendrick's cuz I can't stand her.

But Pa continued talking: "Reverend Blackman said that that Henry and Flora can continue having lunch together but not to spend any time alone until the dust settles on this. The truth will come out and we all should find comfort in Jesus."

I wondered how Jesus can comfort you if people are saying nasty things behind your back. Both Ma and Flora were still sobbing. I bet they have their doubts, too.

Finally, Pa looked directly at me and then over to Nellie. "Our family is going to get over this," he said firmly. "We will hold our heads high and continue to go to church every Sunday. Irene, you and Nellie should walk away if anybody starts talking about this. Just turn around and walk away. Don't say a word. Even if people are asking you questions, just politely say that you need to go home. Do you understand?"

I nodded. So did Nellie.

Flora ran upstairs and locked her bedroom door, but I could hear her sobbing. No Sisters' Club tonight.

Flora
Monday, May 14, 1934
Afternoon

I went back to school today. Henry didn't even look at me. Nor did he look at me at church yesterday. Guess he's feeling guilty that he drove down Lovers Lane on our one and only date. At lunchtime I went over to meet him and make things right, but he saw me, turned around, and walked away. Was I ever humiliated.

Sometimes it feels like it actually was my baby buried down there in the woods. I switch from being totally angry to feeling very, very sad and guilty. But I'm not guilty. Neither is Henry. Whoever buried that baby should be feeling guilty, not Henry or me.

My future of becoming Mrs. Henry Fitch is now as dead as that baby. Well, at least I have one good friend, Jean. She saw me standing there in the hall near the lunchroom when Henry turned away and she pulled me in to eat lunch with her. Her friend Mimi sat with us, too. I guess Jean had told her my story. Mimi was as sweet as could be and kept smiling at me while Jean talked. I don't remember a word.

I managed to sit through all my afternoon classes and I rode home wordlessly with Dan and Dalton. How I longed for old times and their quiet bantering. My world has vanished.

When I got home today, Ma ordered Irene and Nellie to go outside.

"Well, what happened at school today?" she asked.

"It was awful." I started sobbing. "Henry wouldn't even look at me. When he saw me, he walked away."

I just couldn't stop crying. I'm surprised I have so many tears inside me. It's like an endless flow. Ma eased me down into a chair.

"I never had to endure what you're going through," she said quietly while I cried. "You are so young and so innocent. You continue to live your life as a good girl and someday this will be far behind you."

Ma went on: "Flora, whatever happens down the road, you need to keep your self esteem. You deserve the best, and there's no reason for you to take the blame for someone else. You deserve to be happy and someday you will be. Remember that you're not the one at fault here. Neither is Henry. Just continue to be the good girl that you are."

She paused for a moment. "Do you hear me?" she finally asked.

I nodded.

But being happy seems like a long way off. Maybe as far away as Nellie's outer space friend ZeeZee. I'm so glad I have only two weeks of school left this year. Then I'll stay home and work in the garden. All that garden work that used to sound so terrible now sounds terrific.

Nellie
Wednesday, May 16, 1934
Forenoon

I'm still sewing on buttons, darning, and mending since the weather turned wet and cold again. It's not that I hate these tasks, but I'd rather help Pa with the animals. I feed potato peelings to the pigs every night after supper, and I sit with him while he milks the cows. I 'specially like it when he takes one of Bessie's tits and sprays milk at Three Foots, my favorite cat. Three Foots jumps in surprise each time, even though Pa sprays her jist 'bout every night.

The chore I hate is gathering the eggs and washing them. First you have to take a wire basket into the chicken coop where it's all dusty and hard to see. The dust smells like chicken pee. I cough and sneeze and cough and sneeze some more until my eyes water. Mainly I rush in and try to think 'bout something else. Next, I pick up the eggs that are already lying there. That's easy. What I can't stand is grabbing the eggs from under the hens cuz they peck at me. They scratch and claw and are real mean 'bout giving up their eggs. Nasty Ma-Hen is the worst cuz she always pecks and scratches my wrists. Sometimes it makes me mad when there ain't no eggs under the hens. It's no fair having my wrists and arms all bitten up and not even gittin' an egg for all that trouble.

Trying to talk to chickens is like trying to talk to briars and brambles. The closer you git the less they listen and the more they try to hurt you. Chickens don't want you in their house. Talking to them in a quiet voice outside in the yard works better, but those roosters always seem to know they might soon become

Sunday dinner. We only got two roosters left now. Naturally, I go in the chicken coop and try to gather the eggs as fast as I can and then git out quickly.

After I have all the eggs, I take them into the house where I wash and dry them and put them into boxes for Ma to peddle. I git my hands all dirty cuz a lot of the eggs have chicken manure and straw stuck on them. Sometimes the straw is stuck on so hard I have to scratch it off with my fingernails. The rags I use jist don't do the trick.

I try hard not to break eggs. Only once when I was pulling an egg out from underneath Nasty Ma-Hen I jerked away to avoid gittin' pecked and the egg rolled off the nest and fell to the floor. It broke open right there on the dirt. Ma was purty nice 'bout it and only told me to be more careful. If I find a cracked egg, then I put it aside and we use it ourselves. Ma never sells cracked eggs.

Bloody eggs are the worst. Ma always cracks open each egg separately in a little bowl and checks it before she uses it. She don't want one bloody egg to spoil all the rest.

Sometimes the eggs have double yolks. Kinda like twins. Ma always gives Pa the double yolked eggs when she fries them up for breakfast. She knows how hard he works and wants to give him extra food.

Today when I was in the chicken coop gathering eggs, holding my breath so I wouldn't have to breathe that awful air, I heard a rustling outside. Then I heard two men's voices, speaking quietly but not quite whispering. I was curious so I froze and listened. I needed to cough but I held it back. The chickens were used to me and they were jist their dumb selves.

"After dark we can git the cows and horses," one voice said.

"Jee-sus, how are we gonna git away with five cows that bellow and move like molasses?"

"Then only the horses," the other voice replied.

Somehow the second voice sounded familiar, but I couldn't place it.

I stood in that dusty chicken coop, frozen, wondering how long I would have to wait before they left. I heard some noise, but I waited a good long time more before I moved silently to the door, cracked it open an inch or two, and looked all around. No sign of anyone. I flew out the door and made a mad dash to the barn to tell Pa what I heard.

After Irene fell asleep I listened at the heat register, like I usually do. Aunt Hazel was in the parlor with Ma. I kinda figured that Pa and Unc Elmer were in the barn with their shotguns watching for horse thieves. They were probably up at the hay-mow window where you can see the house, driveway, and wind-mill. Nuthin' happened for a long, long time. I musta fell asleep on the floor cuz the next thing I knew Pa and Unc Elmer were down under me in the parlor, both talking at once.

"I fired a warning shot high above their heads as soon as I saw them walking up from the driveway to the barn door." Pa exclaimed. "Both of them turned around and hightailed it back to the road."

"But not before I shouted out that all the farmers in Calhoun County are watching for them, and there won't be any warning shots next time," Unc Elmer blurted out. "Don't want them steal-ing my horses tomorrow night."

"Could you tell who they were?" Ma asked.

"Na," Pa answered. "Way too dark tonight. Too many clouds, no moon. But probably not Gypsies, cuz Nellie understood what they were saying."

"We shoulda gotten the Sheriff to come out with us tonight," Unc Elmer added. "But who's gonna believe a day-dreaming seven-year-old?"

"Me," answered Ma.

"Poor Nellie," Aunt Hazel spoke up. "First discovering the baby and now this."

Flora
Thursday, May 17, 1934
Afternoon

Bad luck is raining down on our family. Like a wet, cold downpour. Every waking moment I walk around with a heavy heart. Ma and Pa confided that we will lose the farm if dairy and crop prices keep going down. I wish there was something I could do about that. I tried to give Pa my two-dollar nest egg a couple of weeks ago but he wouldn't take it. Yesterday Ma told me to use the money to go to the movies with Jean, but I can't do that with our farm in jeopardy.

In the meantime, I've decided to sneak behind Ma's back and go to May Hendrick's house after school to confront her about the baby. I feel guilty about it but, by gosh, May Hendrick was wrong to bury her baby and blame me. I'm going over there and get a confession come hell or high water.

So this afternoon after school I walked over to the Hendricks. It was a long walk and I got madder and madder with each step. Finally I got there and knocked on the door. May and her mother came out. They looked surprised, but I told them we needed to have a serious talk. We sat on the grass in their tiny front yard. May's younger sister JoEllen peaked out the door, but Mrs. Hendrick ordered her back inside the house.

I jumped right in, feeling no need for pleasantries.

"I've been suffering evil rumors that I had a baby that died and that I buried it back in the woods. The rumors are totally false." I looked directly at May with glaring eyes. Now it was the time for her to confess.

May burst into tears but I felt stone cold. I wanted her to blurt out the truth. May was just crying, but not saying a word.

"I should be the one crying," I uttered.

Mrs. Hendrick finally answered, "May has had a terrible experience. Last summer she was raped when she was walkin' home from town. The man had a car and offered her a ride and she got in. But he didn't take her home. He drove way off to a woods north of Albion. He had a knife and threatened to kill her if she told anybody."

Mrs. Hendrick, paused and continued, "He beat her up and had his way with her and then left her in the woods for dead, all bloody and unconscious. She was there for hours. Finally she came to and made her way back to the road. She got a ride with a nice colored lady who drove her all the way home. The lady encouraged us to call the Sheriff, but you know our situation. With Roy thieving and in jail most of the time, the law is gonna say she brought it on herself—that our family is to blame. So we didn't tell no one. I was jist so happy to have May home alive.

"But even though May didn't tell a soul, it was soon evident that she was in a family way. So the nightmare continued. Miss Flatshaw was the only one who knew and she was kind to her."

I was still reeling from hearing the word "raped." It's such an ugly word that people don't say out loud. I was stunned. Then Mrs. Hendrick started crying herself, rocking herself with her arms crossed. As she heaved back and forth, she started to talk again. "You probably heard that May had scarlet fever. That warn't true. She went to Detroit and stayed with my sister Rose and had a healthy baby girl that she put up for adoption. A couple from Detroit took her."

I started to offer my condolences, but I couldn't hold back my tears. All three of us were bawling our heads off.

Mrs. Hendrick, talking between sobs, went on. "We heard those rumors 'bout you and didn't wanna believe them. Our family has been living through such horrors and we didn't know how to help you. And Roy, he's been drinking a lot since he lost his job. Last night he got caught horse stealin' so he'll be in jail for several weeks. I've been trying to work more hours jist to put food on the table."

May hung her head still crying. "I shouldn'ta gotten in that car," she sniffled. I could tell she blamed herself, just like I had blamed myself for something not my fault. There was nothing but sobs again.

"Thank you for telling me and I'm so sorry for you," I finally blurted out.

I could hear the other kids in the house fighting, so I soon left and was walking the four miles home.

Gosh, darn it, I felt sorry for May. I was dealing with word rumors. May was dealing with a horrible experience. I couldn't get anything but May outa my mind.

But then I considered the possibility that it wasn't true. What if she had the baby and brought him home where he died? Or God forbid, her father killed the baby during a drunken stupor? Or what if he sold May's baby to the Gypsies? By the time I got home I was totally perplexed. Should I believe May or not?

As soon as I walked in the kitchen Ma told me about two horse thieves who tried to steal Ace and King last night. Probably Mr. Hendrick was one of them. Gosh darn, life shouldn't be so hard.

Nellie
Thursday, May 17, 1934
Afternoon

After school I asked Ma if the horses were okay, and she answered "Yes" without saying anything else. Guess she didn't wanna scare me 'bout the thieves coming last night. It started pouring rain after I got home from school so I didn't go outside at all. I was jist as happy staying inside helping with ironing and mending since those horse thieves are still out there uncaught.

While mending I noticed we don't have no colored thread. We've been using it up over the past year. All Ma has is one spool of black and two spools of white that she bought from Mr. Goldberg the last time he came by. We ain't ever been without colored thread ever before.

Ma told me to use white thread, the dress being light blue flour sack. I love that dress and hope that I can have it after Irene outgrows it. It didn't take me long to git it hemmed. I'm really good with the blind stitch Aunt Hazel taught me last week. Ma usually uses an overcast stitch for hemming, but I like the blind stitch better. You can't see it after you finish. It's nice to choose which stitch to use. Most of the time I don't have choices: when to git up; what to eat; which chores to do.

That's why I like goin' down to the crick. You can do anything you want and talk to any critters you want. Life's good down at the crick. Pa used to play there when he was a kid, too. He's always asking me questions 'bout the crick. I think it makes him feel young again. If only I didn't have to go through the woods to git there.

After hemming up Irene's dress I baked Ma's bread. Baking

bread is tricky cuz the heat from the wood stove ain't always the same. You have to watch the bread and add more wood to the stove to make sure it gits baked all the way through and not burned. Ma loves to have me and Irene help her with that. We can sit in the kitchen and look at our books and check the bread every few minutes.

You can smell the bread before it burns so that's the warning to not add any more wood. Today when I checked it, the bread was a beautiful golden. Perfect. I love smelling the bread while it bakes. The smell goes up to every room in the house. Sometimes Pa says he can smell it from the tool shed and the granary. Not the barn, chicken coop, pigpen, or sheep shed, though. They all have their own smells.

Nighttime

Tonight I didn't have to wait long for Irene to fall asleep. As soon as she started snorting those short little piggy breaths through her nose, I crept down to the heat register.

"I nailed boards across both barn doors from the inside," Pa said. They won't be able to get in without a crowbar and a lot of noise. The milk house is the only way to git in. I think that's too close to the house for them to risk it."

"Are you going to nail up boards every night?" Ma asked.

"Just for the next week," he replied. "Even if they get in the barn through the milk house, they still would have a job getting the horses out through the barnyard and then down our drive-way. It's real hard seeing inside the barn after dark and I put down a few tools they would stumble over—mainly rakes and hoes. Rover should warn us, too. Lately he's been sleeping on some burlap bags out in the Connector between Old Part and New Part."

Pa was talking 'bout the two parts of our barn. Old Part was the first barn that my grandpa built, and New Part is what Pa added on before my sister Flora was born. You can't tell from the road that there are two different buildings. It looks like one large barn.

Ma didn't reply and there was silence for a while.

"The Dunkles and the Sandermeers both cut back their egg orders," she replied. "They said they can't afford two dozen a week. And none of our egg customers wants extra help with house cleaning."

More silence.

"Sam," she exclaimed, "What if we'd lost the horses last night? What if the well goes dry? What if the cows get sick?"

"Too many *what-ifs*, Dorothy," he answered. "We'll do what we need to do. But we have to be careful. I never smoke in the barn any more. And don't waste water, ever. And we'll be real careful 'bout horse thieves. Hopefully dairy and crop prices won't go down any more."

Silence again.

Then Pa cleared his throat. "There will be problems, Dorothy. There always are. We're coping with the dead chicks. So far we've had enough rain. Hopefully, that'll continue."

Pa paused for a moment. "Dorothy, you can help a lot. People need food. They can skimp on clothes and keep the fire low in the winter. But come fall and winter when their gardens are a memory, we'll be there with cheap food: potatoes, sweet potatoes, squash, onions, carrots, beets, and all kinds of canned goods. No fancy cake or candy. Just good, hearty farm food. We'll make it. We've got good girls and Hazel and Elmer have good boys. We'll all make it."

"Maybe I'll can up some whole meals," Ma said slowly. "Some stews and soups. Not much meat, only for flavor, the way I cook for us. People might like that. I'll need more Ball jars. Maybe Old Man Keller will trade me some of his empty ones for a couple of jars of stew."

"Yup, that's a good idea," Pa replied. More silence. I think married people have more silences than conversation. Pa says you need to be careful not to say the wrong thing or something you'll regret later. Ma says she likes the quiet time with Pa. You don't have to be talking all the time, she says. She likes him close by. I understand that. I do too.

Finally there were some words again. "The mortgage is due first," Pa said. "The spring wheat crop was good. Once we get the mortgage paid off, we'll think 'bout the taxes."

I wonder what the "more-guge" is. It may be the salt that comes in the round blue box. Ma once told me that taxes is money that we have to pay the govmint for schools, roads, and bridges and things like that. I think the govmint lives in a building in Marshall, the town where Flora goes to high school. That's where Pa goes to pay the taxes. I rode with him last summer, but he had me sit outside on a bench while he went in. It was fun cuz Mrs. Geist came by with Jimmy and Fritz and sat down and talked to me for a while. They left when Mr. Geist came out of the govmint building.

Irene
Friday, May 25, 1934
Afternoon

Last night Flora told me May Hendrick's story. Flora feels bad
that she went to May's house without telling Ma and Pa, but
what else could she do? I woulda gone with her if she'd asked me.
But Flora knows that I don't like May.

I haven't told May's story to Miss Flatshaw, but I bet she already knows cuz she's the one who told everybody that May had
scarlet fever. It really was a stupid lie. Telling people she had
consumption would have made more sense.

Still, I'm happy things are back to normal with Miss Flatshaw,
and we are talking and eating lunch together. She stills says I'm
the smartest student at school.

Today was the last day of school for me and Nellie. Flora has
another week of high school. I don't know why the high school
has to go longer than country school. It means that me and Nellie
have to start working in the garden a week earlier. So unfair.

The last real school day was yesterday. Today we had a school
picnic. If it rains on school picnic day we have a potluck inside
the schoolhouse. Believe me, a picnic outside is always nicer. All
the kids go to school at the reglar time and play games out in the
schoolyard before the mothers come with the food and little kids.
The big kids play Anti-I-Over the woodshed before we eat. Then
after eating, we play Crack the Whip and Red Rover and the
little kids play Mother May I and Cowboys and Indians.

Ma brought potato salad cuz I asked her to. It's my favorite picnic food and we have green onions and red radishes from
the garden that give it a real zip. I like it best when Ma puts

hard-boiled eggs in it, but she didn't today cuz we have to sell our eggs. Nellie won't ever know how to make potato salad the right way. She won't ever be a good cook like me.

Well, the school picnic was fun, but as usual I was the last person to get chosen for Anti-I-Over. Next year it's gonna be different. I'm gonna be the team leader and choose who I want on my team. Also, I'll have a boyfriend. School will be so great. Miss Flatshaw and I will make fun of any kid who is mean to me.

Flora
Sunday, May 27, 1934
Forenoon

I'm so tired of being poor. And I lost my boyfriend because of an ugly rumor. We were standing outside church today and Henry came out with his family. I thought enough time had passed for us to have a quick conversation after church. But instead of coming over to talk, Henry just ignored me and walked towards their buggy. Most everyone is back to buggies these days, cars being too expensive and gas is ten cents a gallon.

"We have to feed the horses whether they work or not," Pa said. "But I only put gas in the car when we use it," he says over and over, as if we didn't get his point the first time. It's okay, I think Ace and King like the trip to the church. It's not very far, and they get out of the fields and get their curiosity satisfied. Nellie said as much the other day when she was "talking" to the horses. She mentioned that they love to go to new places and experience new smells, sights, and tastes.

Ma noticed that Henry didn't come over to talk to me. "Why don't you go say hello to his family?" she urged me on. So I went over and said hello to both Mr. and Mrs. Fitch, and smiled at his little brother, Bob. Mrs. Fitch couldn't have been nicer, asking me what I was doing over the summer and if I was going back to high school or to County Normal in the fall. I told her high school. I'm more interested in becoming a nurse than a teacher, I told her. What I didn't tell her is that I'm more interested in becoming a farm wife than anything else.

"I'd have to go clear over to Kalamazoo to learn to be a nurse," I mentioned. "It's not practical these days." Mrs. Fitch is smart and can read between the lines: Kalamazoo and nursing are out of the question because of the expense.

"I think you'd be a fine nurse," she responded. "I wish we had a hospital close by. All these farm accidents are a curse. I had all three of my babies at home; I'll never know if little Charles would have lived if we'd been at a hospital." Mrs. Fitch had tears in her eyes. I wanted to put my arms around her, but I'm nowhere near being her daughter-in-law. So I just nodded in sympathy.

All this time Henry just stood near their buggy. Soon Ma came over and said hello to Mrs. Fitch. Mrs. Fitch brightened up and told Ma what a nice young lady I am. Ma just nodded and said that having two boys at home must be so different from three girls. I knew right then that both Mrs. Fitch and Ma were plugging for me, but unless Henry came around there was nothing they could do. So I excused myself and went over and said hello to Mrs. Vandenberg who was standing all by herself.

"Nice having Reverend Blackman back," I said to Mrs. Vandenberg who seemed to be daydreaming. "That revivalist sure was scary."

She looked up quickly at me and smiled. "You have no idea what was going on with that preacher," she whispered to me. "Brother Johnson took all the collection money himself and didn't leave a penny for our church. And him preaching about thieving and other crimes too horrible to mention."

"I had no idea," I whispered back. "I did overhear some girls at school say he has rattlesnakes at the Camp Meetings."

Mrs. Vandenberg continued. "It's not my place to say, but I don't think he's much of a religious man. There are all kinds of rumors about him having his way with slutty girls back in the woods near the Camp Meeting." I wondered if she had heard the rumor about me. I doubt it or she wouldn't have mentioned these.

"Let's hope there are no more trips away for Reverend Blackman," I whispered back.

Right then Ma walked up to say hello.

"You have the loveliest daughters," Mrs. Vandenberg said to Ma in her everyday, non-whispering voice. "So pleasant, too," she added, totally changing the subject.

"Flora here has a musical gift," Ma replied and looked at me.

"And that little one of yours, she looks like that little Shirley Temple movie star that everyone's talking about. A curly-haired blonde sweetie." I didn't know what Shirley Temple looked like, but Mrs. Vandenberg's comment did seem to please Ma.

"Our middle girl Irene is a smart one, too," Ma replied. "She's already learned to sew quilts. I wish we had some new dry goods, I'd teach her how to make a dress. I'm not using the Treadle much these days. Mending and darning, that's about it."

"You and everybody else," Mrs. Vandenberg sighed. "Then she moved closer to Ma and me and whispered, "Two more farms went under over on the other side of the county. We farmers thought we'd make it through the hard times, but maybe not. At least we haven't had dust storms like they've they've had out west."

Ma nodded as if she knew about the dust storms, but I don't think she'd heard about them.

"I'm worried about summer," Ma responded. "A fox got most of our chicks so we'll have mighty little egg money this summer. Just pray for rain to keep the crops and garden growing."

Mrs. Vandenberg nodded in sympathy, then Mr. Vandenberg came over and said hello. He had been talking to Reverend Blackman. Mr. Vandenberg is about as thin as Mrs. Vandenberg is fat. We passed pleasantries, then Ma and I took our leave and joined Pa and my sisters for the trip home. I suddenly noticed how worn Ma's navy-blue Sunday dress had become. I could see where she had patched it from inside and several worn spots would need patching real soon.

Now I regretted that Ma had given me her other dress to re-make for my one and only date with Henry. I was wearing it today, but I do have a second Sunday dress that's in better shape than Ma's. I'm so ready for that President of ours to get the whole country back into shape. It just isn't right that Ma has to go without. She's a good, hard-working Christian woman and deserves a nice Sunday dress.

Nighttime

After Henry's behavior at church today I think Ma understands that I'm not going to be heading to the altar anytime soon. She was quiet after getting back from church while we were getting dinner. Dinner was going to be two squirrels that my cousin Dan shot in Unc Elmer's woods, right behind their house. Ma and I don't like squirrel. Not only has my love life disappeared, but the rest of my life as well. What girl wants to be alone at seventeen? And who wants squirrel for Sunday dinner?

Whenever I go down into the cellar the shelves are bare. A quart of beef chunks, two quarts of tomatoes, two quarts of green beans, and one quart of peaches, and that's it. The potatoes are in a bin over near the wood pile along with other root vegetables. About two weeks' worth of food if you use lots and lots of potatoes and dried beans. We're going to need the garden to grow fast before these are all used up.

I want rooster for Sunday dinner. I want Ma to have a good Sunday dress. I want to be able to play the piano any time I choose. I want to go on dates to movies and dances.

Most of all I want to marry Henry, but that's not going to happen. Guess I'd better figure out what to do with myself since it looks like I'm on the road to becoming an old maid. People say I could give piano lessons, but the truth is that I can't read music. I hear a song and then plunk it out on the piano.

Tonight after supper I was sitting at the piano in the parlor thinking about life, not playing, just thinking. Hard to believe, but maybe May was lucky if she'd actually been left for dead. Even so, I was still having doubts if May was telling the truth.

I could overhear Ma and Pa talking in the kitchen.

"Taxes are due next month," Ma said quietly. "I'm still trying to get some cleaning jobs in town, but no luck."

"Is anyone well off enough to hire you?" Pa asked.

Ma didn't respond. I guess she was thinking the same thing as Pa.

"We may need to sell stuff from the garden for some quick cash," he said.

"But that will limit how much we can put up for winter," she responded.

"Winter won't matter if we can't live here," he snapped back. I'd never heard Pa use this tone of voice with Ma.

Ma responded immediately. "Okay, we have the largest garden we've ever put in. I'll start peddling produce right away. The lettuce, green onions, and radishes have already come in. No way I can put them up anyway. Then sperrygas and strawberries will be ready in a couple of weeks. I'll start with my egg customers," Ma replied.

"The girls can take care of the garden," Pa said. "You can peddle more days than Friday if need be. If you get lucky and get some housecleaning jobs, you can take Irene with you to help out and Flora can supervise Nellie in the garden. I'll watch out for them, too. We'll change our eating schedule and have a cold dinner at noon. Just put out bread and butter and whatever's in season. Then we'll all be back together for a hot supper."

Pa sighed. "Maybe it's for the best that it didn't work out for Flora and Henry. We need her here to take care of the house and garden if you're gonna be peddling vegetables and cleaning houses most days." I realized that tears were coming to my eyes. I'd never heard Pa talk like this.

"I can double up on washing and bread-making so that Flora don't get stuck with all of it," Ma answered. "We'll do the ironing at night after supper. Irene's old enough to handle a flat iron now."

Pa sighed again. "Then there's Hazel and Elmer," he said. "I can't keep getting help from Elmer and the boys without the girls helping out Hazel. How can we take care of that?"

There was a long pause.

"Wednesdays. There's not much sewing going on these days," Ma offered. "We just won't have sewing day. The girls and I can do the mending and darning in the evening along with the ironing. There's plenty of daylight here in the kitchen all summer long.

She sounded a little more positive. "If the girls go up to Hazel's on Wednesdays they can clean her house and do whatever she wants. She may need to change her schedule a little too, but Hazel's never been a stickler about schedules."

Well, I have to say that my future looks darn bleak.

Nellie
Saturday, June 2, 1934
Forenoon

Ma is teaching Irene to remake clothes using the Treadle. I wanna learn too, but my leg ain't long enough to reach the floor so I have to wait. Irene brags that she knows everything there is to know 'bout sewing. Period. Well, I didn't believe her so I asked her how to make a buttonhole. She got out a pair of buttonhole scissors from Ma's sewing box and cut a hole at the bottom of her shirt. Then she threaded up a needle and sewed all the way around that hole, using an overstitch. Dang, if it didn't turn into a buttonhole.

After that she was feeling so good 'bout herself that she decided I could join the big kids playing cops and robbers in the jailhouse. I was on a team with Alvin and we caught both Jake and Irene and put them in jail. Then we changed sides and I was a robber. Irene caught me and put me in jail. "Bye, bye, sucker," she yelled. "You won't be getting out till nighttime."

I waited for a while until I was sure they were far away, and then climbed up to the top, found the hole in the roof, and climbed down the outside. I decided to stay away from Irene so she'd think I was still in jail. Maybe she'd start feeling bad and worry about me.

Afternoon

I went out to the barn to find Pa, but I kept gittin' interrupted by animals. Rover wanted a bone. Three Foots wanted to show off her latest dead gopher. Patsy, one of the other barn cats, came around to tell me 'bout her latest catch. At least I didn't have to watch her eat it—a small mouse. Patsy also told me that Fancy Fatsy is gonna have kittens. After all these animal conversations I decided to lie down on the grass near the milk house.

I shut my eyes and later opened them when I heard the most unusual music, like nuthin' I'd ever heard before. I looked at the sky and saw all kinds of colors streaking across it, like ribbons. The ribbons were dancing in time with the music. It was so beautiful. Rover saw it too, cuz I asked him. He said it was heavenly music and that a rainbow was splitting up into all its colors.

Nighttime

At suppertime Irene kept looking at me, kinda strange. I knew she was wondering how I got outa jail. I'll never tell. Ma kept talking 'bout the missing girls never showing up and how the Sheriff is worried that they were "ducted." I asked what that meant. "Did they turn into ducks or something?" Ma just looked away and Pa told me I was too little to understand.

So I stuck my finger in my ear. I'd find out from Flora and Irene.

Ma spoke up, "Even though it's summertime and you girls aren't walking to and from school, you still need to be careful."

"Careful of what?" I asked.

Ma sighed. "Always let Pa and me know if there are train riders or other unknown men around. Tell us if you see any strange cars."

"Yeah, like there are lots of cars coming out to the garden, while I hoe onions," Irene blurted out.

"Don't sass me," Ma barked at Irene. "You understand full well what I mean. I don't want anything bad to happen."

"Well, that's already happened to me," Flora muttered under her breath. Ma looked up at her but didn't reply.

Finally after supper cleanup and night chores, us girls gathered on Flora's bed for a Sisters' Club meeting.

"What is this "duck" thing?" I asked Flora.

"Being abducted means that someone kidnaps you and hurts you. You never want to get abducted," she said.

I nodded. "So is that what happened to the Spring Lake girls?" I asked.

"No one knows," she answered.

"So nuthin' to do with ducks?" I asked. I really like ducks, 'specially mallards and wood ducks.

"No ducks of any kind," Flora sighed. "Just be careful."

"So what reports do you have?" Flora asked me and Irene.

"I saw wonderful colors in the sky," I answered. "So did Rover. Maybe ZeeZee is making them out in space."

Flora said nothing, waited and then looked at Irene.

"Wait, wait," I said. "Maybe ZeeZee can figure out who buried the baby. He's good at solving bank robberies. I bet he can figure out dead babies . . . ."

Irene interrupted me. "But Nellie, you make up the ZeeZee stories in your head. It's your imagination. So you either know who did it or you don't."

I felt bad. I wanted an excuse to go play down near the old bus and cabin ruins. I've missed my good times there with my 'maginary friends.

Irene spoke up again. "Maybe it's Mrs. Vandenberg at church. She's so fat you wouldn't know if she had a baby inside her."

Both Flora and I looked at Irene as if she were crazy.

"She's been talking about wanting a baby for a couple of years now," Flora answered. "She would never leave a poor little baby buried down in the backwoods. If she'd had a baby that died she'd be crying all through church every Sunday, just like Mrs. Geist. Poor Jimmy."

I think Flora's right.

Irene
Monday, June 4, 1934
Forenoon

Summer vacation has started and believe me, it's no vacation. Last year I asked Miss Flatshaw what the word "vacation" meant. She thought a moment and said, it's like "vacating," getting away from something like school. I had thought it meant going on a trip to somewhere interesting like a fishing trip in northern Michigan. Folks around here talk fondly about their fishing trips, mainly to places like Houghton Lake, way Up North.

"Well," Miss Flatshaw continued, "Vacation does mean trips, too. For grownups a vacation is getting away from work.

"It's a nice thing," she added. "I took a vacation to Niagara Falls with my aunt last summer. We stayed in a tent at a campground park near the falls where we could actually hear the roar all night long. It took us three days to drive there. We packed a big basket full of food and stopped along the road for picnics and slept in our tent each night beside the road. Someday I'll show you the souvenir plate that I bought. It's turquoise blue with a gold rim and a picture of the falls in the center." Miss Flatshaw sounded so wistful, as if her trip to Niagara Falls was the last good time she would ever have. It's confusing. Some days she's so happy and some days so sad.

Anyway, as I've said, I'm not expecting this summer to be a vacation. It looks like lotsa hard work. Pa has told us that everyone has to pull together in order to keep the farm. That means working in the garden all day long and helping him with chores. Even Nellie has to work in the garden, but she also gets the easy chores like going down to the meadow to bring the cows back for milking, and separating the table scraps, a chore that used to be mine. I taught her how to give Rover the bones and cooked food, and give the pigs the potato peels, apple cores, strawberry hulls and other uncooked scraps. Naturally, Rover follows Nellie around all the time, asking for more food. I liked it better when he followed me around.

Afternoon

Today's Monday so Ma's been doing the wash and Nellie helps her hang up the clothes. I used to love that job, handing Ma the clothespins. Ma saw me in the garden and knew I wasn't happy working there all by myself, so she came out to the garden and told me it would get better next week when Flora is out of school and working in the garden with Nellie and me.

Later Ma told me I could go play with Nellie, but Nellie was just sleeping with Rover near the milk house. I ran over to them and I lay down beside Nellie and closed my eyes, rubbing them until the yellow spots with black squiggly lines appeared. I kept rubbing my eyes so the designs would change. Nellie seemed to wake up and asked me where the music was coming from. Sometimes she asks the most stupid questions. Music in the afternoon out near the milk house? I told her she was dreaming.

Nellie
Tuesday, June 5, 1934
Forenoon

There's no better place to play in the springtime than down at the crick. I'm still scared to go through the woods but I figure if me and Irene can run through it without looking down, we can git there real fast. I don't wanna miss catchin' those slippery little pollywogs cuz they're so fun to play with. So I asked Irene all nice and sisterly and even used "please."

"I don't wanna go down to the crick," Irene answered, but I kept pestering her. She was hoping she could go to Aunt Hazel's and play with Jake and Alvin. But when she found out that Jake and Alvin were helping Unc Elmer clear stones from his back field, Irene finally caved in. Actually, by then I was hopin' to help Unc Elmer, too. I love to go out with the stone boat and find stones and throw them on it. Unc's workhorses, Trixie and Dixie, seem to like it, too. But when Irene agrees to play with me, it's a big deal.

"Me and Irene are gonna go to the meadow," I told Ma. It was kinda the truth. We skipped down the lane, and I saw two blue-birds coming out of a bluebird house. We passed by some yellow forsythia in bloom and entered the first meadow and went to the cows: Bessie, Rosie, Clover, Cocoa, and Moo-Moo. I named Moo-Moo myself. She is my favorite, a beautiful beige Jersey. Irene's favorite is Rosie who's an orangey-colored Guernsey. The other three are black and white Holsteins and they're nice cows, too.

Last summer Irene and I watched Clover cow have a baby. Clover was lying down in a flat green patch on the side of the lane near the first meadow. It was slow going. We watched part of it in the morning seeing 'bout half of the calf come out but it was all covered in wet slime. Then we heard the dinner bell and ran home for dinner. After dinner we both ran back down the lane and saw that the calf had nearly all come out. When the calf was entirely out Clover licked and licked it until all the slimy stuff was gone. The calf was this cute little black and white thing. Clover nudged it until it got up on its wobbly feet and starting sucking on one of her tits. It was a bull calf that Irene named Zaccheus, after the tax collector in the *Bible* who climbed a sycamore tree to see Jesus. Pa sold the calf a couple of months ago.

So after Irene and I stopped to see the cows we ran down the second meadow, past more forsythia, the rusty gate, the old bus, the cabin ruins, and the poison ivy tree. There were lots of daffodils along the fence where Irene and I had planted the bulbs last fall. We walked over and inspected the flowers and I mentioned we could pick a bouquet for Ma on the way back.

Once we passed by the daffodil patch we started running again and came to the stile and climbed over it into the woods. When you reach the woods it's 'bout a fifteen-minute run down the path to the crick. I kept my eyes on Irene who was running ahead of me and I didn't look at the place where I had dug up the baby's hand. Finally we were at the crick, and we both started looking for pollywogs. I saw some near some lily pads. They were too far into the crick to catch, but it was fun to look at them anyway. We were sitting on the bank poking sticks into the crick, looking at anything that would appear. I was hoping to see tiny little guppies. Finally a few swam by.

After a while Irene crawled back onto some rocks in the sunshine and left me with the little crick critters. She likes to do that: jist watch me play. Most of the time I don't care, but it would be more fun if she stirred up some critters, too. So I kept poking and finally found some right near me. I turned around to tell her that I had found some more. "Come over here and play with the pollywogs," I yelled.

That's when I saw it. A GIANT RATTLESNAKE. It was curled up on a rock right behind Irene. I couldn't tell if it was sunning itself or if it was gittin' ready to strike. The only other time I had seen one was with my cousins, Jake and Alvin. That one was a smaller rattler than this ugly fella. When they found it my cousins kept prodding the little guy with a stick until it hissed, rattled, and tried to strike the stick. Irene and I both know to stay away from rattlesnakes and snapping turtles. Joe Frederickson lost the tip of his pointy finger last summer when he was playing with a snapper.

Naturally I was really scared when I saw the snake. I whispered to Irene, "You gotta walk toward me right now. Slowly. Don't run. Don't turn around."

Irene looked puzzled, but slowly got up and started walkin' toward me. That rattlesnake stayed put. But as soon as Irene was close to me, I pointed at the snake. She turned around and saw it immediately. So we both walked backwards up to the path to the woods as far away from the rocks as we could git. When we were on the path and couldn't see the snake no more, we ran through the woods, past the hollow ash tree, the big oak tree and over the stile, past all my favorite places to the barnyard.

Nighttime

I told Irene not to tell Ma and Pa 'bout the rattlesnake or they wouldn't let us go to the crick no more. But tonight as I was lying on our bedroom floor with my ear to the metal register I heard Ma talking to Pa.

"They went all the way to the crick and saw a rattlesnake. Those girls oughta to be whipped." I was suddenly furious with Irene for tattling, but I kept still to hear what Pa had to say.

"Well, it's a fine place to play. I spent my childhood down at that crick," Pa replied. "It's much safer than being on the roads these days, 'specially with those girls gone missing. Besides, our girls did exactly the right thing, getting out of there fast. Irene don't take no chances and Nellie is a real smart girl."

It was the first time I ever heard Pa call me smart. Irene always brags 'bout being smart but not me. My heart filled with love for Pa.

Irene
Tuesday, June 5, 1934
Afternoon

I'm absolutely beside myself with all this garden work. When I grow up I am not planting a garden. Amen. I will marry a rich husband who gives me lots of money to buy eggs, fruits, and vegetables. Maybe I'll even hire a cook to make all the meals while I tend to the animals—goats, mainly. No hens, pigs, sheep, workhorses, and just one cow unless I have enough money to buy milk. Then no cow. This gardening is so unfair. I hoe all morning, pick strawberries mid-day, and weed all afternoon until dark. When I crawl into bed at night and shut my eyes, all I see is onions needing hoeing and strawberries needing picking.

I miss going to school, playing with my cousins, and talking to Miss Flatshaw. I had been looking forward to going to church last Sunday, but Flora was making such a big deal about wearing Ma's rouge and inspecting her face in the mirror that I just wanted to go back to bed.

So today, after gardening all morning, Ma decided that me and Nellie could go play the rest of the afternoon. I was so ready to go up to Unc Elmer's and play with Jake and Alvin. But Nellie wanted to go down to the crick so I said yes, just to be nice. Rarely do my attempts at kindness get appreciated by either Nellie or Ma and Pa.

After stopping to see the cows, Nellie and I ran fast through the woods and got to the crick right away. She usually slows down to do idiotic things like look at the underside of flowers or insects, but today we went straight to the crick, running at top speed.

I went up to a nice warm rock and was enjoying the sunshine heating up my face when for no reason I looked around. There was a rattlesnake right behind me. Slowly I backed up and saved Nellie who wasn't paying attention. We both ran fast up the path back to the house. I was real proud that I had saved my sister and told Ma as soon as we got back.

Nighttime

I was sitting at the kitchen table pretending to read my *Bible Story Book* tonight, and I could barely hear Ma and Pa talking about the rattler. That didn't surprise me, but what came next was a real shocker.

"We could put Flora back in the girls' room with Irene and Nellie, and rent her room. After all, it has its own stairway and side entrance," Pa said.

"No. No. No," Ma replied. "I'm not having any strange man sleeping under this roof with three girls here. It's bad enough with those girls gone missing. Then there are the train riders who come by. Do you think I'm mad? No mother would ever allow it."

"If we had hired men, they'd be sleeping up there," Pa replied.

Ma said nothing.

"How about a spinster needing a place?" Pa continued. "Irene is already too thick with Miss Flatshaw but there are other single ladies who might work out."

"Who do you have in mind?" asked Ma.

"No one. Maybe a school marm. Or maybe a widow who don't want to live alone."

"Would she use our kitchen?" Ma asked, clearly not excited about the prospect.

Pa paused but didn't answer.

"Well, I'm not saying no, but I'm not saying yes either," Ma answered. "I don't like the idea of a stranger using our privy either."

Neither did I. Nor do I want Flora sleeping with me and Nellie. There's not enough room as it is. Nellie's always ending up on my side of the bed. She says she gets cold and needs me to warm her up. I think she just likes hogging the bed. Also, Flora is big, like an adult. She would take up at least half the bed and I would get squeezed in the middle. I just don't like that idea at all.

I started listening in again.

"Well, let's wait until after harvest," Pa finally said. "Then we'll know where we stand. But in the meantime, keep your ears open for a lady needing a room." Nothing else was said after that.

All night I kept thinking of reasons I didn't want a stranger coming to live with us. She might have lice or some awful disease. She might take over the kitchen when I wanted to read my *Bible Story Book*. She might take a long time in the privy and make us wait. She might eat our food when we're not looking. She might have whiskers like old Mrs. Dunleavy. She might be fat and break our furniture. She might cook weird-smelling food and I might vomit.

Flora
Thursday, June 7, 1934
Afternoon

I'm fed up with rumors and fed up with life. Jeepers, I'd like to bury my head in the sand like Ma and pretend that Nellie had never discovered that poor baby. But she did. And I'm suffering the consequences.

So I'm doing something about it. After finishing off the gardening and before supper I took off for the Hendrick house. The second time. This time May's sister JoEllen answered the door. I asked if May was home.

JoEllen nodded and yelled out, "May, Irene's sister is here."

May came rushing out and looked at me as if surprised.

"Can we go outside and talk again?" I asked.

She looked scared to death. There wasn't any sign of Mrs. Hendrick. Guess she must be in town working.

May nodded and we both sat down in a shady spot in their sideyard. I didn't want to be seen from the road.

"I'll come right to the point," I said to her. "We've found no one claiming that dead baby and the rumors about me are still swirling all over town. Do you have any proof that you actually adopted your baby?"

A look of relief swept over May's face.

"Yes, I'll show you the papers right now."

She jumped up, ran into the house and was back with the papers in an instant, handing them to me.

"Guess you knew right where they were,"I said to her as I looked at the pages.

"I keep them under my bed. Sometimes I look at them right

before I go to sleep and I think about my baby in some stranger's house. I sure hope they are treating her kindly."

I thumbed to a page titled, *Certificate of Adoption*. Yes, it was all there with May's name listed as the birth mother of a girl born March 26, 1934. It looked all official with signatures and witnesses.

"I'm sure they are nice," I answered. "People who go to all the trouble to adopt, want a baby a whole lot. I'm sure they're giving your baby a lot of love."

We both teared up.

"Well, now you can go to high school and get a good job when you've finished," I said. "Then you can get married and have all the kids you want."

May seemed to brighten up with that thought, but then frowned again. "I'm not good at school. Remember you used to help me with reading."

I nodded. "There's lots of jobs where you don't need a lot of schooling. Hair stylists, for one. Or working in a bakery. My grandma used to work in the dime store before she died. She loved that. She liked having all the children come in. You do have to know how to make change. I could help you with that."

"That'd be nice, Flora," May answered. "I'd like that."

"Well, I won't be blaming you any more, "I went on. "You've been through way too much already. I'm sorry I thought you were making up the rumors about me."

She nodded and we both burst into tears. Neither May nor I deserved any of this sorrow.

Nighttime

"May's baby was definitely a girl that she gave up for adoption," I told my sisters at our late night club meeting.

"Wait, what?" Nellie asked. "May ain't had no baby cuz she's not married.

"Nellie," someday Ma will tell you about babies. It's not my place to do this. But sometimes it happens that girls have babies first before they marry. Not often, but just in a blue moon. Usually if this happens they either get married straight-away or they give the baby up for adoption."

"Oh," Nellie answered, still looking confused.

"It will all make sense some day," I said to her, but for now we need to focus on those Gypsies and find out more about the missing girls. You should watch the woods any chance you get to see if anyone goes down there with flowers or a gravestone or anything else.

Both of my sisters nodded solemnly. I don't think either of them wants to go there any time soon.

Nellie
Saturday, June 16, 1934
Forenoon

I've been thinking 'bout mice today. Ma screams at them when she goes down cellar. She says they're filthy and she don't want them anywhere near our food. So when I was down cellar today I screamed at one, too. It scared me when it brushed by my foot while I was picking out some potatoes for dinner. I was barefoot, of course, and I felt its furry little body run along the side of my foot.

I know exactly how many potatoes to git for dinner and supper. Two big ones for Pa, and one medium for each of the rest of us. Sometimes I change it up and git two smalls instead of a medium. Ma don't mind at all. Ma says she gives me that job so I can practice counting. But I really think Ma don't wanna go down cellar herself cuz of the mice down there. I told Ma we need to git a cat to live down there.

All our cats catch lots of mice in the barn. Three Foots loves to bring dead mice from the barn out to the yard to show off while she eats them. She says she's a good hunter and she is. After she's eaten, she's a happy cat. She'll let me do anything with her. I can even pick her up and hold her by her tail and she don't care. But Pa told me not to do that cuz it might hurt her. I don't understand cuz Three Foots always seems to like it.

I figured that Three Foots never had a fourth leg, but Flora says not, that it was a horrible accident. She claims she had nuthin' to do with it, but that we live on a farm, after all. What does that mean? Yeah, we live on a farm, but all the rest of the cats have four legs. Once in a while Flora is high and mighty 'bout stuff. Irene is that way all the time.

Pa told me that mice are jist little animals like gophers and I don't need to be scared of them or scream when I see them. In the future I'll try and think of mice more like gophers when I go down cellar to git potatoes. I've never tried talking to them cuz there's so much screaming when they show up. So I'll try harder. And believe me, I'll be going down cellar a lot this summer, with all the canning. At the end of every canning day me and Irene have to carry all the glass jars down to the shelves in the cellar.

I have memorized where everything goes down there. The only problem is when Ma cans something new, it's unclear where to put stuff. Last summer she made some pickled beets and I put them next to the reglar beets, but she wanted them near the cucumber pickles. How was I to know?

Afternoon

Flora gave me two of her real old *McCalls* magazines cuz she knows I like to cut out the pictures. Last week she got three new ones from her friend Jean. I like the covers the best. One of the magazines has a picture of three girls roller-skating on the front cover. Another one has a lady with giant sunflowers. Someday I would like to draw pictures and write stories for a magazine, maybe *Farm Wife* that Aunt Hazel gits in the mail.

One of the *McCalls* Flora gave me a long time ago had a shaggy sheep dog on the cover. The lady was holding long brown straps with the ends in each of her hands. I hope she warn't gonna hit the dog with it, like you do with the reins on a horse. The lady had on a nice blue sweater, but she didn't seem very happy. Pa told me to think up a story 'bout the lady and the dog that has a happy ending. So I did.

This morning I got Ma's shears from her sewing drawer and started cutting out interesting pictures from the magazines. I was laying them upside down on the table thinking 'bout pasting them on an old newspaper that way, upside down. Since I was already in the kitchen I got some flour and put it in a dish and added water to make paste. Then Ma came in and asked me what I was doing, even though she could plainly see.

"Jist making paste for these pictures," I answered her.

"Well, you used way too much flour," Ma snapped. "That flour comes from the wheat that Pa raises," she continued.

Like I don't know where flour comes from. But I didn't backtalk.

Ma shook her head. "Next time ask me before you make paste," she said.

"Okay," I said. I didn't want her taking the paste away from me. So I continued with my cutting and pasting. It warn't until I was almost finished that I noticed the picture I was making was something I saw last night: people flying around in the sky with lots of streaks of color all around them.

Flora
Friday, June 22, 1934
Nighttime

Tonight we had a Sisters' Club meeting in the kitchen after Ma and Pa went up to Aunt Hazel's and Unc Elmer's to play cards.

When I requested reports, Irene answered, "Well the strawberries and onions haven't been telling me nothing. Maybe the lettuce will have something to say tomorrow."

"Enough of the sarcasm," I responded. "Nellie, what news do you have?"

"Jist the colors and music in the sky," she answered. "Maybe it's that baby's soul making music for us to enjoy."

"Nellie, you're such a simpleton," Irene piped up. "That dead baby's not gonna tell us who buried it in the woods with music, colors or anything else. You need more common sense."

"Okay, okay," I interjected. "No fighting or saying bad things about your sister. Let's figure this out intelligently."

"That's what I meant. Intelligently. Not stupidly," Irene answered looking at Nellie.

"Meeting's over," I announced, annoyed with Irene. Both of my little sisters ran out of the room. I'm getting discouraged about the lack of progress we're making.

I need to do something bold. I think I'll visit the Gypsy camp.

Nighttime

Right before bedtime I went out to the privy. The sky was peppered with stars. That's when Nellie ran up and caught me.

"Turn around and look way up above our heads," she sang out. So I turned around and looked straight up. There were all kinds of bright colors buzzing around. Both of us kept looking and looking until the colored ribbons slowly faded away.

"What is that?" Nellie asked.

"I don't know," I answered. "Maybe the Northern Lights." I wished they hadn't disappeared so soon because I wanted Ma and Pa to see them. I also wished we had a telephone so I could tell Jean about the colors in the sky.

We always accuse Nellie of making things up but this was real. Yet I wouldn't have believed her if I hadn't seen it myself.

Nellie
Sunday, June 24, 1934
Forenoon

After church today everyone was talking 'bout seeing the colored shooting stars. The whole Geist family had seen them as well as Mr. and Mrs. Vandenberg and all the Katz family which includes five kids. Everybody was so excited 'bout seeing all the colors, 'specially since no one's never seen them before. Never ever. Kinda like we never ever had bears in our part of Michigan until this year.

Since I saw the colored stripes first, I was disappointed that Ma and Pa didn't say that I had discovered them. When I told our family 'bout all the people flying around in the colored streaks of light Ma warned me not to talk 'bout the flying people. Guess it's okay to see colors in the sky, but not people.

However, Ruthie Katz, who is four, started talking 'bout the flying people and Mrs. Katz ignored her, too. After church Ruthie was telling this to Mrs. Vandenberg who nodded politely. I don't think she believed Ruthie, but Mrs. Vandenberg is one of the nicest ladies. Both her and Aunt Hazel are good that way. Mrs. Geist, too.

I walked over to Ruthie and asked, "Where did you see the people flying around?"

"Out above our hayfield."

"How many were there?"

"Way too many to count. I think they were kinda dancing in the sky,"

"Was it at night?"

"Sunset. They were up there dancing and floating and having

a gay old time. There were lots of colors behind them, but I guess it was the sunset or the Northern Lights that made the color. I got Mum and Pops to come look at the people, but they couldn't see 'em."

"How 'bout your brothers, did they see 'em?"

Ruthie looked up and saw that her parents were leaving and ran to them without answering me. Ruthie's like that. At church picnics she quits in the middle of a game, or she'll jist run away whenever. It's good she's not starting school this year. You gotta pay attention in school.

Flora
Monday, June 25, 1934
Nighttime

At supper I signaled Nellie and Irene for Sisters' Club. As soon as they both appeared in my room, I started talking.

"Listen up, Jean told me some news that affects you girls. But I don't think Ma and Pa know about it yet, so you have to keep it a secret."

"Is it about the baby?" Nellie asked.

"No."

"Well, what?" Irene insisted.

"Jean told me the Parson Creek School Board is going to have a hearing to decide whether to fire Miss Flatshaw."

"But she's the best teacher ever," Irene almost shouted. "Why would they even think of firing her? And what's a hearing?"

"Just a meeting," Flora answered.

"Has she done something wrong?" Nellie asked. "Did she steal something?"

"No, nothing like that. Jean said she'd been seen at the Camp Meeting all last summer and all this spring. She takes sweets to Brother Johnson and snuggles up to him and kisses him after the service, every week. In front of everybody attending."

"This sounds like an ugly rumor," Irene spoke up. "You've been the victim of a rumor, Flora, and it's cruel. Miss Flatshaw wouldn't do that."

"Maybe it's true," Nellie said. "She does talk a lot about going to Camp Meeting and how it makes her feel closer to Jesus. She always smiles when she talks about Camp Meetings."

"Jean said Miss Flatshaw was being too friendly with the

preacher. She painted herself into a corner by chasing after him every single week. In public."

"I don't believe it. So what's gonna happen at the hearing?" Irene asked.

"The School Board is going to meet with Miss Flatshaw and see what she has to say about her behavior, but they're not going to tell her about it in advance. She'll be going into the meeting not knowing what it's about so she doesn't have time to prepare some lies."

Irene kept shaking her head. "Maybe the preacher is actually her cousin or something like that. I sure would hate for her to be a victim of rumors, like you, Flora."

There was silence for a long time. Irene finally said, "This ain't fair. Someone needs to warn her."

We all sat in stunned silence for several minutes.

"Now let's get down to the real business of this meeting," I went on.

"Whenever I can get out of the garden, I'm going to the Gypsy camp and spy on them."

"No, no," Irene breathed heavily. "What if you get caught? Ma and Pa would never forgive you."

"Well, they'll just have to. It's about time we figure out what really happened and quash all those rumors. I've taken enough blame for something I didn't do. Aunt Caroline would want me to figure this out."

Nellie
Tuesday, June 26, 1934
Forenoon

I've been thinking up all kinds of games to make the garden work go faster. Find the smallest weed. Find the biggest weed. Count the strawberries I pick. Count the strawberries I eat. Still, I jist git tired of workin' in the garden. The dancing people and colors haven't been in the sky for a while, so I don't even look forward to them no more.

Flora is nice to me, 'specially on the days that Irene is gone with Ma. She tries to help me with my games. She and I have strawberry picking races. She has to pick two rows of strawberries to my one. The rest of the rules are that you have to pick them all. You can't leave any ripe ones unpicked or you lose. You can't bruise any of the berries or you lose. It's okay for me to eat strawberries as long as Flora don't see me do it. I like that rule, cuz Flora knows that I eat them, but she don't wanna lie to Ma. So far I've won every race. I think it's impossible for her to pick two rows to my one even though she has grown-up arms and legs.

Today Irene isn't in the garden with us cuz she and Ma are up to Aunt Hazel's helping with window washing. Wish I was going there instead of gardening. Even though I hate window washing, it's better than strawberry picking. There are mosquitoes and other bugs all over the strawberries, so by the end of the afternoon you are bit real bad. Also, if you eat too many strawberries you git the runs. Then, sometimes it starts to rain and you still have to pick 'em. Ma says to come in the house only if there's lightning. Well, picking strawberries in the rain is purty miserable.

Finally, something happened. I found a small black arrowhead, not in the strawberry patch, but off to the side, lying there on the plowed-up garden bed. This was the first arrowhead I've ever found, even though Ma, Pa, Flora, and Irene have found some. We keep them in a box on top of Ma and Pa's cherry bureau. This one was small, an inch long, and in perfect condition. I'd never seen a black one before. The Indian who carved it musta wanted an arrowhead that could be used for squirrels, rabbits, and possums. Most of the ones in our box are larger and light colored, probably for deer hunting, very different from this little black one. I showed it to Flora and she really liked it, too.

"Have you ever seen any black rock like that?" I asked her.

"No, but Mr. Lutz says he found some black ones over on the other side of Johnnycake Ridge," she answered. "Let's show it to Mr. Lutz tonight and see if he has ever found any like this."

"Okay," I said. Mr. Lutz kinda scares me the way he swears at his cattle all the time, but Ma says he's a real good guy inside, and Ma usually is right 'bout these things.

Nighttime

After supper while Irene was in the kitchen reading her *Story Book*, Flora and I walked over to Mr. Lutz's house with the arrowhead. I knew he was there. I'd heard him swearing at his cattle before supper.

"Mighty nice, mighty nice," Mr. Lutz said inspecting the small arrowhead, "Where did you find it?"

"In the garden near our strawberry patch," I answered.

"Have you found any black ones like these?" Flora asked him.

"Yes, I have. About a dozen from down by the crick on the other side of the ridge," he answered. "But they're all larger than these. Old Man Keller told me they're black obsidian from the

Pottawatomi Indians. They built wigwams along the crick and raised their crops here where we have our farms. Real nasty fellows. One chopped off the head of an early settler right in front of everyone, Indian and White. He used a long blade. No doubt about it. Lots of people saw it. Savages. Glad we're not dealing with them no more."

"Pottawatomi," I repeated, having never heard that word before. "I like how 'Pottawatomi' sounds."

"It's the name of their tribe," he said.

"Like Gypsies or pirates?" I asked.

"Kinda, Sweetpea," Mr. Lutz laughed. "Did you know there are lots of different Indian tribes that all had different languages? Indians from Michigan don't understand Indians from Florida or Indians from California."

I felt a chill. Maybe the black hand I found buried in the woods was an Indian, not a Gypsy or pirate baby.

"Can we look at your arrowheads?" Flora asked, totally unaware of my thoughts. Mr. Lutz went off to find his arrowheads, coming back with a boxful. However, none of his black obsidian arrowheads looked like mine. Mr. Lutz's were larger and less evenly carved. Mr. Lutz seems like a nice guy after all. Maybe he jist swears at his cows outa habit.

Later in the evening after Irene fell asleep I slipped down to my usual listening spot and waited to hear Ma and Pa. I waited a long time.

"Nellie found it," Pa whispered. "I don't think Charlie told them anything about their savage ways. I knew that "Charlie" was Mr. Lutz.

"Flora said he told them about the Indian who cut off the settler's head with one swipe of his knife," Ma whispered back. "Nellie is gonna have nightmares the rest of her life."

Irene
Tuesday, June 26, 1934
Nighttime

I can't think of nothing except finding Miss Flatshaw and warning her about the School Board hearing. But I don't know where she lives. Why didn't she ever tell me that? We're close friends and I should know. I gotta tell her that she could lose her job if she keeps going to those Camp Meetings. But has she really been seeing Brother Johnson after the service? She never told me about that.

Maybe this thing about Brother Johnson is a vicious, ugly lie. People can be so mean. Just think about the two nasty girls at my school who won't play with me. Sugar and Clara Weston, sisters. Sow and Cow, I call them. I'm glad my initials are IY. That don't spell nothing.

Now I'm glad I go to town with Ma every Friday to peddle eggs. I'm hoping to run into Miss Flatshaw and I'm sure I could get a few minutes alone with her. Ma don't particularly like her, so Ma could call on a few houses by herself while I talked to Miss Flatshaw. But last night at supper Ma lowered the boom.

"You have to work in the garden the next two Fridays while Flora and Nellie each have a turn peddling with me. It's not fair that you get every Friday away from the garden."

So I will be on my hands and knees, hoeing, weeding, and picking strawberries all day long, just like every other day. When I finish that I will be washing, hulling, and canning.

How am I every gonna find Miss Flatshaw? Then the thought occurred to me—the Camp Meeting. I could sneak out at night and go to Fonsha. I know that I would be crossing Ma and Pa, but

I think everything that Flora said is true. I need to do the right thing, even if it means going against my parents' wishes.

How long would that take me to walk to the Camp Meeting? I'd need to go about a mile down Parson Creek Road and then maybe four or five miles down Fonsha Road. About six miles all told. I'll measure how long it takes me to walk one mile and then times it by six. I'm glad I'm so good at arithmetic.

Once I find the Camp Meeting and Miss Flatshaw, I'll ask her to drive me home. She has a spiffy Model T. There's no time to waste. I'll go tomorrow night.

Flora
Tuesday, June 26, 1934
Nighttime

Irene kept asking me questions about the Camp Meeting to-night. Like I've been there. There was a time when I wanted to go with Henry, but only because I thought it would be a date that didn't cost anything. But when Brother Johnson preached at our church, I saw his true nature. I'd have to have a mighty strange boyfriend who would want to go to the Camp Meeting, so it's un-likely I'll be a-hooting and a-hollering down in Fonsha any time soon.

I answered Irene by telling her that Camp Meetings are on Wednesday nights at seven o'clock, but that I would never go with her. I told her that it would be so much better for her to read her *Bible* stories and think about becoming a better person rather than going to Camp Meeting. She didn't like that at all. She said she was trying to find Miss Flatshaw.

Why Irene likes Miss Flatshaw is beyond me. I wonder if she knows that the kids all call her "Miss Fatshaw" behind her back? Irene thinks they're best friends. Rather weird friendship in my estimation. Maybe Miss Flatshaw feels sorry for Irene; I don't know. But it's mighty strange for a teacher to be a friend with a student.

Irene
Wednesday, June 27, 1934
Nighttime

I am so excited cuz tonight I am secretly gonna go to the Camp Meeting in Fonsha to warn Miss Flatshaw about her teaching job. This afternoon I figured out I can walk a mile in eighteen minutes. I did this by going back and forth from the lane to the road, which I know is an eighth of a mile. I walked it eight times in eighteen minutes, using the kitchen clock. That means that I can walk to Fonsha in less than two hours if it's six miles away. Not everyone my age could figure this out.

So right after supper I told Nellie that I was gonna stay downstairs and read the *Bible* and that it might take me way into the middle of the night to finish it. I didn't want her to go blabbing to Ma and Pa that I wasn't around when she goes to bed. She can be a little brat without even knowing it.

The first thing I did was put on some shoes. I didn't wanna be walking barefoot down those stony roads. I still have some winter tenderfoot left. I also put on a sweater in case it gets cold after dark. You might say I'm well-prepared for this little adventure.

I left by the side door off the kitchen when no one was around, right after supper cleanup. Ma and Pa would be settling in the parlor where Flora would be playing the piano and Nellie sitting on the floor reading her *Pirate Book*. I snuck around the side fence row to the road so no one would see me walking down the driveway, although I did hear Mr. Lutz swearing at his cows. He wasn't as loud tonight; the cows musta been better behaved than usual. I heard a few "damns," and only one "goddammit."

I climbed over the fence with no problem and started walking down the road until I was near Aunt Hazel and Unc Elmer's farm. Then I went to the other side of the road and walked down through the ditch. I figured if they'd finished eating supper I'd be hidden from their parlor and upstairs windows while in the ditch. Once again I'm using my smarts.

After I got by Unc Elmer's farm I walked on the road towards the church. There are three big hills before you even can see the church so I walked them kinda fast and got thirsty. I wished I had brought some water, but there was nothing I could do 'bout that now. By the time I got to the church it seemed like I had been gone an hour, but I knew that it was only a mile from our farm to the church. Shoulda been just eighteen minutes. I then realized that I hadn't counted in any extra time for climbing fences, walking in the ditch, or going up and down hills. What I had measured this afternoon was flat. This trip was gonna take me longer than I had figured. Miss Flatshaw had better be grateful. I'd only gone a mile and already I was tired and thirsty.

Walking by the church cemetery was spooky. I could see my grandparents' graves from the road, Irma and Jacob Yoder, Pa's parents. I only remember my grandparents a little bit and I don't recollect my other grandparents at all. We always put flowers on all the graves on Decoration Day at the end of May. This year Ma made bouquets of iris, poppies, and spirea in Ball jars. I saw that they were still there, but wilted. Ma would be collecting her Ball jars real soon.

Looking again at the cemetery I spotted the Geist plot and saw Jimmy's fresh grave on the front side of the church. It had more flowers than any other grave. Then walking on, I startled when I saw a woman standing on the far side of the church, in the middle of the cemetery. She was so quiet just standing there at a grave. What was she doing here? Could this be "our baby's" mother? I froze for a couple of minutes and watched her. She didn't move much, but I thought she was crying. The Sisters'

Club needs to find out about her. But I didn't have time to talk to
a crying lady right now. I needed to find Miss Flatshaw.

It was getting kinda dark by then so I picked up the pace and
ran for a while. I was out of breath when I heard a car coming.
Who would be out at this time of night? Maybe someone going
to the Camp Meeting? I considered hitchhiking, but I decided to
hide behind a tree instead.

I was standing behind the tree with my hands on some vines
when I realized I was touching poison ivy. I wanted to swear like
Mr. Lutz does, but I just kept quiet. I might as well have sworn,
the car was so loud puttering down the road. I finally looked at
it when it was farther away, but it was just too dusty and too far
away to tell if it was anyone I knew. I wondered if it was the lady
at the cemetery, but I hadn't see a car parked anywhere near the
church or the cemetery.

I jumped back onto the road and started walking again, and
wouldn't you know, another car came by so I got right back into
more poison ivy. After that car drove by I started running down
the road to make up for lost time, but I just started panting and
getting thirstier so I slowed down to a fast walk. My legs and feet
were getting tired, too. This worried me cuz I hadn't even gotten
as far as Fonsha Road.

Finally, when it was getting really dark, I reckoned about my
bedtime, I reached Fonsha Road and turned right, heading south
toward Fonsha. The road was tree-lined and dark. I wished the
moon was full so I could see better. I knew there was a one-lane
bridge ahead so I pushed on. I would be able to get a drink of water from the crick. After about a half an hour I got to the bridge. I
stumbled down the roadside to the crick, slipping into briars cuz
I couldn't see clearly, but I found myself at the water's edge and
cupped my hands and dipped into the crick. Water never tasted so
good. I musta drunk enough for an Angus bull. I decided to pee since
I was totally out of sight, then I made my way out of the bushes to
the road, scratching my arms and legs on the briars along the way.

No longer thirsty, I rushed on. I walked for miles and miles seeing nothing but the road ahead of me and not too much of that. I tried playing little games like counting to one hundred over and over again. Twice I stopped to rest when there was a boulder by the side of the road. I sure wanted another drink of water, but there wasn't any sign of a crick or a well.

I was so tired. No one had ever told me how hard it is to walk after dark when everything is practically invisible. My legs were all scratched and my feet throbbed.

Finally, after forever, I came to a clearing with three houses, the village of Fonsha. Where was the Camp Meeting? Flora had told me it was near Fonsha, but she didn't know exactly where. All three houses were dark, sunset and bedtime being hours ago. I didn't see any tent near the village, so I decided to keep walking in case it was on the other side of the clearing. I walked and walked; my legs had become so tired that I had to tell myself to put one foot in front of the other. Finally I reached a corner road where there was a big patch of dirt. A couple of log benches were off on one side, and a couple more on the other. Near one corner were the remains of a campfire.

I kept wishing there was more light. Near the dead campfire was a scrap of burned paper. The best I could tell it was from a hymnal. Then I found some more paper. Yes, definitely bits and pieces of hymns. Next, I got an awful feeling in the pit of my stomach. I started dry heaving but nothing came up.

I wanted to scream and maybe I did. I had found the Camp Meeting, but no one was here. Had I got there too late? Was the revival meeting over? The embers in the campfire were cold. They hadn't had any fire tonight. Then I sat on one of the log benches and instead of screaming I started to cry. I had come all this way, gotten into poison ivy and been scratched by briars only to find no one here. My legs and feet were aching like they'd never ached before. Where was Miss Flatshaw and, more importantly, her car? I needed a ride home.

Nellie
Wednesday, June 27, 1934
Nighttime

Even though Irene hadn't come up to bed tonight, I decided to listen in on Ma and Pa as usual. If Irene was gonna read the whole *Bible*, it would be a long while before she came up to bed. I remember Mrs. Geist telling me that reading the *Bible* would take a coon's age. I 'spect Irene won't be able to finish it even if she stays up mosta the night.

I've watched Ma read the *Bible* many times, and the words are tiny and the pages thin, so it takes her a half-hour to read only two or three pages. Thinking 'bout that I carefully climbed out of the bed with my pillow down to the register. I figured I'd tell Irene that I rolled out of bed if she came up unexpectedly and found me down there.

The scene was the usual: Ma darning socks in her rocking chair and Pa smoking his pipe. I couldn't see them, but I knew they were down there and what they were doing by the sounds and smells. There warn't no conversation for the longest time. I was hoping that they'd talk 'bout the Indians some more.

Finally Ma said, "Irene's been asking Flora 'bout the Camp Meeting, trying to get all the details about where it is, what time it is and whether kids can go there. She might have it in her head that she needs to go there and confess her sins or something."

"Don't need to worry about that," Pa answered. "Brother Johnson done picked up and left. All his collections were coming up empty so he decided to move on. I heard it from the guys at the gristmill this morning."

I heard Ma's soft chuckle. Sometimes she holds back a big laugh if she thinks it ain't proper.

"Well, what about Miss Flatshaw?" Ma asked.

"Rumor is, she went with him."

"Well, if that don't beat all," Ma replied.

"I'll tell Irene at breakfast tomorrow that the Camp Meeting is gone, so she can get all those notions out of her head," Pa answered.

That's all I heard. My pillow was so nice and comfy that I musta fell asleep on the floor. When I woke up it was real dark, and I was still on the floor and I was cold. I crawled up in bed and rolled over to snuggle up to Irene to git warm. I rolled all the way over to the edge of her side of the bed but she warn't there. Then I remembered she was gonna read the whole *Bible* tonight; she was probably downstairs reading by the kerosene lamp. But dang it, I was so cold. I lay there awhile and couldn't git warm or go to sleep without Irene beside me.

After a while, I decided to go downstairs and git in bed with Ma and Pa. I hadn't done that in a long time, but I knew I could git warm between them, no problem at all. When I opened the door to their bedroom Ma raised up and looked at me. My eyes could see better now and I could see she was surprised. "I wanna sleep with you; I'm cold," I stammered. "Irene's still reading the *Bible* and our bed is awful cold," I said pleadingly. By then Pa had raised up too and was looking at me. I jumped over Ma and climbed into the middle of the bed. Sure 'nuf it was wonderfully warm in there.

But Pa said, "Why is Irene reading the *Bible*? It's the middle of the night," he said. Like I didn't know that. I'm seven, after all.

I wiped the sleepy out of my eyes before I said anything.

"She never came to bed," I answered. "And I'm so cold." Ma and Pa both jumped out of bed and ran out of the room. I jist snuggled down in the warmth under their covers. However, they were soon back questioning me again.

"Did she come up and put on her nightgown?" Ma asked.

I shook my head. "She told me she was gonna read the whole *Bible* so she would be up late."

Then without speaking Ma and Pa both got busy, Pa lighting a little candle on top of the bureau. Then they both got dressed hurriedly.

"You stay here in bed and don't leave," Pa commanded me in his sternest voice.

Pa then said to Ma, "Wake Flora up to help us look for her. Check every nook and cranny of the house, including the cellar. Check underneath the bed in their bedroom, too. Maybe she was hiding from Nellie and fell asleep. I'll go check the barn and other buildings. Could be she wanted an adventure and decided to sleep in the barn with Rover. Then meet me in the kitchen."

This kinda scared me, but the warm bed felt so darned good. I was asleep in no time.

Flora
Wednesday, June 27, 1934
Nighttime

"Flora, Flora," Ma shook me out of my sleep. It was the middle of the night and I couldn't understand why Ma was in my room waking me up. Only once, eleven years before, Aunt Hazel had awakened me and she took me to her house to sleep on their davenport. When I woke up in the morning, she told me I had a sister named Irene. Nellie was born during the day when I was in school so there wasn't any nighttime drama.

But tonight Ma was looking down at me in the darkness. "Where is Irene?" she demanded.

I was confused. Why was Ma here in my bedroom asking me about Irene? Irene sleeps on the other side of the house with Nellie.

"Isn't she in bed?" I answered, confused.

"No, according to Nellie, she never went to bed."

I sat up, suddenly awake. "Probably she fell asleep in the kitchen or parlor," I answered. "She does that all the time."

Ma just looked sad and shook her head. She was close to tears.

Jumping out of bed, I told her I'd look for Irene. I pulled on the brown dress I had worn to school and hadn't hung back up. Ma told me Pa was out searching for Irene in the barns and outbuildings.

Ma lit a candle for me, and I proceeded to search the whole house, starting with the parlor where the *Bible* lay unopened. When I finished I met Ma and Pa in the kitchen.

"Maybe Aunt Hazel and Unc Elmer's," I suggested feebly.

"The Camp Meeting," Pa answered. "Didn't you say she was asking lots of questions about it?"

I nodded, too dumbstruck to think that my little sister would go off to the Camp Meeting in the middle of the night.

"Gypsies," Ma answered. "They took Irene."

This was all getting very frightening. I shuddered. Irene gets on my nerves. She is a little know-it-all. But still, she is my sister and I love her.

"Okay, Ma and I are going to take the car down to Fonsha. If she's not there we'll wake up Hazel and Elmer. They wouldn't let Irene sleep there without telling us, but maybe she snuck into their house. Flora you stay here and put that latch on the backdoor. If Gypsies already came to the house once tonight, we don't want them trying again." Ma shuddered when Pa said that. I may have also.

Irene
Thursday, June 28, 1934
Before Dawn

When the car drove up I was too tired to move. I had settled down in some leaves near the old campfire just wanting to rest enough to get energy to walk home. I figured I could drink some more water from the crick to revive me, but I had a long walk ahead of me before I would even get to the crick. I drifted off a few times and would wake up again, cold and scared. I figured I had all night to get home, so I might as well wait until I was rested. When the car drove up, I decided to jump up and run into the woods and hide. But my body wouldn't jump.

The car door opened and I could see two people, and then a dog popped out and ran right over to me. It happened so fast I couldn't get away, but soon I realized the dog was Rover and I could hear Ma and Pa calling my name.

"Over here," I answered, surprised at how weak my voice was. I guess all that crying had taken it out of me. Rover was jumping all over me, licking my arms and legs that had blood all over them from the briar scratches.

Pa ran over and scooped me up, even though he hadn't lifted me in a couple of years. I clung to him, never so happy to have Ma and Pa come get me. Ma was crying. Then she kept asking if a bad Gypsy man had carried me off.

I won't go into what happened next. I had to tell the truth, even though I would have escaped a bad whoopin' if I had lied and blamed a Gypsy man. I don't think Ma and Pa totally understood I was doing this for a good reason. They thought I wanted to go to the Camp Meeting to meet up with Miss Flatshaw and have a jolly old time. Miss Flatshaw had better appreciate all I went through for her. I will tell her the whole story next fall. In the meantime, she'll have to figure out how to save her job herself, cuz I've done all I'm willing to do.

Nellie
Thursday, June 28, 1934
Forenoon

After all the scariness of Irene not being in bed last night, I woke up hearing her whimpering beside me. It musta actually been early morning cuz it was still dark and I could hear the roosters starting to crow—our two and Mr. Lutz's half dozen or so, across the road. They seemed to be crowing back and forth to each other. I couldn't quite figure out why I warn't still in Ma and Pa's bed. Pa musta carried me upstairs to bed after they found Irene.

Later when I woke up again, Irene was already down in the kitchen and Ma was washing her up. Irene sat still in the wash-tub. She had welts and scratches all over her arms and legs. Apparently her bottom, too. I could tell she was trying to be brave but Ma's scrubbing warn't gentle. Finally she got out, wrapped in a towel, and Ma ordered her to go back to bed. She went upstairs obediently wearing a long, sad face.

Ma looked me and sighed. "Nellie, if Irene ever isn't in bed again, you come tell Pa and me immediately. And don't you ever go off by yourself like Irene did last night. It's a wonder that we even found her. Thank goodness she had asked Flora all those questions about the Camp Meeting. And we're lucky Rover sniffed her out. It was so dark out there. Any Gypsy could have grabbed her and taken off with her." Ma shuddered.

"Why do Gypsies take people?" I asked.

"Only children, not grown-ups," Ma answered.

This was confusing. Why would Gypsies want more mouths to feed? The three Gypsies I'd seen looked tired and poor, and their horses looked worse than they did.

"Well, they steal things and sometimes they steal children," she answered. Again, I jist couldn't figure it out. A Gypsy might steal something like food cuz he was hungry or a horse cuz he needed to replace one of those old sick ones. But why steal a child? It don't make no sense. A child needs food and a bed, and parents to explain the rules. Where were Gypsies gonna git more food, beds, and parents? Any fool knows we're in bad times, and it takes all summer to grow and put up food. Stealing a child is gonna make more work for them Gypsies.

"That's the way it is," was the only answer I got out of Ma when I asked her again. She warn't making no sense today, but she'd been up all night looking for Irene. It's hard to make sense when you need sleep.

Flora
Thursday, June 28, 1934
Forenoon

Because of all of the happenings with Irene last night, Ma said that I could have a break from gardening today. So I immediately decided to go over to Jean's house and maybe even go spy on the Gypsy camp afterwards. I hadn't seen Jean since school was out, so I was excited to see her. When I got there Mrs. Spinatti greeted me warmly. Then Jean appeared and gave me a hug. People in our family don't hug much, but Jean's parents are Italian so she is always hugging me. I've gotten used to it and I like it.

"What a nice surprise," Jean said. "As usual, I want you to play the piano."

"Okay, but I haven't heard any new songs," I responded.

Jean asked her mother if we could listen to the radio. When Mrs. Spinatti nodded, we both ran into their parlor where she tuned in the radio. Jean and I listened to *I Only Have Eyes for You*. I listened carefully went over to the piano and plunked it out. When I tried it for the second time, I played much better and Jean started singing along. We were singing and laughing so hard that Mrs. Spinatti came in and started singing with us.

Jean interrupted, "It's time to teach you how to Lindy Hop."

"Lindy Hop," I repeated, confused.

"It's a dance," she said, grabbing my arm. Then she proceeded to guide me through the fast-paced steps while Mrs. Spinatti played some music. If we were laughing before, we couldn't stop laughing after that. Lindy Hop, I love you.

"You deserve to have a day off, too" Mrs. Spinatti said to Jean.

Mrs. Spinatti certainly was a wonderful mother. Every Friday she worked for Dr. Holzer in his office in town. Every now and then she'd bring home old magazines for Jean who, in turn, gave them to me.

Jean, excited at the prospect of the whole day off, pulled my arm and we ran up to her bedroom.

"So are you feeling better?" she asked.

"No," I answered with the painful truth. "The sting of those false rumors isn't so bad anymore but all this lonesome gardening makes me ponder it."

Jean smiled. "You should go to some dances. That will cheer you up."

"Where are the dances and how much do they cost?" I asked. Clearly I was totally uninformed regarding social activities, particularly since the Red Barn Dance Hall had closed down for good.

"The closest one is the White Rabbit," she answered. "It's near Battle Creek and they have different bands every week. Admission is five cents," she continued. "Every now and then it's free for ladies. I've gone twice with Mimi."

"Who drives?" I asked, knowing that Pa would never give me the Model A when we weren't even taking it to church.

"Mimi's father lets her drive," Jean responded. "I think the cost of gas isn't a problem because her father has a steady job with the railroad. She's made two new dresses since Easter."

"Well, I want to go," I answered.

"Great," Jean said. "We're going on Saturday night. You'll love it. We can dance together until some boys ask us to dance. It's so much fun."

Then I started worrying about the money. I remembered my nest egg of two dollars that I've saved from helping Ma peddle eggs over the years. I quickly figured out I could go to the White Rabbit forty times with my two dollars. Not bad, particularly if we went on some free nights, too.

Feeling so good, I whispered to Jean my plan for the afternoon: I was going to walk over to the Gypsy camp and spy on them. Did she want to join me?

YES.

Afternoon

It took Jean and me about an hour to walk to the Fairgrounds near the Gypsy camp. There were a lot of trees and brush along the fence row between the Fairgrounds and Gypsy camp and we approached from the Fairgrounds side.

When we got there I realized the fence was six feet high with barbed wire atop it. We'd need to do the spying from the Fairgrounds side of the fence. Jean pulled out an old pair of binoculars, an heirloom from her grandfather who fought in the Great War. She spent a couple of minutes twisting them to come into focus. Then she handed them to me.

I could see four women sitting near a campfire, peeling potatoes, and putting food into pots to cook their supper. One of them was old and only watching the kids. The others were cooking. There were seven children of all ages who ran around through their campsite, but the women made them slow down whenever they got near the fire."

Then if happened. I had to sneeze from all the dust, and even though I tried to hold it back, I just couldn't. It was a quiet sneeze, but two women looked up towards us and slowly walked over to the fence. They acted like they were breaking branches off the trees for kindling. Both put the kindling down in front of a tent and walked inside it. I didn't see them leave the tent but all of a sudden they were at the fence right across from Jean and me.

I tried to smile and act pleasant, but my heart was pounding. Jean stood right beside me and I could see her hands shake.

The younger of the two had very long dark hair, black eyes, and brown skin. She was pretty and looked to be about sixteen or seventeen, my age. The other was older, maybe forty or forty-five.

"Why are you here watching us?" the younger one whispered with a marked accent.

I decided to get right to the point. "A baby died and I wondered if it was from your people," I answered.

"Baby?" both women repeated.

"No," the younger woman replied. "No baby. It is very sad when a baby dies. We have these children, no baby," waving her hand at all the kids who were running around.

We talked for a couple of minutes about their camp. They had come here every year for the past three years, which is unusual for them. Usually they head out for new places. But she told me that people here leave them alone, and only the Sheriff stops by now and then to ask questions. Apparently the men get accused of stealing and the Sheriff has to investigate.

I mentioned that we go to the high school in town and asked her if she ever goes to school. She said no, that they move around too much for school and her father wants her to get married. Her voice trailed off.

Then she stepped close and whispered very softly, "I'm lonely and would like to become friends with both of you, but I am not allowed to make friends with anyone not Gypsy." The other lady drew near, obviously trying to find out what she said.

The moment was awkward and I wasn't sure if she was telling the truth, so I looked at Jean and we decided to leave before any more ladies came over to the fence. We exchanged names with the younger lady. Hers was Patya. I looked at her and smiled, but said nothing. The other lady scowled at me. Jean had tears in her eyes.

We said goodbye and ran back through the fairgrounds to the road and came home. On the way home Jean and I talked about whether Patya genuinely wanted to become friends or if she wanted an excuse to come to our houses to steal things. Jean believed her and wanted to befriend her. Me, I just don't know.

Nighttime

Later when I was helping Ma get supper, I told her about the dance at the White Rabbit on Saturday night. I think she was pondering the fact that I wasn't going to become Mrs. Henry Fitch. She went quiet for a long moment.

But then smiled at me and said, "We had a huge scare with your sister last night running off to the Camp Meeting, but that don't mean you can't go out and have some fun with your girl-friends. Just be very, very careful. You remember what I told you when you had your date with Henry. Well, be even more careful with other boys. Always stay close to your girlfriends, and never accept a ride home with a boy."

Ma kept going on and on without pause. "If Mimi's car breaks down, all three of you should stay together. Don't one of you go off to get help. I just can't imagine that Irene was by herself on those lonely roads last night," she sighed. "You must be home before midnight, and Mimi needs to drive you right here. Don't even think about walking back from Jean's house after dark."

I got the message loud and clear. Have fun but don't take any chances.

Irene
Friday, June 29, 1934
Forenoon

Well, it finally happened. When I looked and felt my worst. Ma insisted that I go with her today to peddle eggs and vegetables. I hadn't wanted to go with Ma cuz my whole body was busting out with poison ivy rash. It's all over my face and even on my bottom and on most of my arms and legs. Even in my private parts so it stings when I pee.

The rash is worst around my right wrist and both legs where it is so totally red that you can't see any skin, just the tiny red bubbles. I must have some in my mouth, too, cuz it hurts way too much to eat. The rest of my body itches so much that I can't stand it, but Ma says if I scratch the watery rash it will spread all over. As if it ain't all over my body anyway. I've been rubbing the sleeve of my dress against my arm and that helps a bit, but I can feel it wet underneath the fabric, probably spreading up and down my arm.

So Ma and I went into town and I tried to hide behind Ma while she went from door to door. It didn't make sense for me to be there. Who would wanna buy food from a farm lady who has a daughter covered head to toe with poison ivy? People might think it was small pox or, worse yet, something that I got from eating our eggs and vegetables. They might never buy food from Ma again. I think this whole thing was Ma's anger coming out. She knows how ashamed I am of how I look.

If I hadn't been tortured enough, just as soon as we walked down High Street to Main, there stood Miss Flatshaw on the corner, looking just like she was waiting for me and Ma to appear.

She extended her hand to Ma who was slow to reach out and shake it. Then she smiled at me and asked me how I was. I shrugged, knowing that I looked red, raw, and miserable.

Ma smiled what I thought was a fake smile at Miss Flatshaw and said that I had run away to the Camp Meeting a couple of nights ago, hoping to find HER. I winced. I didn't wanna talk about that at all.

"Camp Meeting?" Miss Flatshaw questioned me. She was acting like she'd never heard of it.

I just stood there stunned. What did Ma want me to do? Break down and cry? Finally I nodded. There was another awkward moment of silence.

"Well, Irene had heard that you often go to the Camp Meeting," Ma finally responded. Ma was clearly angry at me for running away on Wednesday night. Maybe she was getting some pleasure out of this encounter, but I simply wanted to git in the car and hide.

"Oh, I only went to Camp Meeting a few times," Miss Flatshaw replied. "It seemed like the right thing for a religious woman to do."

Ma glared at her like she had turned into an onion.

Finally, I blurted out, "I wanted to see you and know that you are okay and will be back teaching in the fall."

Miss Flatshaw stiffened but didn't say a word. Her lips pursed up and she looked straight at me.

This wasn't going the way I wanted it to. Again, I wanted to run and hide.

"Why wouldn't I be back?" she finally asked in a loud, slow voice, emphasizing every word.

"I dunno," I mumbled. Please God get me out of this situation. This was worse than being in the empty Camp Meeting in the middle of the night.

Ma grabbed the sleeve of my dress and turned me around, saying to Miss Flatshaw in her fake nice-person voice, "Nice to see you."

Miss Flatshaw didn't respond so Ma and I walked down Main Street and looked in the windows of the shops. I think she was hoping for more people to look at me and make me feel ashamed. Fortunately, no one else appeared.

Nighttime

I wanted to hear Ma and Pa's conversation but I knew they would be watching to see if I was in the kitchen. So I carefully went into their bedroom and lay down on their bed in the dark. I figured I could leave when they went out to the privy before bed. To my surprise I could hear better here than from the kitchen.

"She was standing right there on the corner of High Street and Main, just like she was waiting for us," Ma said.

"So she didn't run off with Brother Johnson after all," Pa replied. "Or maybe she decided she was better off without him. Nobody seemed to like him. Even those who went to Camp Meeting regularly quit after all that nonsense with snakes."

I couldn't believe what I was hearing. I thought I was her friend but she sure hadn't told me her secrets. She was so cold and unfriendly today, like she had never met me before. She shoulda been happy cuz I walked all the way to Fonsha to see her. But she seemed not to care at all. I won't make that mistake again.

Nellie
Saturday, June 30, 1934
Forenoon

Irene is so miserable with bruises and poison ivy rash that she hasn't been able to work or play with me. Maybe Ma was feeling generous or maybe cuz I didn't go with Irene on her trip to Fonsha, Ma told me I could go play. I kinda wanted to go down to the crick cuz it's my favorite summertime place to play. I love spotting the guppies and waterstriders. The pollywogs probably have turned into frogs already. You really have to hit the right time with them. I love their long tails and slippery skin.

I wish I didn't have to go through the woods to git to the crick. The woods scare me cuz of all that's happened. But that's the only way to git there. So I decided to go to the meadow and play with the cows for a while and then figure out if I have enough courage to run through the woods. When I got to the first meadow all five of the cows nosed up to me, but quickly got bored and walked off to a new grazing spot. Even Moo-Moo walked away.

Since the cows were no fun, I decided to climb one of the cherry trees in the fence row to see if I could see beyond the woods to the crick. I chose what used to be Flora's climbing tree. It has low branches so I could git an easy start.

I got up to the top branch and, dang, I could see our whole farm if I looked south, and Aunt Hazel and Unc Elmer's farm if I looked east. I craned my neck looking towards the crick. It looked like Unc Elmer was down on his back forty near the crick. I couldn't quite tell what he was doing, maybe dragging a gunnysack. Then I realized that something warn't quite right. The man warn't Unc Elmer who's really, really thin. This man was taller and a lot wider than Unc Elmer. It warn't Pa either; this guy was much heftier than Pa, more like that nasty Brother Johnson, the rivalist preacher. But Brother Johnson is long gone, or I would have said it was the preacher.

I had seen Pa pitching manure into the spreader in the barnyard right before I walked to the meadow. Pa warn't in sight now cuz the granary was in the way. So I sat in the cherry tree and watched. I was glad the tree was all leafed out. I doubt if even the cows could see me, let alone the man down in Unc Elmer's back forty. I wondered how he got there. Maybe he snuck down Unc Elmer's lane or more likely he took Old Man Keller's lane from Keller Road and walked across the river to git there. The lane has a gate at the road and is 'bout a half mile from Old Man Keller's house, far enough away that you can't be seen going through the gate. I 'spect the Gypsies use that lane with their horses, too.

Jist then I noticed Unc Elmer. He was up in his barnyard. It looked like he was gonna spread manure today, too. Unc looked like he had finished loading it into the spreader. My oldest cousin Dan was hitching up Dixie and Trixie and then Unc started toward one of his cultivated fields toward the road. He wouldn't be going nowhere near the crick.

So I looked back to see if the stranger was still there. He warn't, thank goodness. I wanted the crick to myself so I could play with the little water critters. I'd like to see some baby turtles. I'm always gentle with them and I'm always careful to throw them back in the water real quick. I don't wanna hurt any of them. Sometimes they're scared of me, but I usually sing a little song to them and they calm down.

So I waited a long time to leave my hiding place in the cherry tree. Then I scooted down the tree and set off towards my favorite part of the crick to explore. After I climbed over the stile I got to the path in the woods and started running at my fastest speed, but something tripped me and I fell to the ground. At first

I thought I'd tripped over some tree roots but two large hands pulled me up.

I was 'bout to thank whoever belonged to those hands, but before I knew it my neck was being squeezed and it hurt real bad. I gasped for breath and I twisted to git out of the hold of those big hands. But they shoved me down to the ground and pulled down my drawers. It was so fast I didn't have time to think. I started screaming but the hands grabbed my head and started squeezing my neck again. The man stunk like he'd never had a bath. A terrible, horrible stink.

I struggled and struggled but those hands held on tight. I fought hard kicking and pulling myself away. In a couple of minutes the hands loosened their grip as one hand stayed on my neck and the other seemed to be unfastening his suspenders. For an instant my neck was free and I looked at his face. It was that horrible rivalist preacher. I was so mad. I coughed and shouted, "I know who you are, and God is gonna send you to hell." Then I coughed some more.

He looked at me quizzically like he had never seen me before, holding me tight. Suddenly, he slackened his grip on my body as he fumbled with his pants. I decided to use every bad word I had ever heard Mr. Lutz use on his animals.

"You goddam son-of-a-bitch," I cursed at him. "Goddammit, let me go," I continued. "Shit. Shit. Shit." I had run out of cuss words, then I remembered some more. "Damn you to hell. You goddam son-of-a-bitch," I repeated. Then he tightened his grip again. I don't think he liked my cussing at him.

Finally he freed up my legs and I kicked and kicked at him. He had managed to pull off his suspenders and his pants were down to his ankles. A body part I had never seen emerged. What was this deformity that stuck straight out? I pulled myself up again with the idea of running off, but he struck my head and pulled me down to the ground again.

"Goddam it to hell," I shouted as I kicked at his ugly

protuberance. "You'll burn in hell." I wanted this preacher to know how angry I was. He was hurting me bad. Fortunately I was wearing shoes. I kicked harder and harder. Finally I hit underneath his privates and he screamed out in pain, letting go of me.

I took off not looking back. I wanted to git into the wild part of the woods where there was enough thicket for me to hide. Before running I pulled up my drawers so I could run faster. For a long time I simply ran, not really sure where I was going. I listened but couldn't hear him behind me.

I kept in the woods, keeping clear of the path, looking for the heaviest brush. When I got to a blackberry thicket I kept going even though I was gittin' all scratched. All I wanted was to find a safe place away from his horrible, strangling hands. I twisted through the briars, figuring the scratches warn't near as bad as the strangling.

I continued on for a long, long time until I fell on the ground in Ma Bear's sleeping place, a nice round low spot under a boulder and I lay there curled up in a ball catching my breath. I knew I'd made it all the way to the swampy pond cuz that's where Ma Bear lives. I strained to hear the horrible preacher, but there was only the sounds of the breeze in the woods and my own panting. I lay there a long, long time, resting and hoping the evil preacher was nowhere near.

It seemed like hours before I got enough courage to git up, and only after Ma Bear returned and told me to be careful going home. I made my way to the hollow tree where I hid for a long time, worried that the preacher would come walking by and snatch me again. I've never been so still in my life. Lying on the heat register eavesdropping on Ma and Pa had been good practice. Then gittin' bolder, I climbed the large oak tree to see if he was anywhere near. Sometimes ZeeZee and I fly to this tree and I was hoping he would appear today. I looked in all directions but I saw nuthin'. No ZeeZee, no evil preacher.

Finally, after what seemed like hours, I slid down the tree, staying clear of the path, and followed the crick northwest until I crawled through some more briars to reach the west lane back to the barn. I ran straight to the house and into the kitchen.

Ma warn't there. Maybe she was up at Aunt Hazel's. I looked around for something to eat. Not much but I stuck a knife into the butter dish and licked off the butter. It was so warm and sweet and comforting. All I wanted was to taste the sweet warm butter and forget what happened. I licked and licked and let it roll down my throat. That butter was so darn good.

Afternoon

Finally Ma got home. I was still crying so Ma came and sat with me in the parlor.

"Ma," I started, "I wanna tell you 'bout today when I went down to the meadow and the woods."

"You went down to the woods?" Ma repeated with alarm.

"Yup. Irene was too miserable from the poison ivy, so she couldn't play with me and I really miss goin' to the crick and playing with the guppies and waterstriders."

"So what happened?" Ma sat down on the bed and waited.

"Remember the rivalist preacher who preached when Reverend Blackman was gone?"

Ma nodded.

"Well, he pulled me down to the ground and tried to strangle me. Then he pulled down his pants and I could see his privates."

Ma gasped. "What?" She looked at me with a face I had never seen before. She was scowling and her eyes were so wide open they looked like they were gonna pop out. "He tried to strangle you and hurt you?" she repeated.

"He choked me so hard I couldn't hardly breathe. He pulled down my drawers and I thought I was gonna die. It was only when he was taking off his suspenders that he let go with one hand that I kicked him and got away."

"What happened next?" Ma asked.

"Well, I ran and ran and finally rested in Ma Bear's bed. When she finally came back, she whispered that I should be very careful going home."

Ma scowled again but didn't say anything.

"I stayed there for a long time, then climbed the ZeeZee tree to see if the preacher had gone away. I couldn't see him so I ran back along the west lane."

"Tell me again what happened," she asked. "Just repeat what happened."

I told the story again as best I could remember.

"And what about that bear?" Ma seemed calmer now.

"I rested in her nest where she sleeps, until she came back and told me to be careful."

"Was her nest like a bird's nest up in the tree?" Ma asked.

"No, like a deer's nest," I answered. I'd seen lots of round deer's nests when going down to the woods with my sister and cousins.

"Well, after supper I want you to tell this story to Pa."

I agreed, but I have to say that telling it made me feel worse. This warn't one of my frigments.

Nighttime

I couldn't eat supper thinking 'bout having to tell Pa 'bout the rivalist preacher trying to strangle me. Ma didn't believe my story and I was afraid that Pa would make me go down and then show him where it all happened. I sure don't wanna walk down there again. Why were all these awful things happening down in the woods? I used to love the woods. No more.

Pa's reaction was different from Ma's. He kept asking me more and more questions and I did the best I could to answer them truthfully. He even seemed to take me seriously when I explained 'bout Ma Bear being my friend and how lonely she is without Pa Bear. Ma jist shook her head slowly back and forth with a frown when I talked 'bout Ma and Pa Bear.

"So how did you know it was Brother Johnson?" Pa finally asked after a long time.

"Well, I seen him at church."

"You know for sure it was him and not an imaginary person?"

I nodded.

"Well, let's get you tucked in bed, safe and sound," Pa said. "I'll have a talk with the Sheriff. No reason for you to have night-mares, little girl." He gave me a hug. Ma warn't as generous. She jist went upstairs with me and tucked me into bed as usual.

Flora
Saturday, June 30, 1934
Nighttime

Ma and Pa were upstairs with Nellie a long time tonight before I left for the dance with Jean and Mimi. But, gosh darn, I want a fun night out with my friends so Nellie's drama can just wait. We'd already had too much this week with Irene going off to Fonsha.

When Jean, Mimi and I got to the White Rabbit I danced the Lindy Hop with Jean. Mimi said she was fine sitting by herself and then she started talking with some other girls.

When the next song started Jean and Mimi danced together. I was just sitting on the side feeling awkward when a tall, handsome boy named Tom introduced himself and asked me to dance. That was the beginning of an absolutely dreamy evening.

Tom and I danced several dances together and we introduced each other to our friends. Turns out that Tom is a farm boy, but he's been working with the CCC building a dam in the Battle Creek River. We talked for a bit about whether it was a crick or a river.

"I'm sure it's a river cuz there's usually not enough water in cricks to dam up," he said.

"Well, I think a river named after a crick is a little strange," I answered.

"Yeah, me too."

"My littlest sister Nellie would have fun with this. She's always getting words mixed up. Nellie also talks to animals and she spies on people while she's hiding."

"Well, that settles it. I must meet Nellie," Tom replied. "When

I was little I used to do a lot of talking to animals. I think she and I would get along great."

This made me laugh.

"How about a Coke?" Tom took my arm and steered me toward the refreshment window.

I simply nodded and went along. Tom bought sodas for Jean, Mimi, and me, but he kept asking me to dance. I simply floated through the evening. I like the fact that he talks a lot more than Henry. He told me about the other boys working on the dam, about his parent's farm, and the schools he's gone to. He talked more in one evening than Henry had in four months.

Tom asked me lots and lots of questions about myself. I surprised myself when I told him how much I wanted to become a nurse, but how that was out of the question. He understood.

On the way home Jean and Mimi teased me about Tom, but I didn't care. He had asked if I was coming back the next Saturday, and I told him it depended on Mimi, because I didn't have a way to get to the dance by myself, and she's the only person I know who can get a car on Saturday night. He said to try hard because he is saving for a car. I think that means he will ask me out on a date when he gets a car.

When I got home just a little before midnight Ma was waiting up for me. I smiled and told her I'd had the time of my life. Ma seemed relieved that I was home safe and sound. I didn't ask her about Nellie and her drama because I wanted to go to bed with my happy feeling.

Irene
Sunday, July 1, 1934
Forenoon

I guess Ma figured I had my comeuppance on Friday when we ran into Miss Flatshaw. She said I didn't have to go to church today and told me to stay inside and not go down to the woods. Then she made me repeat that I wouldn't go down to the woods. Why would I go down near the baby's grave? That's the last place I would go.

I look and feel so ugly with all the poison ivy blisters all over my body. Last night Ma had me take my Saturday night bath in soda water to help ease the itching. Ma just kept sighing and crying. Guess she was still upset about my going to Fonsha.

Before the rest of the family went to church, Ma told me to wear my nightgown all morning and let my skin be exposed to the air. The rash is still all watery and she said it would help dry it out.

After the family left, I got my pillow and a blanket and crawled onto the kitchen roof from my bedroom window. It's all nice and sunny and warm up there and the roof is mostly flat. In fact it was so warm and quiet up there that I pulled up my nightgown and let the sun bake the tops of my legs. It felt good to be up there in the hot, hot sun. My only worry was if a bird would fly over and drop his johnny on me. That sometimes happens walking to school and out in the schoolyard.

This morning I was so itchy that I wanted to scratch all the watery bubbles but I forced myself not to. The hot sun did make my skin feel better. After a long time I turned over onto my stomach and let the sun burn the poison ivy blisters on my backside.

I have a lot on the back of my neck and around my ankles so I particularly wanted the sun to dry them up.

I musta fell asleep with my face down in the pillow cuz all of a sudden I heard voices and a dog barking. I thought I was waking up in my bed and hearing people talking downstairs as usual. But no, as I woke up I realized I was still on the roof. There were people down under the windmill. I saw three men pumping water into their cups and playing with Rover. I slowly and silently pulled my nightgown back down past my feet. Still, no one looked my way.

I figured that if I got up to sneak back into my bedroom someone would see or hear me, so I lay flat watching them throw a stick for Rover to fetch. Their cups were metal and reflected the sun's rays. I think they were train riders, not Gypsies, cuz they were young and speaking English, and they didn't have horses. They were in a good mood, drinking water and playing with Rover.

I caught only pieces of their conversation.

". . . back from church . . . up the road. . . .Palmer farm . . . ."

That caught my attention. The Palmer farm is Unc Elmer and Aunt Hazel's farm up the road. Unc Elmer and Aunt Hazel were probably at church, too. They don't always go, but there was a good chance there was no one at their farm this morning. Still, these guys didn't look like thieves. I think they were just trying to figure out whether to stay long enough for Ma and Pa to return so they could get a sandwich.

I turned, looking up at the sun trying to figure out how long I had been asleep. Would Ma and Pa and my sisters be returning soon? The sun was pretty high in the sky. When I turned my head one of the guys musta spotted me cuz he yelled up to me, "Hey, girl on the roof, could you make us some sandwiches, please?"

Suddenly I panicked. I was wearing my nightgown. Ma would be furious. I'd get another strapping and I have poison ivy all over my hind end. It would hurt like the devil.

"Sorry," I finally responded. "I'm sick and can't come down. You might catch my disease. Anyway, we're out of bread. Why don't you go try somewhere else?" I paused thinking about all these sins and it was Sunday, to boot.

Not only did I not go to church today, I'd turned into a liar. Yesterday was bread-making day. We had lots of bread and it was fresh and delicious. Actually a bean sandwich sounded mighty good to me right now since I hadn't had any breakfast.

"Well, what disease do you have?" a tall guy wearing a blue shirt asked. "If it's chicken pox or measles I've already had them." He musta been able to see my blistered face more clearly than I thought. "What do you have?" he asked again.

"Appendicitis," I answered after a long pause. It was something Aunt Hazel had a long time ago and was very serious. Everyone was scared she wouldn't live through it. A perfect pretend disease.

"Well, I think you could make a few sandwiches then," Blue Shirt called up to me. He had walked up close to the house and I could see his face clearly now. He had a nice smile and was very tall, taller than both Pa and Unc Elmer. I'm sure he could see the poison ivy and knew that I was lying. Still, he kept smiling.

"Okay, but you'll have to wait until my family gets back," I yelled down to him. "They should be back soon. That way, I won't touch your sandwiches. You don't wanna get appendicitis."

Right then I saw some dust down the road. Probably the family. I breathed a sigh of relief and quickly scooted through the window and shut it behind me. I threw on my shimmy shirt, drawers, and my old blue dress. Then I ran down to the parlor window to see if it was Ma and Pa. No sign of them. But where did the dust come from? No car or buggy drove by.

Next, before I could figure out what to do, I heard the outside cellar door opening. Were these train rider guys gonna sneak down the coal bin and come up the cellar stairs? My heart started pounding. I would have to act fast.

Pa's guns were hidden in the closet under the stairway but all of us girls have strict orders never to touch them. Should I now? I thought these guys just wanted sandwiches but what if they wanted to steal stuff from the house?

I snuck out to the kitchen and looked out the window to the windmill. All three guys were still there, just waiting and drinking their water. What was going on? Had they thrown Rover down to the cellar just to be mean? But no, I could see Rover bringing a stick back to one of them and now he was drinking water out of one guy's cup.

Maybe I was imaging things. But no, I heard someone shuffling in the cellar. I don't think whoever was down there had a candle cuz there was too much noise. Then I heard a crash. There was definitely someone down there. I sucked in a big breath and ran out to the well.

All three of the young men looked surprised and startled to see me there. I was glad I was wearing a dress.

"Thieves are down cellar," I said quickly. "I think they're trying to steal things."

There was a long pause before anyone answered. I looked crazy sick with all my poison ivy all over my face, arms, and legs. Then I guess they saw how scared I was.

"Where is your outdoor cellar door?" one of them asked.

"Around on the other side of the house across from the hen house," I answered.

"And there's only one stairway inside your house that goes down to your cellar?" another one asked.

I nodded.

"What's down in your cellar?" another guy asked.

"Just coal, the furnace, root vegetable bins, and lots of lots of shelves for canned food."

They all looked at each other and nodded. "But anyone knows that June is when the shelves are empty," I answered. "Most of the garden hasn't come in."

"Depends on how stupid you are," the short guy in a gray shirt answered. "I once met a guy who thought rabbits were hatched from eggs. He thought baby bunnies appeared every Easter."

I smiled at that.

"Fred and I will go around to the cellar door, and you two keep the inside door at the top shut tight," the blue shirt guy said to me and the short guy. "It's probably a possum or raccoon or something, but if it's still in there, it will probably try to come back up through the outdoor cellar door, as long as it can see daylight."

So that's how the short, gray-shirted guy and I ended up at the top of the cellar stairs yelling to the animals or thieves to get out. We heard a rustling and shouting. Gray Shirt and I kept waiting at the top of the stairs. More noise. Then the other two guys yelled out that they got the thief, but to go down cellar and make sure there wasn't anyone else down there.

I quickly lit a kerosene lamp and Mr. Gray Shirt walked down the cellar stairs first. I followed him with the lamp. We checked every nook and cranny of the cellar and behind the furnace. There was a lot of broken glass on the floor near the coal bin, probably glass jars of tomatoes and peaches as best I could tell. Since I was barefoot, I was real careful. Mr. Gray Shirt yelled up to his friends that there wasn't anyone else down there.

We both ran back up the steps and then out the door and around the house. Knocked out cold on the grass by the cellar door was dirty old Mr. Hendrick, May Hendrick's father. He was all black from coal and had a grisly beard, smelling bad. He had used a rope ladder to get down from the cellar door to the coal bin. There was a quart jar of green beans and one of beef on the ground near him.

"You know this thief?" tall blue shirt asked me.

"Kinda," I answered. "He lives about six miles away. He's not a farmer. They rent a house on the Blankenship farm." The tall guy tried to tie up Mr. Hendrick's arms with the rope ladder, but it wasn't working, so I ran to the tool shed and got some binder twine which worked great.

Thank goodness, just about then Ma and Pa and my sisters came up the driveway. I couldn't wait to tell them the whole story and how I nabbed Mr. Hendrick with the help of the train riders. I think this may have been the best day of my life. Neither of my sisters have ever caught a thief red-handed.

Pa went up to Unc Elmer's and called the Sheriff. Ma looked forlorn cuz of the broken jars of food, shaking her head. Finally, she smiled and said she was so happy that the train riders had helped me out.

We had three guests for Sunday dinner all joking that they had caught appendicitis from me. Nellie kept looking at my hands and stupidly asked which was the red hand that I used to catch Mr. Hendrick. She wanted to know if I was wearing a glove. That made everyone laugh.

Nellie
Sunday, July 1, 1934
Afternoon

Today was a fun day, so different from yesterday. When we got home from church we found that Mr. Hendrick had tried to steal several quart jars of food from down cellar. Ma was mad cuz he had broke three quart jars full of food all over the cellar floor near the coal bin. That means not as much food for us and believe me, we need the food.

Sheriff Devlon came out and took Mr. Hendrick to jail after Pa called him from Aunt Hazel and Unc Elmer's house. We don't have a phone, so we use their telephone if we have a problem. Well, this certainly was a problem, having a thief go down cellar and steal food.

I asked Pa if Sheriff Devlon had caught Brother Johnson. Pa shook his head. I want him to be thrown in jail with Mr. Hendrick. Most of all I want to be able to go down to the second meadow and the crick without being scared.

Ma made me and Irene clean up the mess in the cellar. There were little bitty pieces of glass and it was hard to clean up so we used wet rags until we got it all. I wanted to throw out the rags, but Ma insisted that we rinse all the glass out of them, wash them, and hang them on the line to dry. She warn't gonna lose any rags after losing all that food and three Ball jars. But that warn't the fun part of the day. The fun part came later when the train riders told stories.

Ma invited the three train riders to stay for dinner and gave them each a slice of bread to eat right away, since dinner was gonna be at least an hour later. Ma had me git lots of extra potatoes from the bin cuz the three men were real hungry. Then Irene and I picked two quarts of strawberries while Flora made a shortcake. She was in such a happy mood today cuz she met a new boy at a dance last night, a farm boy named Tom.

Next, I went out to the garden and picked lots of lettuce, green onions, and radishes for a huge salad, the biggest one I've ever made. Ma showed me how to make salad dressing out of vinegar and sugar. It sure did look good.

Before dinner we all sat around the dining room table and Pa said grace. The train riders seemed to be downright happy to be having a Sunday dinner, and they said they were mighty grateful for the good food. Ma had made a beef stew with the quart of beef that had been spared. She put lots of onions, carrots, and potatoes in it so there was plenty. And for the first time this summer we had strawberry shortcake. There warn't a crumb left after we'd finished.

After dinner Unc Elmer, Aunt Hazel and my two younger cousins Jake and Alvin, the twins, came over and we all went outside under the maple tree and sat on blankets. My older cousins, Dan and Dalton, were rabbit hunting so they didn't come. It was one glorious summer day, and the stories began. I loved sitting on the blanket next to Aunt Hazel, closing my eyes and listening to everyone talk.

When the train riders told their stories I jist listened. The three had come from near Chicago and stopped off at a lot of towns along the tracks looking for work. They'd found a job near Kalamazoo putting shingles on a roof, but that ended. Now they were at our house. I wished they could stay with us and be hired hands, but I knew from all my spying on Ma and Pa that we couldn't pay them one cent.

My cousins Jake and Alvin kept asking them questions 'bout riding the rails, thinking it sounded fun. But they talked 'bout being hungry all the time, and the dangers of riding with other crazy men who carried knives. They'd seen a fight where one train rider got hurt really bad and it was all bloody. They also talked 'bout not being able to take baths and how most train riders had itchy lice. They'd only been riding the rails for four weeks and were hoping they might find work once they got to Detroit. Aunt Hazel was glad that they talked 'bout the bad parts of being train riders cuz Jake and Alvin seemed to git purty excited 'bout it. Course, they're only ten and I think you have to be thirteen to be a train rider. These guys were old, maybe eighteen.

Jake asked our guests if they had met John Dillger, the bank robber, cuz he had robbed a lot of banks near Chicago. They said no, he was still on the lam. I wondered why a bank robber was on a lamb but Jake asked so many other questions I didn't git a chance to figure out whose lamb it was, or even if he knew. I have a feeling that it ain't a real lamb, possibly a nickname for a horse or car. No one could sit on any of the lambs I've ever seen.

Alvin asked the train riders if they had ever seen any shanty towns along the way. They all nodded yes, and said it was very sad that whole families didn't have houses to live in and people didn't have food. They did say that some shanty towns are better than others. They stayed a couple of nights at one that had friendly people, and warm fires where they sang songs at night, and the children played in the fields during the day. All the rest of the shanty towns they saw were miserable. No one talked for a long time after that.

Ma wrote down the names and hometowns of all three train riders before they left. She asked Irene to make sugar sandwiches for them to eat the next day. Finally, Ma told them that she would say a prayer for each of them every night. They thanked her and all of us. At sunset the three men headed toward the tracks in town.

All three of us girls went to bed without supper, not even asking. We'd had a huge dinner and I for one didn't wanna eat when I knew our train rider friends wouldn't be eating a crumb until they had their sugar sandwiches the next day.

I suspect Mr. Hendrick was having bread and water at the jail. Later after the train riders left, me and Ma took some food over to the Hendricks' house. Mrs. Hendrick was grateful but surprised. She said she hadn't seen her husband in several weeks. She thought he was still in jail from the horse thieving. Guess he wasn't stealing food for his family.

Flora
Monday, July 2, 1934
Nighttime

"Time for Sister's Club" I announced as my sisters joined me in my bedroom.

"Why are we meeting if no one has anything new?" Irene asked, clearly annoyed.

I drew in a big breath. "Well, I met a wonderful boy Saturday night and he's going to hear the rumors about me soon if I don't miss my guess. We GOTTA figure this out. Otherwise Tom will never want to date me."

"Well, I forgot all about this," Irene was stammering. "But on my way to Fonsha that night I walked by the church cemetery. There was a strange woman with her back to me. She was standing there on the far side of the cemetery. I think she was crying. I meant to tell you both as soon as I got home. But that trip didn't turn out as planned."

"What did the woman look like?" I asked my sister.

"Her back was to me and I didn't see a lot—it was getting dark. But she was about as tall as Ma and was wearing a dark dress. I guess her hair was dark. I don't remember."

"Was it Mrs. Geist?" Nellie asked.

"No, she was nowhere near Jimmy's grave," Irene answered. "I would have recognized Mrs. Geist, anyway."

"Well, we'll be going to the church Fourth of July picnic on Wednesday night. Irene, I want you to show my exactly where this lady was standing. We'll find the gravestone and get the name off it."

Both my sisters nodded.

"Anything else from either of you?" I queried my sisters.

Both shook their head. So I started speaking.

"Well, I'm getting closer to finding out about the Gypsies. There's a teenage girl in the camp who wants to become friends with Jean and me. I'm going to try to make friends with her and find out what she has to say. Right now no one in the camp is admitting that there has been a new baby in the past three years. Hopefully we'll get to the bottom of this very soon."

Nellie
Wednesday, July 4, 1934
Afternoon

Today's the Fourth of July and I jist couldn't wait for six o'clock to come. I've been ready all day to go to the church picnic, hoping Reverend Blackman would make some more ice cream again this year. I asked Ma if we could take some cream in case he does.

"No," Ma answered. "If he wants to make ice cream, he'll let us know if he needs cream. Besides, it's not just frozen cream. You add sugar and vanilla and lots of egg yolks. Most folks don't have that. You know that we're short on eggs." I could tell Ma was tired and ornery.

At noon we took dinner down the field to Pa, Unc Elmer, Flora, and Irene. They all were sweaty with hay dust all over them. Ma had put some beef, cheese, tomatoes, and lettuce between some large chunks of bread. It looked so good as they gobbled it down. She'd brought lots of jars of water and had one pitcher of cherry juice mixed with sugar water that we'd made this morning.

Later, back in the kitchen Ma and I ate our dinner. There warn't no beef left over, but Ma was cooking up a fresh batch of beans for church tonight, so we ate bean soup with hard bread dipped into it. Ma had left a small glass of the cherry water for me. It was mighty good.

Ma saw me smile when I drank the cherry water. "Honey, if I had my way you could have cherry water and ice cream every day."

I nodded. I knew she meant it.

Nighttime

So finally, after everyone had cleaned up after haying, we went up to the church. I helped Ma and the other women set out the food. Mrs. Geist asked me to stir up her creamed potatoes and peas. I liked doing that and I was careful not to break any of the peas. She put it down right beside Aunt Hazel's scalloped onion casserole, one of my favorite dishes. Aunt Hazel had also brought scalloped corn (last year's corn) and two cherry pies.

Mrs. Vandenberg had brought a dessert called wacky cake. She whispered to me that it's called that cuz there's no milk or eggs in it. It looked so delicious. Mrs. Vandenberg also brought a sugar milk pie. Again she whispered to me that since she saved the milk and eggs from the cake she could make the pie. I sure do like Mrs. Vandenberg.

All the food got put out soon enough but Reverend Blackman still hadn't said the blessing. I guess he was waiting to see if anyone else was coming. That's when Flora poked Irene and me to go over to the cemetery. I told Ma where we were going and that we'd pay our respects at Jimmy's grave.

Irene led the way to the far side where the graves were old and the stones hard to read cuz they were so weathered.

"Around here," Irene pointed. "I think she was standing about here."

We all looked around. There was an empty plot or maybe a grave with no stone. All three of us groaned and we walked back to the picnic.

Finally, after Henry's family arrived and apologized for being late cuz they were haying, Reverend Blackman said grace and thanked God for our country and the food in front of us. Then we ate. It was so amazing to eat all this food. I couldn't stop. Even Ma was eating lots and lots for a change, and she always saves the food for other people.

To my disappointment Reverend Blackman said nuthin' 'bout ice cream, but I loved the wacky cake and cherry pie. The kids were organizing a game of Blind Man's Bluff so I ran with my cousins Jake and Alvin to join in. Irene stayed on the blanket with her eyes shut. I think she was listening in on the conversations all around her, but she was too tired to play cuz the haying had taken it all out of her.

Jist as it was gittin' dark Ma came to the field where us kids were playing. I told her to look up and see all the colored shooting stars. There was no yelling or kid noise for a good long time as all of us looked up to the sky. Ma picked me up (which she never does anymore) and carried me back to the churchyard, mainly keeping her eyes on the night ceiling.

I kept on watching the sky, too. Lots of other people were seeing what I have seen on and off all summer long: colorful shooting stars streaking all across the heavens. When we got back to our blanket, Irene was still asleep. She was the only person not looking up. As we sat back down with Pa and Flora, Reverend Blackman thanked God for His beautiful sky and with his "Amen" the colors faded away until we had our usual starry show overhead.

Flora
Wednesday, July 4, 1934
Nighttime

After finishing the hay baling today we went to the church picnic. I was worried that Henry would be there and it would be so
obvious to everyone attending that he wasn't speaking to me.
How humiliating. I kept telling myself that I'd met another boy.
Ma musta understood how I was feeling because she invited
Mrs. Vandenberg to sit with us. Mr. Vandenberg had wandered
off with Reverend Blackman going through the cemetery stopping in front of several graves, talking about the occupants. Mrs.
Vandenberg was happy to join us since her husband had left her
alone once again.

They're close friends, Reverend Blackman and Mr.
Vandenberg. Sometimes Mrs. Vandenberg just rolls her eyes
when people ask where her husband is. Sometimes she says, "He
thinks he's getting closer to God, but really he's spending time
with an old friend. They've known each other since they were
both ten years old."

Finally we saw Henry's family pulling up and getting out of
their wagon so I hurried back to our blanket and lay down by
Irene. Ma brought me a plate of food so I didn't even have to walk
down the food line. I just ate and talked to Ma and Mr. and Mrs.
Vandenburg.

After everyone had eaten, Irene fell asleep. She snorted and
moaned and then outright snored. It had been a hard day of haying. Mrs. Vandenberg just smiled and said our family was lucky
to have such good, hard-working children. I never thought about
it that way. We don't have a choice. Ma and Pa expect us to do

our part. On the farm everyone has to work; even Nellie has lots of chores and she's only seven. She and Ma milked the cows, gathered the eggs, and did all the other chores today before the picnic, since the rest of us were haying.

I think it was Mrs. Vandenberg who noticed the shooting stars first. Pa was lying beside Irene, either asleep or resting with his eyes closed. It was early dusk before the mosquitoes were beginning to bother. Ma had gone to check on Nellie who was playing with the older kids in a field across the road from the church.

"Look up there, dear," Mrs. Vandenberg said to me, "Shooting stars, and are they ever amazing. I've never seen them so bright or so colorful."

I looked up and saw what Nellie and I had seen once before: colorful stars shooting across the heavens in all directions. The sky, still tinged with the colors of sunset, was filled with magnificent bursts of colors.

"It's like our own fireworks," Mrs. Vandenberg whispered to me. Since I had never seen fireworks, I couldn't quite compare. But, I could hear others whispering and pointing upwards. Ma arrived back with Nellie in her arms and woke up Pa. Now everyone except Irene was awake, looking up at the burst of colors.

Next, I heard Reverend Blackman's voice.

"Dear Father, we thank you for this wonderful family gathering tonight, and we are honored with your beautiful display in the sky overhead. It reminds us that we are mere mortals while your majesty can be seen throughout the heavens. Lord bless all the people here who are here observing your wonders. We are members of your community and we understand that we are not here for self-glory, but to worship you and love and help one another. As we all struggle to keep our children fed with roofs overhead, let us not forget that money cannot buy the wondrous show you have given us tonight. In the name of Jesus Christ. Amen."

Irene
Friday, July 6, 1934
Forenoon

We've all been working so hard. Every morning except Sunday we get up an hour before daylight, around five, and many hours later go to bed with the sun, around nine, or later. Most of those sixteen hours are spent working in the garden, kitchen, and fields. No one complains, not even Nellie. I think that's cuz she saw how hungry the train riders were and saw how much food we raise on our farm. All of us are too dead tired to complain anyway. Complaining takes too much energy. July and August will be extremely long months before school starts again.

Ma has been selling some garden vegetables to her egg customers. She could be selling a lot more eggs but we just don't have any more to sell, so overall she's making less money than last summer. We don't eat eggs for breakfast. Milk toast is what Ma mainly makes, and the toast is sometimes burnt cuz the heat in the oven is uneven. If Dan and Dalton catch any extra bluegills from Green Lake, we have them for breakfast. That's my favorite breakfast along with fried mush, made out of ground corn. But those breakfasts are few and far between.

School will be starting the day after Labor Day and I'm so ready to quit working in the garden. We're gonna have a new teacher but I don't know her name yet. I wonder how long it will take before she realizes that I'm the smartest kid in school. I'm so ready for her to be my new best friend and share secrets with me.

Afternoon

I can't stand going to town with Ma to peddle eggs. Each time she tries to be cheery but underneath I can tell that she hates it as much as I do. First, we go to the nice part of town with the big brick houses and lots of old elm trees. This is where most of her egg customers live. We go up and knock on doors, and Ma begins by telling them what she has that particular day. I'm always surprised at how nice people are to Ma even when they can't buy anything. She always ends the conversation by asking when would be a good time to return. People who say maybe three or four weeks never buy nuthin.' But the "come back next Friday" people often buy stuff the next week.

I can see children playing around the neighborhood, and I wish I could stop and play with them. Sometimes they have swings. I love those. But more often than not they are playing games like we do at school. Hide and Seek is my favorite.

Ma sometimes sighs when we pass a group of kids playing cuz I know she wishes I could be there. I might as well be, as little good I'm doing helping her. Us girls come along cuz she thinks she's gonna get some cleaning jobs that we can help with, but that hasn't happened. I think the ladies in town would feel bad paying for a cleaning lady even if they had the money. These days everybody complains about having no money. Even the ladies in the nicest part of town. I wonder if they actually have money but don't want others to know it, or if they really don't. Ma says they don't.

Today Ma drove to the south side of town where I had never been, across the train tracks. The houses and yards are smaller and we walked down several streets trying to peddle eggs and vegetables. Only one woman said she would buy some eggs, lettuce, and a bunch of green onions. She was real thin and had on a well-worn cotton dress faded to gray. I could hear a child crying inside the house when she went back inside to get her money. After a long time she came back and said she couldn't buy the eggs after all and gave Ma a penny for the green onions and lettuce. Ma said to keep the eggs and she could pay for them another day. The lady thanked us and took the eggs into the house. As we walked away I could hear the lady pulling a pan out of her cupboard. I imagine she was gonna fry up some eggs.

Ma and I walked back to the Model A, we got in, and we both cried.

Flora
Saturday, July 7, 1934
Afternoon

Today I returned to the Gypsy camp. It was unexpected as Ma and Aunt Hazel had gone to an orchard to pick peaches; they were going to pick Red Havens since it's too early for the Elbertas, my favorites. They'd be gone all afternoon. My cousin Dan stopped by and asked me if I wanted to ride to town with him. I said yes and left a note for Pa that I was with Dan. He dropped me off at the town cemetery right near the Fairgrounds and I told him to pick me up there in two hours.

As soon as Dan was out of sight I walked to the Fairgrounds and over to the fence row where Jean and I had been. I came right up to the fence. Since it was early afternoon there were no meal preparations in progress. I think the women were napping because only two little girls sat outside of one tent, both sewing and talking Gypsy.

I wanted to see Patya so I walked along the fence near the tent that she had gone into that day. I pretended to sneeze. The little girls looked up but didn't come over. Guess they thought the sneeze came from a tent.

However, in a couple of minutes Patya emerged from the tent and started breaking off branches, like she was collecting kindling again. She saw me and smiled but continued walking away collecting more and more branches. I walked along the fence in the direction she was walking and suddenly I found her right beside me near a large hole in the fence.

"This way," she said, as we walked down a path that led to the river. "We camp here so we can carry the water," she explained.

We walked along the river until we came to a clearing and we both sat down.

"My English is bad," she apologized. "But I never get to talk English. Only men go to town. All women stay in camp."

I nodded. I know what it feels like to be housebound.

"What happens if you just leave and go into town?" I asked.

"I would be treated bad, maybe have to leave the camp. The only way for girl to get out is to get married."

"Is there someone you want to marry?"

She shook her head. "Only one boy in camp. He is cousin and I don't like him anyway. I must marry Roma man."

"How will that happen?"

"My father will find someone and then I must go to his camp." Tears came to her eyes. "I want to be like you. I want to walk around and see everything. I want to meet man on my own."

"I'm still trying to find the mother of the dead baby," I said, changing the subject.

"Not here," Patya responded. "When anyone dies we get sad and make . . . . "She moved her fingers to indicate people walking.

"A procession," I said.

"Yes, to the burial place. We have no dead baby, no procession."

"If a baby comes to your camp unexpected, what happens?"

Patya looked confused. "That never happened."

"No stolen babies or stolen children?"

"Never. We have enough children." Patya smiled, like it was a joke.

"Can I come visit you and your friend?" Patya asked.

I shrugged.

"How long will you be camped here?" I asked.

Patya shook her head. "Maybe the fall. We follow good weather. "Please come back with your friend many times. I am lonely."

She hesitated. "I, I want to get away. See other places. Not be married to a man I don't know. I want to see other people, learn new things. I want to live in house, not tent."

"Have you told your mother that?" I asked.

"She tells me to be quiet. That I must live my life here."

"I'm sorry it's so hard. Surely other people have left your camp. What happens if they do?"

"We don't see them again. I don't know. I hope they find work and food."

I knew I needed to get back to the cemetery to meet Dan.

"Can you walk with me to the cemetery?" I asked. She thought about it for a while and then nodded.

"So no babies here in the past year?" I asked her.

"No," she said. "We like babies and we like children, but no new babies here. Come back again. Bring Jean."

Dan was pulling up when we got to the cemetery.

"This is Patya," I said to him as he jumped out of the car and shook her hand. I could almost feel the electricity between them. We said goodbye and Dan and I drove off.

"Wow," he exclaimed. "Where did you meet her?"

"Better not ask," I answered. "I'm trying to find out that dead baby's mother to stop all the rumors. Patya is someone I met trying to get it all figured out."

"Is she the mother?" he asked.

"No, not even close," I sighed.

Nighttime

I was so worried about telling Tom about "the rumor." But tonight was our third date and it seemed like I should tell him. Even though Ma says I shouldn't say anything to anyone, I feel like the rumor is this huge sword hanging over my head.

So while we were taking a break outside the White Rabbit, I just bit the bullet. "Tom, I gotta tell you something real important," I said. "It makes me so unhappy."

Tom looked surprised and nodded for me to go on.

So I started with the whole story, just like I did with Jean. I told him about the buried baby, the rumors, and how Henry and I had had only one date in the city park. I also told him how I'd gone to Iowa last year to help out Aunt Caroline. But I never was in a family way, then or ever.

Tom frowned. "So you're totally innocent?"

I nodded. "The rumor has made my life unbearable," I replied.

"What else?"

"Nothing else. That's it. An awful, terrible lie."

"Well, I believe you," he replied. "Try not to let rumors get you down."

I felt so relieved. Tom wasn't the least bit alarmed. Why was everyone else in my life taking these lies so seriously?

Then Tom paused. "Well, are you telling me you want your old boyfriend back?"

"No, no, no," I almost shouted. "He is a very nice boy, but we only had that one date."

Tom frowned again. "But do you want him back?"

"No," I replied, much more calmly this time. "I don't want him back."

Tom smiled at me and gave me a little kiss on the cheek. "Don't worry about it, sweet girl. These things have a way of working themselves out."

I sure hope he's right.

Irene
Thursday, August 2, 1934
Afternoon

All three of us girls have been working in this gigantic garden for weeks on end now. We all fight to go up to Aunt Hazel's house to clean. Anything to get away from the hot, humid garden and the worms and insects living there. Now and then a garter snake slithers by, but I like that. It breaks the monotony.

Actually, when we all are together, hoeing, weeding, or picking we sometimes have a Sisters' Club Meeting where we simply make up a story about the baby. Even though it was Nellie's idea it's kinda fun.

Nellie made up the first story. "Once upon a time," she started out, "there was a beautiful princess who married a handsome prince." Nellie went on and on about them living in a castle in a faraway kingdom until finally an ugly witch killed their baby and took it to a faraway woods and buried it. Nellie then proceeded to have the prince and princess hunt down the witch and burn her at the stake. She finally had the dead baby come alive and go back to the kingdom. Stupid story but it got our minds off picking peas.

My story was a lot better. The baby belonged to a preacher and his wife who lived right next door to the church. When their baby died they decided they wanted to bury it far away from the church so they wouldn't see the grave every day and be sad.

Flora's story was about a Negro couple who were trying to find the path her grandparents took while running away from a plantation in Virginia. The couple found the old cabin ruins, and then their baby decided to be born right then and there. But the baby didn't live so they decided to bury him near the path of their ancestors.

Those were the first stories. In one of my stories the baby was born in our manger, like Jesus. Another like Moses, was left in the bulrushes, only it was in the brambles near the pond. Nellie told stories about her imaginary friend ZeeZee dropping the baby down from an imaginary moon named Gabriel. As usual she got it all mixed up. Gabriel was an angel, not a moon.

Well, it was kinda fun for a while, then we all got tired of the stories and started making weird noises while we picked. Nellie started with her rooster sounds, and Flora and I joined in with all kinds of farm animal sounds. Then we added coyotes and any other animal we could think of. We finally ended up making monster sounds. Those were the best cuz they were the loudest and scariest.

Nellie
Sunday, August 12, 1934
Afternoon

I'm busy playing a trick on Irene. Any time she's not around I
look at the stories in the *Bible Story Book* and figure out where
the stories come from in the real *Bible*. It's purty easy since the
stories go from beginning to end and the real *Bible* has head-
ings at the top like "Adam and Eve" and "Christ is Risen." I already know how to use the two little dots to separate chapters
and verses in the *Bible*, cuz I've seen it at church. I'm 'bout half
done but I'm waiting to write them in the book when they're all
done. The biggest trick is that I'm gonna make my handwriting
look like Irene's so she'll think she wrote them herself but can't
remember.

Flora
Monday, August 13, 1934
Nighttime

Tonight after my sisters went to bed I stayed in the kitchen knitting by the last light from the west window. Ma came into the kitchen and interrupted.

"They've found the bodies of the two missing girls from Spring Lake. They were buried in a soft loam forest up near the lake."

A shiver ran through my body.

"How old were they?" I asked.

"Both were nine, younger than Irene. They were friends who disappeared walking home from school."

My mind was racing. Both girls were too young to have had a baby. But I also thought about May's story. She had gotten into a car, been taken to a forest, raped, and left for dead.

"Where was the forest where they were buried?" I asked.

"Up near Spring Lake, about eight miles from their homes. The farmer who owned the forest was taking a walk with his wife yesterday afternoon. They went into the woods since it was so hot. When they found a lunch pail and hair ribbon they called the Sheriff who later found the bodies."

Tears were welling up in my eyes.

"Flora, you need to keep an eye on your sisters. You hear me?"

"Don't you think that you and Pa should do that?" I answered. I really don't like how Ma tells me to watch out for my sisters.

"First, don't sass me," she sputtered. "Of course, we've told Irene and Nellie to be careful. But with these girls found dead, everything is so horrible. Just warn your little sisters." Then she added, cautiously, "Sheriff Devlon can't find that revivalist preacher who tried to have his way with Nellie. Everybody says he left town long before that day, but I'm scared he didn't."

"Okay, Ill warn them," I answered before Ma left the room. It wasn't going to do any good arguing with her. I felt heavy with despair. Nothing like having the weight of the world on your shoulders. All the horrible rumors about me. Disobeying my parents when I visited both May and the Gypsy camp. And now I have to keep my little sisters from being murdered. What next?

Irene
Tuesday, August 14, 1934
Nighttime

Right during supper Flora said to both Nellie and me, "Meet me in my bedroom after your chores." She said it right out loud with Ma and Pa right there. No finger in ear signals. No explanation. Ma and Pa just calmly sat there as though this was normal.

Of course, Nellie and I zipped right through our chores and were up in Flora's bedroom before she finished hers.

"This is serious business," Flora said before we even got situated on her bed. "Those two Spring Lake girls were murdered and buried in a forest up near Spring Lake. You girls have to be careful about strangers even more than ever. And around people you know. Come to me even if you think something's just a little bit off. Or if you're not sure. Don't take any chances. Ever."

"Okay," Flora hesitated for a moment. "So those girls were too young to have babies.

"So without May and the Spring Lake girls where does that leave us?" I asked.

"Gypsies, mainly," Nellie replied. "Unless you think ZeeZee dropped the baby from outer space."

"The baby was buried, not dropped from a spaceship," I scolded Nellie. She's nigh on to stupid some days.

"Well, I'm beginning to believe it wasn't a Gypsy baby," Flora answered. "Not that they don't have their own problems," she muttered. "Maybe we need to find some new suspects."

"Where?" I asked. "Until school starts I only see people at church. No one there is talking about lost babies."

"So do Ma and Pa know about Sisters' Club?" Nellie asked. "How come you didn't use our ear signal at supper?"

"Oh, that," Flora answered. "Ma wanted me to warn you to be careful around strangers. She's real worried about those murdered Spring Lake girls. So that's what we talked about up here tonight. Got it?

Nellie and I both nodded.

I went to bed feeling so discouraged. As much as the Sisters' Club seemed like a good idea early this summer, I think it's been for nothing. And those poor murdered girls from Spring Lake. I'd really hoped that they were having a gay old time in California.

Nellie
Wednesday, August 22, 1934
Forenoon

Pa told me and Irene that they've hired a new teacher named Miss Swanson. I think that is such a purty name, like a beautiful swan with a song. I hope she's as beautiful as her name. Irene has warned me that Miss Swanson may do things differently than Miss Flatshaw. I wonder if Miss Swanson knows how to speak different languages. I'd sure like to learn some new ones like German or French. Or maybe even Gypsy or Pottawatomi. Then I might find out why Gypsies wanna steal children. That's still a mystery. Or I'd listen in on private conversations 'bout dead babies. That'd make Flora happy.

Nighttime

Tonight I started listening down the heat register as soon as Irene fell asleep. She was snoring very, very loudly and I was as still as a mouse.

"I do believe that Irene snores louder than you," Ma said. I could hear her rocking chair squeaking back and forth.

"Yup," Pa answered.

"You hear anything about Roy Hendrick?" Ma asked.

"No. He's still in county jail. He only has one more week. Apparently Maud don't want him back."

"Who would?" Ma replied. "Next week after he's out we need

to watch out for the horses. Sheriff Devlon's been warning all the farmers."

"Yup."

I listened some more to the silence. Then more. Then more.

"I need to find Nellie a pair of shoes for school. I always forget how much young feet grow in the summertime," Ma's voice rose up from below. I looked down at my feet. The bottoms were all toughened from going barefoot all summer.

"I'll pull out Irene's old ones and have her try them on in the morning," Ma continued. "I imagine I can put some cardboard in the soles just like ours."

I've never had a new pair of shoes, always hand-me-downs from Flora and Irene. Same with my clothes. Only once I got a new homemade dress at Christmas that was too big so I could "grow into it."

Flora
Wednesday, August 22, 1934
Afternoon

Ma's warnings to watch over my sisters no longer makes me feel blue. Mainly because I simply can't stop thinking about Tom. It's like I'm dancing in the sky amidst those beautiful colors we saw on the Fourth of July. When I wake up in the morning I think about Tom and I just float out of bed. It makes working in the garden so much nicer. I think about each of our dates and remember what he has said to me. Then I focus on the future, dream about being married to Tom and think how my name would be Mrs. Thomas Sharp. That has such a beautiful ring to it.

I have a boyfriend and I'm in love! I'm no longer obsessing about that buried baby and instead I daydream about my next date with Tom. Life has suddenly become good.

Tom bought a used Model A from a friend so now we can go to the White Rabbit every Saturday night. He's not a great dancer, but neither am I, so we go outside and talk a lot. He smokes and I just sip a coke. Most of the time I'm thinking about our goodnight kiss. I think he does, too.

Why I spent so much time with Henry is beyond me. Sheer stupidity, I guess. Henry never once told me that he loved me or even said that I am special. I always brought up topics of conversation with Henry because he rarely had anything to say. Tom, on the other hand, always tells me he's glad to see me, and he saves up stories to tell me from week to week.

Some good news: Ma and Pa told us girls that after the corn picking they should have enough to pay the taxes. We got lucky with rain. We could have used more, but the crops got by. Pa said that we need to save up in case we have dust storms, a drought, or other problems next year. But I just don't see how we can save any more than we already have.

There were a couple of weeks this summer when it got real dry and Irene and I hauled water to the garden to prevent the tomatoes, potatoes, onions, and carrots from drying up. A few days later we had an amazing thunderstorm and that helped everything including the muskmelon, watermelon, and pumpkins planted between the rows of corn in the west field. Pa put them in the cornfield since last year the squash crossed with the pumpkins in the garden and no one liked the result. We ate it anyway. Ma boiled it up and mashed it and we ate it with salt and pepper. Stringy, horrid stuff.

The Sheriff is still looking for Brother Johnson in case he was the one who tried to hurt Nellie. With those girls' bodies found, everyone with daughters is in a panic. The Sheriff has questioned Nellie three more times now, but he seems to have gotten nowhere, but he did say the baby had died of natural causes—not murder.

Ma's so dreading the beginning of the school year when Irene and Nellie will have to walk to school. She keeps telling them that they have to wait for Jake and Alvin. No running ahead like they used to.

Pa told us they're replacing Miss Flatshaw with a new teacher. Even though she wasn't the world's best teacher, I still feel sorry for Miss Flatshaw. She was my teacher from fifth through eighth grades. She knew the Three R's and taught them. She was good to the kids who struggled, like May, and she was so nice to poor little Jimmy Geist. But then her weight made her so unattractive. That can't be easy. I think she was the victim of rumors and believe me, that's no easy row to hoe.

Irene
Tuesday, September 4, 1934
Nighttime

Today was the first day of school and geez, how I hate the new teacher Miss Swanson. She's nothing like Miss Flatshaw. I knew from the moment I set eyes on her there'd be a problem. She wouldn't look me in the eye and she seems scared of us older kids. She's overly strict cuz she's young and she's shorter than some of the older kids including Fritz, Earl, and me. She seems to know I'm smarter than her so she ignored me most of the time.

When I took my dinner pail up to Miss Swanson's desk to eat at lunch, she smiled and said I couldn't eat with her. She said she can't play favorites and that she needs a few minutes to herself. Well, why can't she eat with me? Miss Flatshaw did all the time. What makes Miss Swanson so high and mighty?

This is Miss Swanson's first year of teaching and you can tell. She didn't seem to know what to do most of the time. I had to tell her about all the chores I do and about bell ringing and dinner hour and recess. She didn't know how to space out the classes, so today she only got through fifth grade. Us seventh graders didn't even get called up.

This morning Miss Swanson told the big kids to write stories about their summers. Then she didn't even choose mine to read out loud. My essays are always the best. But her topic was crummy, too: "My summer." Like I had anything to write about. Too much work and too little play.

Hopefully next summer will be different and more interesting. But as Ma says, "The garden don't grow by itself, and the cellar don't fill up by itself." My essay would have been the best if

I had gone off to the State Fair or seen the circus. Then I woulda had something to write about rather than hoeing onions and canning tomatoes.

At recess Miss Swanson went out and helped the little kids on the merry-go-round so they didn't fall off. I still got chosen last for Red Rover and Keep Away. It's no fair. I wish Miss Swanson would figure out what's going on and change the rules.

At this point anyone, even Flora, sounds like a better teacher than Miss Swanson. But Flora's not gonna go to County Normal for teacher training; she's doing another year of high school. Flora told me that she's never wanted to be a teacher. If she had her druthers she'd be a nurse. She says that's the most important job of all: nurses save people's lives.

"Well, what about when you break an arm or leg?" I asked her. "You're not gonna die from that."

"If not treated properly, you could die," Flora answered. "Think about lockjaw; you get that from stepping on a rusty nail. Stepping on a nail isn't such a big deal, but getting lockjaw it is a BIG DEAL and you die from it."

I thought about it and agreed. Maybe I'll become a nurse.

Nellie
Tuesday, September 4, 1934
Nighttime

Today was the first day of school and I got to meet our new teacher, Miss Swanson. I think I'm gonna like her a lot. She thought up lots of fun things for us to do like writing 'bout our summers and drawing pictures of the fall flowers along the roadside, like goldenrod and gentian. She even went out at recess and played with us little kids, making sure no one fell off the merry-go-round.

Miss Swanson asked us to 'magine some made-up stories and I told her 'bout ZeeZee who flies around in our old bus. She really liked that and told me to write a story 'bout ZeeZee when I have extra time at school. That sounds so much better than all the penmanship we had to do with Miss Flatshaw.

We haven't done much with Sisters' Club, but I'm hopeful we can get it going again with the new school year. Flora will be at high school with her friends to git information. But she don't seem to care much 'bout the buried baby anymore. She's more interested in talking 'bout her boyfriend Tom.

Flora
Saturday, September 8, 1934
Forenoon

I started back at high school this week, but it's so different from last year. I'm so in love with Tom that I don't care about ugly rumors. Surprisingly, this fall everyone is treating me great. I eat lunch with Jean and Mimi every day and we joke and have fun. Those horrible rumors seem to have disappeared. I rarely see Henry; he keeps to himself and never says hello at church or at school.

Today, being Saturday, Ma and I are canning more tomatoes and making bread-and-butter pickles. We haven't missed a single item in the garden. Not one pea, not one string bean. If we have extras we take them to Aunt Hazel, the Blackmans, or to Mrs. Hendrick. Ma says Mrs. Hendrick is so grateful since she don't have but a tiny little garden that fills up their itty-bitty backyard.

Since Ma didn't grow any flowers this year, we put squash in the zinnia bed and more potatoes in the old petunia bed. Over the summer Ma said she felt bad about having no flowers, but a few came up from last year. We had one iris that came up from near the backdoor. Also one red poppy plant near the steppingstone. That was a nice surprise. Irene and Nellie brought Ma a few daffodil bouquets from the fence row in the meadow. But the daffodils didn't last long, only a couple of weeks in the spring.

All our neighbors grew food rather than flowers this summer. The Floral Hall at the County Fair had only a few flowers this year. Three of the four wings were empty and the fourth was only half full. Ma was hoping to take a few cannas or dahlias that had self-seeded, but they were too scraggly to enter for any prizes. Instead we took a couple of items for the baking competition, a cherry pie and a no-bake Top Cake that we cooked in a pan on top of the cook stove. The cherry pie won a blue ribbon and a dollar, but the cake just didn't hold up and crumbled all over the cake plate. No ribbon for it. Still, we got to bring it home for a dessert with the Blackmans. They all thought it tasted wonderful—and it did.

Tonight Tom and I are going to see a movie, *It Happened One Night*. We'll meet Jean and her date there and probably go over to her house after the movie. I'll wear my summer gray linen dress. Tom's seen it before, but I know he likes it. He told me so. Tom cares about me a lot. He's always interested in my opinions, whether it's Roosevelt's policies, farm news, or books I've read. Now I know what falling in love is all about. They could make a movie about Tom and me. I'd like Clark Gable to be Tom and maybe Loretta Young would be me.

Nighttime

When Tom brought me home tonight, Ma and Pa were still in the kitchen playing pedro with Aunt Hazel and Unc Elmer. They invited us to sit down with them and have some of Aunt Hazel's walnut pie. It was so delicious and it felt so grown-up to sit there with them and tell them about the movie. Aunt Hazel already knew how handsome Clark Gable is. She'd seen pictures of him in a magazine. She called him a "dreamboat." Claudette Colbert is cute, too, but not beautiful.

"So when are you gonna teach Flora how to make this wonderful walnut pie?" Tom teased Aunt Hazel. Tom always makes everybody feel good.

"Well, these are last year's nuts," Aunt Hazel answered. "So I'm using them up before the new ones are ready in a few weeks.

I can teach Flora next week if you'll be around next Saturday night."

"I think I can arrange that," Tom answered and winked at me.

I just wanted to kiss Aunt Hazel. Now I already had a date lined up for next Saturday night and I'll learn how to make walnut pie, as well.

Irene
Tuesday, October 16, 1934
Forenoon

Miss Swanson has been teaching everyone about the Indians that used to live along Parson Creek. They are the Pottawatomi tribe and they lived in wigwams. We're posta bring in something to school that belonged to the Indians, so Nellie and I brought our family box of arrowheads. Some of the other kids brought arrowheads too, along with beads, pieces of leather, broken dishes, and some old mangy fox furs.

When Miss Swanson asked if any of the items had family stories to go with them, Fritz Geist said his piece of leather had been given to his great-grandfather in exchange for some oats and molasses. JoEllen Hendrick said her grandfather found arrows down by the crick where some awful massacre had taken place. She said she didn't know nuthin' about the massacre, though.

Nellie then pulled a little black arrowhead out of our box.

"I found this in our strawberry bed," Nellie said. "See how perfect all the teeth around each one are."

"Do you know what kind of rock it's made of?" Miss Swanson asked.

"I think it's opposite," she answered.

"Obsidian, obsidian," Fritz yelled out. "That's the kind of rock those black arrowheads are made out of. Not opposite, it's obsidian. The whitish ones are flint."

Miss Swanson smiled at Nellie, like she was her pet. Then she smiled at Fritz, too.

It was almost too much to bear, having the teacher being so

nice to Nellie when she had made a mistake. It also irked me that Nellie knew about this Indian stuff when I didn't.

Nighttime

Tonight I signaled my sisters for a Club Meeting. It had been so long since my walk to Fonsha, but the mystery woman at the church cemetery had long been on my mind.

Finally, on Sunday, I simply asked Reverend Blackman if he might have known who this mystery lady was. After I showed him where she was standing that night, his eyes lit up.

"That's Mrs. O'Neil. Her husband died several years ago when they were moving to Dearborn. She didn't have any money for a funeral or burial, so the church took care of it. She comes back every now and then to visit his grave," Reverend Blackman informed me.

"Well, one more possibility marked off the list," Flora announced when I told her, not really seeming to care about poor Mrs. O'Neil or our dead baby. I liked it better when she was really passionate about Sisters' Club.

Flora
Tuesday, October 16, 1934
Forenoon

Golly, gee, the school days go so darn slow and the weekends go so darn fast. I've seen Tom just about every weekend since he got his car. Even when we don't have enough money for the movies or a dance, we still get together and drive around town or go for a walk. Last weekend we walked down to the woods to look at the fall colors. It was so lovely. Tom picked out a red sugar maple leaf, an orange oak leaf, and a yellow poplar leaf and gave them to me. My heart melted. This weekend Nellie and I will paste them on a sheet of paper to keep forever.

I rarely see Henry at school, and then yesterday he came up to me early in the morning when I was standing alone in front of my locker. "Flora," he said. "I really miss you. I'm sorry all those things happened."

"It wasn't your fault," I answered.

"I felt guilty about taking you to Lover's Lane," he answered.

"Nothing happened." I answered. "We turned around and went back into town."

Henry looked thoughtful. "I hear you have a boyfriend."

That surprised me. How did he know?

"Yes," I responded slowly. "He's from the west side of the county. His parents have a farm near Burlington."

"Well, I'm happy for you," Henry replied, but he looked sad, not happy.

I decided to change the subject. "I don't see you much at school anymore."

"No, I just have two classes this fall and two in the spring before graduation, so I've been helping my dad with the farm. But next week I start a job down at the grain elevator replacing Old Man Smiley. He and his wife are moving up to Lansing to live with his kids. He says he just can't lift those bags of grain any more. That's why they hired me." Henry's voice was calm and even.

"That's wonderful," I responded. "Keep those cats healthy. I always loved going there with Pa and playing with the cats. Nowadays Nellie does the same thing."

Henry smiled at me. I thought he was going to say something else, but he didn't.

"See you at church," I finally said to him.

"Yup," he replied, turning and walking away.

I wondered if he was sad that I have a boyfriend now that he's starting a job and will have some money for movies and dances. He's always been so quiet, so I wondered if it took a lot of nerve coming up to talk to me. But last spring we ate lunch together almost every day before that horrible baby ordeal. He's a nice boy. But Tom is THE ONE.

Nellie
Wednesday, October 17, 1934
Afternoon

I really like school. Miss Swanson is so pleased that I know all four directions. Today she had us all draw a map of our farms with all the fields and buildings using north as the top and south as the bottom and east on the right side and west on the left. It was so much fun. She even gave us some colored pencils to use.

JoEllen Hendrick, May's sister, is the only kid who don't live on a farm so she drew a map of an 'maginary farm. Miss Swanson told us to take our maps home to show our parents cuz we all did such a nice job. I was 'specially happy with mine.

This afternoon, after Irene, Jake, and Alvin had come home from school, they all told me that we were gonna go to the crick. No choice for me, they'd already decided it. Jake and Alvin had gotten into their heads that they wanted to spear some fish in the crick and wouldn't consider anywhere else to play. Irene said we warn't telling Ma and to jist tag along.

We took the only way to git there, down the lane, through both meadows, to the main path in the woods to the crick. We ran the whole way. We didn't stop to talk to the cows or climb the cherry trees. In the second meadow we passed by the poison ivy tree, the rusty gate, the old cabin foundation, the old bus, the hollowed-out tree, and ran over the stile into the woods. We ran as fast as we could down that long path to the crick. They're all bigger than me, so I was in the rear, as usual. Since I hate those scary woods, I ran extra fast and stayed right behind Alvin.

Once we got to the crick, Jake and Alvin took out their jack-knives and made spears out of oak branches. I wanted to use a willow branch but Alvin said it would bend too much and that oak branches are stronger and better for spearing. I wanted to make my own spear but neither one of them would let me use their jackknife. I jist warn't happy at all.

Then we went down to the clearing at the crick where we always play. Jake, Alvin, and Irene bent over the water trying to spear some little fish. I knew full well that if you want good bluegills you need catch them out of Green Lake—never from the crick. Irene told my cousins that, too, but they wanted to spear the fish anyway. I tried it a few times, but it warn't no fun.

Finally I decided to climb up high on my favorite oak tree at the edge of the woods. I kept climbing up higher and higher to find a good branch where I could see across the crick. I'm glad I was wearing shoes cuz oak bark is real rough. Irene finally quit spearing and went over to the rattlesnake rock and sat on it, watching Jake and Alvin who were whooping and hollering, telling the fish to swim slower.

I don't like being down there on the ground no more. Too many bad things happen down in the woods. My favorite place is way up high in the trees and the oak tree is the highest one in the woods. It's on the east side of the woods overlooking the crick, so it gits to see the sun first every morning. Lucky tree.

When I reached the top it felt so good. I love being up high where no one can reach me, like being on top of the world. I looked down at the crick and could see Irene sitting and my cousins trying to spear those quick-swimming little fish. But here I was, way up high, jist like a big buzzard. I decided that I would draw a picture of this for Miss Swanson someday. A bird's eye view of the woods and crick.

As I looked around I could smell the faint odor of smoke, but I didn't see anyone smoking. Across the crick was another woods and beyond that some more pasture land belonging to Old Man

Keller. Over to the east is Unc Elmer's farm. I could see his pastures and Unc Elmer's seven cows grazing. The lane to his barn
is bordered with bright red sassafras.

I looked back at the crick. Still no fish, but Jake and Alvin
were pushing each other, each one trying to git to his favorite
spot. Not a serious fight, jist boys pushing. To the west I couldn't
see anything but the woods.

Then I looked to the north and our own farm. But what I
saw seemed distant and unbelievable. Pa was running toward
the barn where a plume of white smoke was drifting upward. Ma
ran to the dinner bell and started ringing it. That's our warning
signal to Unc Elmer and Aunt Hazel that something is wrong,
being that we don't have a telephone. I've never heard the dinner
bell ringing for anything but meals. I could hear it, too. I yelled to
Irene and my cousins and they looked up puzzled, not seeing me
at the top of the oak tree.

So I scooted down the tree yelling at them, "Run fast, there's
something wrong!" I screamed at the top of my lungs.

Irene rolled her eyes and exclaimed, "Yeah, like a seven-year-
old knows these things. Keep fishing."

Irene
Wednesday, October 17, 1934
Forenoon

Today started out like just a normal day. Milk toast for breakfast. My toast was on the burnt side but Ma just won't tolerate complaints these days so I ate it, burnt and all. The last time I complained about breakfast, Ma took my bowl and ate it herself. She said we were lucky to have bread in the pantry and told me to fix my own breakfast. I was almost late for school.

School was awful today. Miss Swanson had everybody draw maps of their farms. What a waste of time. I was finished in just a few minutes, but some of the kids took forever, Nellie being one of them. Miss Swanson let everyone have an hour to do the assignment. Being smart I always finish first.

I was dumbfounded that over lunchtime, Miss Swanson had already graded every map. She picked out the three best to show everybody. You can imagine my amazement that mine wasn't included. She picked out JoEllen's, my cousin Jake's, and Nellie's. If that don't beat all. Each of them took their map up to the front and talked about it to the entire school.

JoEllen's map, being imaginary since the Hendricks don't own a farm, featured lakes, mountains, oceans, and a huge three-story house with towers. Miss Swanson said the house looked like a castle in a storybook. JoEllen was grinning ear-to-ear by the end of the discussion. Jake's map had all the farm buildings plus all their animals, including their cows, pigs, chickens, sheep, the goat, the ponies, and the bull. I have to give him credit as he had done a good job of coloring all the buildings and animals as well as the corn fields, oat field, wheat field, pastures, and sky.

Nellie's map was way out of proportion and maybe since Miss Swanson has never been on our farm, she didn't know the map was wrong. Nellie's map showed the house and buildings as way too small, and the lane, pastures, fields, woods, and crick as way too big. When Nellie got up to talk about it, I pointed out that the woods and crick don't actually belong to our farm, but Miss Swanson shushed me and said it was Nellie's time to talk. I've never had a teacher shush me before. Miss Swanson ain't gonna last very long as a teacher. Maybe to the end of the school year at most.

Nellie talked a lot about the meadows and our five cows who were grazing under the pink-flowered cherry trees on her map. But those cherry trees only bloom in the spring, certainly not now in October. Then she talked about how much fun it is to catch pollywogs in the crick. But you couldn't see any pollywogs in her picture. Then Nellie explained how you can take the lane from the barn to the first meadow, run across it to the second meadow and through it, then use the stile over the fence to get to the beginning of the woods, and run down the trail through the woods down to the crick. She didn't say anything about the dead baby she found. She did mention the lilacs, the poison ivy tree, the rusty gate, the old bus, the cabin ruins, and the row of daffodils. Next time I'll take the entire hour and draw the best one, for sure, and it won't have cherry trees blooming in October.

Afternoon

It was after school that things changed from ordinary. My cousins Jake and Alvin wanted to go spear fishing in the crick. So we all went down there and made spears and tried and tried. But the fish weren't cooperating. Nellie was off somewhere doing her little-kid thing when I heard the dinner bell being rung

over and over and over. So all four of us raced back to the yard
where Ma was ringing the bell. There was a faint odor of burning wood in the air.

"Go help Pa," she yelled. "There's a fire in Old Part." The old
part of the barn is where we keep the bull and any sick heifers
and steers. There's also storage for grain in there. If an animal
gets sick Pa puts it in its own special room in Old Part. Then I
saw Aunt Hazel, Unc Elmer, Dan and Dalton pulling up in their
Model A, then running toward us. I could see a ribbon of white
smoke rising above the barn and the burning smell was getting
stronger.

Ma started pumping water into pails and we made a "fire brigade" with Ma handing the pail first to me, then I handed it to
Aunt Hazel and she ran into the milk house and ran back with
an empty pail. Dan and Dalton and their twin brothers ran out
to the barnyard and brought out the bull and tied him up near
the horse tank. Then they started taking pails of water from the
horse tank into the back door of Old Part in the same kinda brigade. We were all running at once trying to even out the brigade
as we passed pails of water into the fire and empty pails back to
the windmill pump.

That's when it struck me. Our barn was burning up. We
wouldn't have enough money to rebuild it. What if Old Part, the
new barn, and the milk house all burned up? They were all connected. Even if Pa and Unc Elmer could rebuild it by themselves
there was no way we would have money to buy lumber or nails or
anything. I think this was on everyone's minds as we frantically
ran the pails of water into the barn.

Ma had been pumping water into the pails for a long time. I
heard her groaning and Aunt Hazel took over doing the pumping.
Ma then traded places with me. She was the first runner as she
tried to catch her breath. She gave the filled pail to me as I ran it
into the milk house. I was ready to run it all the way to Old Part
if necessary, but Unc Elmer came running into the milk house

from the Connector and handed me an empty pail as I handed him the full one.

Unc Elmer was wearing a red farmer's handkerchief over his mouth and nose like a bank robber. He was coughing underneath it and the smell of smoke was a lot stronger. I wondered about Pa. Would he get burnt up fighting the fire? My mind was racing as I ran to give the empty pail to Ma as she handed me the full one. What if Pa died and all the barns burned up? What would we do? I ran faster and faster thinking all these awful things.

Suddenly it struck me that maybe Pa had already died. That's why Unc Elmer was the only one coming back from Old Part with empty pails. Maybe the flames swallowed him up just like the ones the revivalist preacher screamed about.

After these thoughts, I ran and ran so hard I didn't think about anything else. My heart was beating so fast I thought it was gonna come out of my chest. I was sweating to beat the band and my legs hurt from all the running. At one point when I was doing the switch off, I noticed that Ma was now doing the pumping again. She and Aunt Hazel seemed to be switching off much more frequently. Pumping must be harder than running, I thought.

After two more runs I ran up to the pump and told Ma I'd pump for a while. I was right about it being harder than running. After only pumping one pail my arm was aching. But I managed three more pails before Aunt Hazel came to my rescue.

Once when I looked over at the barnyard I could only see Jake and Alvin carrying pails from the horse tank. Dan and Dalton must be dousing the fire inside. After glancing at the barnyard I started running full force again, panting and handing off water to Unc Elmer. Then a thought struck me outa the blue. Nellie wasn't here helping. What was that lazy, stupid girl doing?

As if by magic my question was answered. Mr. Lutz was in his wagon with a fire hose racing up our driveway. Nellie was sitting beside him as Chief and Star charged up to the horse tank.

Mr. Lutz jumped off his wagon and took a long hose and put it into the tank, instructing Nellie to adjust the height so the water could flow downward through the hose toward Old Part. Jake and Alvin helped Nellie and cheered when the water came out the other end of the hose.

Mr. Lutz had already put a red farmer's handkerchief over his nose and mouth and was running the hose into Old Part.

"Quit gawking," Ma yelled at me as she and Aunt Hazel switched at the pump again. I didn't even answer Ma. Instead I ran my pail as fast as I could into the milk house and met Unc Elmer in the Connector. When I ran out to meet Ma and exchange pails I could see that Nellie, Jake and Alvin were still holding up the hose so that the water would flow downward to the barn.

We kept doing this. My arms and legs ached more than when I walked to Fonsha. But everything was at stake. If we lost the barn, then we'd lose the farm. We'd have nowhere to go. I kept huffing and puffing and helped Ma and Aunt Flora pump the water every few minutes.

It seemed like forever when Dan and Dalton came out and said the fire was out, but they were dousing it good so that it wouldn't start up again.

"Is Pa okay?" I yelled at Dalton. I hadn't seen hide nor hair of him since this whole horrible thing began. I was still worried that he might have died in the fire.

"Yup, he's hosing down all the floors with Mr. Lutz," Dalton answered. "He should be out soon, then Dan and I will finish up in there."

Finally, when Pa appeared, he walked slowly to the pump and Ma handed him some water in the metal cup we always keep at the well. Pa coughed and coughed, struggling to drink the water. After he got it down he handed the cup back to Ma for more and more, until Unc Elmer and everyone gathered under the windmill.

I wondered why Pa wasn't smiling. After all, it was a close call and we'd put the fire out. Still he had a frown on his face. Pa and Unc Elmer walked back to the Old Part, both coughing, yet talking quietly. He had said none of us could come back there except Dan and Dalton. We were all to stay away, too many hot embers.

I asked Ma how the fire got started and she didn't know. She said fires start from lightning or sometimes just start on their own. Well, there wasn't no lightning today so I figured this one started on its own, but that seemed real strange, too.

Flora
Wednesday, October 17, 1934
Afternoon

When I got home from school today I learned there had been a terrible fire in Old Part, the oldest part of the barn. I was extra late because I'd walked home today. That's because Dan and Dalton had stayed home to help Unc Elmer with corn picking. Ma was still sitting at the well, exhausted. I kept asking her how the fire got started and she said it started all by itself. When I looked at her skeptically she just shook her head.

I got supper ready without Ma even asking me. I fixed boiled potatoes and heated up some navy beans mixed with molasses. Pa ate some bread and butter, too. All during supper neither Ma nor Pa said a word. It was clear without asking that they weren't willing to talk about the fire.

After supper when I was walking out to the privy I decided to go look at the Old Part. What I saw made me cry. The manger and stanchions were all burnt. It looked like the loose hay in the manger was the first thing to go, where it was darkest and most burnt. The floors that Pa kept covered with straw were all black. Even the main beams holding up the roof were dark with smoke and soot stains. The smell of smoke permeated the entire area including the stalls for sick cattle.

While the damage looked terrible, it could have been so much worse. When I was a little kid I saw the Watsons' barn go up in flames. Ma kept pulling me back farther and farther away from it, worried that the it would fall over on us. I was totally spellbound. Finally, when we were way out in the road it collapsed. I will never forget the sight. The red roaring flames dancing up and down the building, the smoke curling up in the sky, and finally the skeleton of the barn falling inward. I've been scared of fires ever since.

But how did the fire get started? Ma and Pa aren't talking. That says a lot. I think they don't know. I sure hope Irene and Nellie weren't responsible; that would be a heavy load. But Irene insisted they were both down at the crick when she noticed the smoke. Jake and Alvin, too.

Nellie
Monday, October 22, 1934
Forenoon

No one's talking much 'bout the fire in Old Part. It's not forbidden like the buried baby, but jist nuthin' to say, I guess.

Yesterday Flora's boyfriend Tom came over for Sunday dinner and he told us that if he didn't work at the CCC he would come over and sleep in the barn in case whoever started the fire came back. Tom thinks someone was smoking in Old Part and fell asleep. But how could you fall asleep when you're smoking? Pa always smokes his pipe in the parlor and never in the barn. And who would be sleeping in the afternoon? You have to either go to school or work during the daytime.

Tom showed me and Irene where the fire most likely started, a very black part in the manger that used to have hay in it. He said he thought whoever was in there was using the manger for a bed and was napping when the fire started. The person could have thrown a match down in the hay, or emptied a burning pipe, or thrown out a cigarette. Tom's a smart guy and I see how he may have figured out what happened, but I can't picture anyone taking a nap in the afternoon. No one does that, there's jist too much work to do, 'specially now during harvest season.

Irene and I have played in the manger a lot; mainly we bury ourselves in the hay, hiding from Pa. He always finds us, usually cuz we can't stop laughing and the hay jiggles. But no one ever falls asleep there. Pa says he will rebuild the burnt part of the manger and stanchions this winter. People think that farmers don't work in the winter. Little do they know.

Tom believes whoever started the fire snuck out the back door of Old Part. He showed us where the tall grass was trampled down back by the old grapevines and raspberry bushes. There was an empty whiskey bottle on the ground, too. Tom picked it up.

"It looks like whoever was there made a path through the tall grass, then cut back into Mr. Lutz's south field and went to the road or kept on going across the road down toward the ridge," Tom said. But he couldn't find any trace of him after the road.

When we got back to the house Tom handed the empty whiskey bottle to Pa who stared and stared at it, then went up to the kitchen cupboard and swept his hand across the top shelf. It's way too high up there to keep much of anything so I wondered why he was doing it.

"That Roy Hendrick stole my whiskey and then purt near burned up the barn," Pa said shaking his head.

Ma looked up in surprise. "First trying to steal the horses, then the stuff in the cellar, and now your whiskey. Don't he know enough to leave us alone?"

Pa soon left to call Sheriff Devlon from Unc Elmer's house.

Irene
Thursday, October 25, 1934
Afternoon

Miss Swanson is beginning to figure out how smart I am. Finally. This morning she asked me to help the three second-graders with their arithmetic when I was just sitting there looking for something to do. I'd read all the books on the shelf. Seems like I know *The Boxcar Children* by heart cuz I've read it so many times.

I pulled my desk over near the second graders and asked them what assignment they were working on. It turns out that they're learning how to multiply. Easy as pie. At first they didn't understand what multiplying meant. So I started with easy stuff and showed them the difference between adding and multiplying. Then we worked on two times two, two times three, and two times four until everybody understood. By the time we got to three times nine they all were nodding their heads. I hope Miss Swanson asks me to help them tomorrow. If she does I will help them memorize their times tables, going up to nine times nine and I'm already thinking about how to teach them division.

Nighttime

Tonight I overheard the most amazing news and I'm just bursting to tell someone. I was in the kitchen trying to find something good to eat and I heard Ma and Pa sitting outside on the stoop. They rarely do that but last night was gosh-darn summery warm. The moon was big and beautiful, no longer full, but shining bright. I couldn't find anything to eat. Stale bread was it. Nothing in the pie safe or cupboard so I just stood there wondering if I wanted stale bread. I was kinda thinking I'd give a piece to Rover.

Then I heard Pa talking. "He came to ask me for her hand in marriage."

"Well, I guess we've been expecting that," Ma answered.

"But not so soon," Pa answered. "I was hoping it wouldn't happen so fast. She was just getting over Henry when Tom appeared. I'm thinking it would be better to wait till next spring. There's no hurry. She'd be eighteen by then and graduated from high school."

Ma seemed a little irritated with Pa. "But she's in love with him and there's no reason for her not to get married now. Making them wait don't do anyone no good."

There was a long pause before Ma continued. "Besides it's different now than when we were young. There's cars and Lover's Lane and so many girls getting themselves in trouble. I know Flora's a good girl, but there's no supervision when they're courting. That rumor was so hard to endure."

"Tom lives clear across the county," Pa spoke up. "We'd really be losing her, Dorothy."

Ma muttered something back to Pa that I couldn't understand.

"I already did," Pa said. "I knew what you would say, so I told him that we would welcome him into the family."

"Wonderful," Ma answered. "I need to get the wedding dress out of the attic and get it fitted to Flora. It'll look so nice on her. A winter wedding would make everyone so happy." Ma's voice held more excitement than I had heard in a long time. Since their conversation was ending, I figured it was time to get out of the kitchen before they came in and found me listening. No stale bread tonight.

Nellie
Thursday, October 25, 1934
Forenoon

Irene and I ran all the way to school this morning without stopping. We were the first ones there. Miss Swanson said hello and asked if we could grab some wood from the shed to put near the stove cuz it usually gits cold around this time of year. So in 'bout fifteen minutes we had piled up enough wood to last a week or two.

Then as the rest of the kids were arriving Miss Swanson told me and Irene that she's gonna go to the Carnegie Library next Saturday and she could check out some books for us. Irene seemed to know what Miss Swanson was talking 'bout and said she wanted science books. I told her I liked maps, so she said she would try to find an atlas, which is a book filled with maps. Later I was thinking 'bout Indians and asked her to git some books 'bout Indians, too. She said she would. I think Miss Swanson is the best teacher ever. Even Irene seems to be liking her a lot more these days.

Miss Swanson is helping me write down my stories. I've written a story 'bout the people dancing in the sky with all the rainbow colors in the background. Flora loves that one. She says being in love is like dancing in the sky. I can't wait to be in love and dance up there with all those colors around me.

I also wrote a story 'bout the Indians who used to live down by the crick near Johnnycake Ridge. There are lots of words I don't know how to spell, so sometimes Miss Swanson has an older kid help me, like Fritz Geist, or my cousins Jake and Alvin, but never Irene. I don't think Irene would like that.

At first I was worried 'bout not having paper for writing but Miss Swanson gave me a lined tablet like the older kids have and I write small on both sides of the paper. She says to always keep my stories cuz someday when I'm grown-up I will wanna read them and think back on these days when I was seven. I'm not so sure 'bout that, but she says I have a wonderful 'magination, and she don't want me to lose it, ever.

I'm not so sure I understand 'bout how people lose their 'magination cuz it's not really a thing like a little seed or button that you could drop on the ground and not find again. She says it's inside your head. It's the voice that makes up the stories. I don't think you'd lose your 'magination unless someone cuts off your head and that's not likely to happen as long as you stay away from Pottawatomi Indians.

Flora
Friday, October 26, 1934
Afternoon

It's been almost two weeks since Tom figured out that Mr. Hendrick had started the fire in Old Part. When Tom first heard the story about the fire he was ready to stand guard for our family and shoot any intruders himself. I guess Tom and my cousin Dan are a lot alike. They both know how to handle a rifle and aren't afraid to use it. Tom's a good shot and provides lots of game for his family. Last year he and his dad both bagged eight-point bucks. They had venison all winter long.

I myself prefer six-point bucks. They're younger and the meat is more tender. But believe me, these days, no one is complaining about eight-point venison, 'specially when most of the time our Sunday dinner is squirrel or rabbit. Also, Aunt Hazel knows how to cook venison with a pressure cooker so that it tastes fresh and tender. Ma has a pressure cooker she uses for canning, but it's old and she's afraid of it exploding, so she just uses it when she has to. Just for canning, nothing else.

Nighttime

I have a secret, and I am so excited I'm about to burst. Tom has asked Pa for my hand in marriage and tonight, after Irene and Nellie went to bed, Pa told me he said yes to Tom. I was a little concerned that he and Ma would think I'm too young to get married, not having finished high school and being seventeen, not eighteen. But both Ma and Pa understand how much we love each other and what a perfect match we are.

Aunt Hazel married Unc Elmer when she was seventeen. Ma married Pa at seventeen, although she was just shy of eighteen by a few days. Tom told me last weekend that he's saved enough money so we can get married in late December. His father really struggled with the crops this summer because he couldn't afford to hire any farmhands while Tom was working for the CCC. Mr. Sharp had really needed Tom's help and Tom's mother had been beside herself with worry about her husband, concerned that he might have a heart attack.

Ma still worries about money and what we'll do if there's an unexpected expense. She's not making enough egg money. For the past three years she has only bought salt, sugar, and baking powder from the store in town, and a few little things from Mr. Goldberg, the peddler. She and Nellie go through the button box and count buttons. They both know exactly how many we have and what color they are. Same with thread. But now we've run out of all of the colors. Ma says black and white thread will fix anything. I have to say I miss the good old days when we went to Sallin's Dry Goods store and bought material for a new dress and got buttons and thread to match.

I think Mrs. Roosevelt understands about us poor farmers. I've listened to her on the radio with Jean and her mother and with Mrs. Sharp. Seems like all the women around the country tell Mrs. Roosevelt about their lives and she talks about us on the radio. She has even built her own factory near her house so women can have jobs there. Imagine that. Tom thinks that she's a homely woman, but so what? We should judge people by their deeds, not whether they have pretty faces and I told him that. I gave him the example of Mrs. Vandenberg at church. She's the fattest lady I know, but also the kindest.

Irene
Monday, October 29, 1934
Afternoon

Stupid Nellie forgot her dinner pail today, so Miss Swanson told me I needed to walk home with Nellie for dinner cuz she didn't want Nellie walking by herself. When we got home Nellie got her dinner pail that she'd left on the kitchen table and I opened mine and we both began to eat our sugar sandwiches. Yummy.

Then Rover started barking and Ma walked to the window. "Oh, it's Mr. Goldberg coming up the driveway with his cart."

Both Nellie and I rushed outside to meet Mr. Goldberg. He was grinning and waving, looking the same as he always looks with his long black beard and black suit flapping in the breeze. But his horse, Ferd, looked a little long in the tooth. Ma invited Mr. Goldberg in for a bean sandwich, and Nellie took Ferd to the horse tank for some water and got the horse a pail of oats from the granary.

"You girls are growing so fast," Mr. Goldberg said as he sat down to enjoy the sandwich.

"And how are your wife and daughters?" Ma asked him.

"Oh, doing fine," he answered. "And we have a new son, Levi, born July 14."

"Congratulations," Ma said. "Your wife must be mighty tired with you away so much. She must work very hard."

"Yah, she's a gut *froy*," he answered in his other language, Yiddish. "We want to save up in order to start a store in Toledo so I can be at home at night. That may take a while."

Ma nodded. "These are hard times and nobody can save money."

"Whatcha got that's new?" Nellie excitedly changed the subject. Her social graces ain't too good.

"Well, I've got a cart filled with new things, Bubbelah," Mr. Goldberg answered her. "I know your Muter likes sewing items. I have threads, needles, thimbles, and some pieces of fabric. I've got lots of cooking things like pots and pans, knives, and spoons. There's an umbrella in my cart. You ever seen one?" Nellie and I both nodded. We'd seen them in town on rainy days, even though no one in our family owns one.

"I'll show you so many things. I got a little vial of vanilla for flavoring cakes, cocoa in a tin, and aspirin powder for headaches. I've got some new combs, brushes, jewelry, and books," which he pronounced *bukes*.

Mr. Goldberg could see that Nellie and I wanted to see the books. "If your mother agrees, I'll show them to you as soon as I finish my sandwich," he said. As far as I was concerned, Mr. Goldberg couldn't finish that bean sandwich fast enough. Nellie, too, was chomping at the bit to see the stuff in his wagon.

When we finally got outside Mr. Goldberg showed us the hair brushes, jewelry, and toys, and saved the books for last. The books he showed us were *Peter Pan, Anne of Green Gables*, and *Girl of the Limberlost*, and he told us a little bit about each one.

"I read these at night when I'm homesick for my own children," Mr. Goldberg told us. You could tell he really misses his family.

"Time for you to get back to school," Ma said before me and Nellie had time to beg for anything. "Go off right now so you're not late."

I knew Ma wanted to buy some things for us, but we have no money. It's been a tough year with so few eggs and all.

"Bye, Mr. Goldberg!" we yelled as we ran down the driveway to the road. Mr. Goldberg nodded to us solemnly like we were grown-ups. We both ran as fast as we could beating the one-o'clock bell by a few seconds.

Nellie
Monday, October 29, 1934
Forenoon

I've been worried 'bout people not believing me cuz I like to make up stories. Last night Pa told me that all of us girls have gifts. Flora has musical talents. Irene has a great memory and I have a superb 'magination. Irene does well in school cuz she quickly memorizes spelling words and history dates and other subjects. But Pa told me that my 'magination will be a big benefit when I'm grown-up. So for now I need to pay attention to what's real and what's 'maginary so people take me seriously. He said I should continue making up stories 'bout ZeeZee, the Indians, pirates, and other 'maginary friends, writing them all down in my book at school.

This morning I used my Reader to find words that I already knew and made up a story using those words. The story was 'bout a boy who lives in a school bus that could fly and helps out people around the world. I told Miss Swanson what I was doing, and she said that was a great idea and that she was gonna ask the other kids to make up stories using words from their Readers.

A special surprise came today when me and Irene ran home to eat our dinners. Mr. Goldberg the peddler came with his buggy. It was so fun looking at all his wares, specially the books and toys. Mr. Goldberg is always so nice 'bout showing us all his stuff, even though he knows we don't have any money. Ma always gives him a bean sandwich, telling him there's no salt pork in the beans. I don't know why she says that. We haven't any had salt pork in two or three years.

If I didn't have Ma and Pa, I would want Aunt Hazel and Unc

Elmer to be my parents, and if I didn't have them, I'd wanna live with Mr. and Mrs. Geist, and if I didn't have them I'd wanna live with Mr. and Mrs. Vandenberg, and if I didn't have them I'd wanna live with Mr. and Mrs. Goldberg. I know she's nice even though I've never met her. Mr. Goldberg always tells stories 'bout her and his children. Four girls and now a baby boy. Pa says he's a Jew. I think that means he has a lot of jewelry; I've seen some of it in his cart. That would be nice too.

Nighttime

At dinner I signaled for Sisters' Club to meet so there we were, all three on Flora's bed. "I jist wanted to get together," I said. "I miss the Sisters' Club."

"I'm afraid Sisters' Club has gone nowhere," Flora said quietly. "We still can't find out anything about that baby."

"But now I know it wasn't a Gypsy baby," Flora added. "Patya has said so over and over and over again. There's no reason for her to lie now. She and Jean and I have become good friends."

Flora had already told us that Jean and her parents are letting Patya live with them when the Gypsies leave camp next week. Jean's so excited—she always wanted a sister. Patya will stay with the Spinattis until next spring when the caravan comes back. She's going to earn her keep by doing sewing and needlework. They figure by spring she'll know if she wants to return to being a Gypsy or not.

"So we have no more suspects and Sisters' Club was all in vain?" Irene said, angrily.

"No, Irene, it wasn't," Flora answered. "If I Jean and I hadn't met Patya she'd continue being miserable. Now she's got an opportunity to experience a different life to see if she wants it. God works in mysterious ways."

With that we officially ended the Sisters' Club.

Flora
Monday, October 29, 1934
Nighttime

My heart is filled with so much joy at the thought of my upcoming marriage to Tom. Ma and Pa have given consent and we're thinking about a wedding right before Christmas. What a wonderful time to celebrate our wedding anniversary. Every year when the church is all decorated and people are happy and excited about the holidays, and everyone's baking special Christmas recipes, we'll be celebrating our marriage.

When I got home from school today, Ma whispered to me that Mr. Goldberg had stopped by for his fall visit, and that she had bought a book for each of my sisters for Christmas.

"I got Nellie *Peter Pan* and Irene *Anne of Green Gables*," she confided after my sisters had gone outside to do their chores. She got out the books and I looked through them. Nellie's book will suit her fine as it is about a boy who flies through the air, just like her imaginary friend ZeeZee. Then Ma and I looked at Irene's book which is about an eleven-year-old orphan girl who ends up on a farm in Canada.

"I know I was using good money," Ma said, "but life is short and all three of you girls worked so hard all summer long."

"Yes," I agreed. "I can't think of any better present for both of them. Maybe you don't have to put an orange in their stockings this year. They'll be so happy with the books they won't even miss the oranges." I was trying to help Ma feel okay about her purchases. Usually she won't spend an extra penny on anything, so this was a huge departure. I wished she'd bought something for herself, but that wasn't going to happen.

Nellie
Thursday, November 22, 1934
Forenoon

How I love school. I've written two more stories 'bout ZeeZee and his flying airship. One story is 'bout how ZeeZee flies all over the world to bring medicine to children who have diseases. The other story is how he went to Mars and found people living there.

Irene says she's fed up with my stories 'bout ZeeZee. She says it's more important to write real stories where people can learn things 'bout history, like George Washington or Abraham Lincoln. But Pa tells me to write stories that I wanna write. He says he likes the ZeeZee stories and that I should keep writing them. So I do.

Flora has been gittin' ready for her wedding for weeks. She's been asking Ma to show her how to do everything from cleaning milk cans to cooking pot roast to making cheese. Tom's mother is a good cook, so she's been particularly worried 'bout that, cuz Ma herself says she's not the best cook. Ma's ma died when she was ten, so Ma knows basic stuff like bread, pies, and reglar meals but she says she missed all the special stuff, like Christmas cooking.

Flora goes up to Aunt Hazel's house every day and helps her make supper so she learns how to cook lots of things that Ma don't make. One day she brought back some shortbread cookies for me and Irene. They were the best.

When I git married I think I'll have Aunt Hazel give me lessons, too. I'm not sure what all you need to know in order to git married but it seems like a lot. Flora hates to dress chickens, but she has been having Ma show her how, jist pretending they have a rooster. When Aunt Hazel gave her a real rooster to dress out,

Flora tried not to throw up, but she upchucked anyway. Same with cleaning fish. All these marriage lessons. Flora says she's lucky she knows how to sew, so she can spend all her time learning other stuff.

Last night Ma and Pa sounded so sad, talking 'bout Flora when she was a little baby. Ma said she had always hoped that Flora would end up with Henry since they live so close. Then she could see Flora every day, but if not every day, several times a week and at church. She said they could come over every week for Sunday dinner, too. I guess Ma was forgetting that the Fitches have Sunday dinner, too.

All of these conversations 'bout missing Flora before she is even gone are kinda sad. I wish Irene would run off again. That made for great stories.

Irene
Friday, November 23, 1934
Forenoon

Miss Swanson has become so much nicer in the past few weeks. She has been bringing me books about history and science that she checks out of the Carnegie Library. She said she's gonna find me books about each of our country's presidents, too. I'm learning a lot about how our country began and how slavery caused the Civil War. I really like reading about the underground railroad and how the slaves escaped to Canada. There was a route that went near our farm, from Marshall to Albion and on to Detroit, across the river into Canada.

Pa's family, the Yoders, were Amish people in Pennsylvania before they came to Michigan. Miss Swanson said that many Quakers, Mennonites, and Amish were opposed to slavery. Pa's folks were simple, quiet farm people and Pa said they tried to live their religion. I'm not sure how that's any different from what Ma and Pa do, but I wonder if they hid slaves. Ma and Pa don't know.

Pa's family owned that old log cabin that now is ruins at the back of the second meadow. Nellie and I have explored it lots of times. You can see where the walls and chimney were. It was a strange place to have a log cabin cuz it's not on any road, just near the crick. Maybe they took the slaves down the crick rather than on the roads and hid them in the cabin. That might have fooled the slave catchers. I asked Miss Swanson about it but she couldn't find a book about it, probably cuz it was all kept a secret.

Miss Swanson took out a book from the library for Nellie that explains the stars, sun, moon, and planets. I've been helping

Nellie with it cuz I wanna know about all the sky stuff too. Turns out that the moon goes around the earth and the earth goes around the sun. I still can't figure out why we don't feel like we're upside down part of the time. Neither could I find anything about the Fourth of July colors that danced in the sky. Miss Swanson says that one day we will be exploring all the planets and stars. I can't wait. I wanna know all about the stars up in the sky and if there are other people living up there. Nellie's stories about ZeeZee might end up being kinda truthful even though she made it all up.

Nighttime

I was sitting in the kitchen with my *Bible Story Book* and noticed that someone had written in the actual *Bible* chapters for all the stories. I decided to check and see if they were correct. I started with the first story, Adam and Eve. To my surprise Genesis 2:4 – 3:24 was right. Then I checked the rest of the stories and they were correct, too. Who did this?

I walked to the parlor and asked Ma, Pa, and Flora. None of them knew. Flora looked closely at the handwriting. "Isn't that your handwriting?" she asked me.

"Well, yes, it does look like mine, but I would remember if I had done this," I answered. Right then Nellie walked into the parlor.

"Do you know who wrote this?" I asked her.

"You did," she replied. "Last summer when you had all that poison ivy and stayed inside, you looked up all the stories in the *Bible* and you wrote them in. Why are you even asking?"

I didn't know what to say. Why wasn't anyone concerned about this weird stuff?

Someone has played a trick on me. Nellie's too little and

Flora's too busy with all this wedding stuff. Well, maybe it was Nellie after all. She knows enough words to do this. So I'm gonna play a trick on her and write a ZeeZee story that she can find somewhere. Maybe in her *Pirate Book*. That would be a good payback.

So I proceeded to write a story about ZeeZee and his flying bus. It's a story of a little girl saying goodbye to him as his bus flies up into the sky. I'd just as soon have Nellie give up on ZeeZee stories. Why write such nonsense when you can learn science?

Nellie
Saturday, November 24, 1934
Forenoon

I've been wanting to go down to the log cabin ruins and see if I could talk to my 'maginary friend, ZeeZee. Mosta the summer and fall I had to work in the garden and didn't have much time for ZeeZee or the pirates or Indian boys. Also, Ma wouldn't let me go anywhere alone cuz of those murdered girls in Spring Lake.

But dang it, I really wanted go down there cuz winter's almost here and today may be the last warm day before it gits all icy cold. But Irene said, "No." She wanted to go up to Aunt Hazel's and play with Jake and Alvin. They're trying to figure out a place for a new jailhouse now that the corncrib is filled to the top with corn. They never did figure out how I was escaping from jail. They kept looking on the floor for loose boards, but they never climbed to the top and found the hole in the roof. I love those slatted corncrib walls—so easy to climb up and down.

"Irene won't go with me to the meadow," I yelled to Pa who was putting on his boots to go fix the pigpen. "I always do what she wants to do and she won't even let me play with her and the twins. She wouldn't let me help build the jailhouse and she never lets me read her *Bible Story Book*, even though I let her read my *Pirate Book*."

Pa came over and looked down at me. I was sitting on a high stool washing eggs. "Irene, come here," Pa yelled upstairs. Irene came bounding down the stairs in an instant. She knows that Pa can't be ignored, ever.

"Is that true that you didn't let Nellie help you build the

jailhouse?" Pa turned and glared at Irene. Then Ma walked in to see what was going on.

Irene nodded. One thing 'bout Irene. She tells the truth. Even though she's a sneaky tattletale, she always comes clean with Ma and Pa.

Pa started to speak, "Well, Irene you keep Nellie company down in the meadow. You girls stay together every minute, even if you fight. You need to be able to see each other all the time. No running off, either of you. Don't you dare go in the woods and don't walk down the road. Nellie gets to decide when to come back to the house. I don't want you hightailing it back early, Irene. Do you understand?"

Irene and I both nodded.

"Let's go now," I urged Irene.

She tied up her shoes and said okay. I think she was trying to figure out how to ditch me without disobeying Pa. As far as I was concerned she couldn't. Then we both took off running down the lane through the first meadow, past the cows and into the second meadow. We finally got to the corner with the cabin ruins and old bus.

"I wanna lay down here and talk to my 'maginary friends," I told Irene.

"Go ahead, baby Nellie," Irene answered. She never had 'maginary friends and ain't too patient with me when I talk to them. She walked to the rusty gate and checked to see if it still opened. It did.

So I didn't bother with her and I lay right down near the fireplace ruins and closed my eyes hoping to see ZeeZee. When he didn't come I wished for my 'maginary Indian friends, Yellow Feather and Broken Wing. Then I wished for pirates. Still, no one came so I opened my eyes and saw that Irene was weeding the daffodil plants along the fence row.

I ran over to the big oak tree and climbed to the top. I went all the way up to the top branch where I talk to ZeeZee. I was up there looking down and I could still see Irene so Pa would be happy. I was hoping ZeeZee would show up, but he didn't. Pa says that someday I will outgrow my 'maginary friends. I think that must be what's happening these days.

Pa says, "When a door closes, a window opens." Maybe it's time for my new window to open up. Wouldn't it be nice if the new window leads to a potful of money, like at the end of the rainbow?

Well, I was kinda enjoying the view from the top of the oak, thinking 'bout my windows. I could see smoke coming out of Unc Elmer's chimney. Then I heard somethin' on the ground. I looked down at Irene and saw a large man leaning over her. He put his hand over her mouth but I could see her struggling to git away. From behind it looked like the evil preacher, Brother Johnson. I wanted to run up to the barn to find Pa, but he'd made it very clear that Irene and I were to stay together. Besides what if the evil Brother killed Irene before Pa could come back with his shotgun?

Now the Brother was carrying Irene into the bus as she was kicking and flailing her arms. He never looked up my way. I don't think he knew I was up in the tree. Still, he might be pretending so he could come back and git me.

My mind was racing. I needed to help Irene. I needed to find something to throw at him. Maybe some of the rocks and bricks from the cabin foundation. Or maybe a long stick that I could jab at him. But what if he killed Irene right away? He had almost strangled me to death before he took down his suspenders that day last summer. I had to do something right away before he hurt Irene real bad. But what?

First, I decided I needed to git him out of that bus and away from Irene. I pulled a few acorns that hadn't fallen off the limb I was on and threw them on the bus roof. He wouldn't know what was happening. I pulled more off and threw them on the bus roof again. Maybe he would think it was a tornado. Then I heard Irene scream so I knew that she was still alive.

Then the Brother came out the door of the bus and looked towards the woods. Guess he couldn't tell what direction the acorns had come from. I lay flat, still on the limb, and sure enough he turned around and looked my way. But he only looked at the sky, not towards me. He turned back around and walked into the bus, slamming the door.

Well, the acorns would only work to git him outa the bus and no more. I needed to give him a real scare, enough to convince Irene to run out of the bus and head for home. So I started making some Indian war noises. I yelled as loud as I could using all the nasty noises from playing cowboys and Indians. This time Brother Johnson came out of the bus carrying a garden hoe. I lay flat cuz I didn't have anything to use against that kinda weapon.

But I kept my eyes on the Brother as he walked around the bus. After he circled around he walked over to the stile that leads to the path through the woods. If only he would walk down the path, then I could git to the bus, grab Irene, and leave. But no, the Brother turned around and started walking back toward the bus.

As soon as he slammed the bus door I started making Indian sounds again, but suddenly they changed into angry monster sounds. I wanted to be totally ready to scoot down the tree if he decided to go over the stile to the woods. So I was no longer lying flat on the branch but near the trunk. The Brother came out of the bus again, and this time walked right under the tree, looking straight up at me.

"You little whore," he yelled. "You ready to atone for your sins?" He was panting, breathing as if he had run a mile. "Now I git to decide which of you goes first."

I stuck out my tongue at him and hoped he wouldn't start climbing the tree.

"You'll never be able to climb up here and git me," I yelled at the top of my lungs. I needed to let Irene know where he was so she could git away. "Jist try," I added, catching my breath. "You're a fat old man and can't climb trees."

Then I started using Mr. Lutz's swear words. The Brother looked up at me, seemingly amused.

"It won't work this time, Girlie," he shouted up.

I kept swearing anyway. "Damn, damn, damn. Damn you to damnation. Go to hell. God dammit."

Out of the corner of my eye I saw Irene sneak out of the bus leaving the door open. But instead of running down the lane to Ma and Pa, she came around the bus carrying the hoe. I knew I needed to make a lot of noise so the preacher wouldn't hear her. I started making the Indian sounds again. The Brother jist looked up at me and laughed.

"You think you're scaring me?" he growled. "You're jist a Satan kid who has a loud voice. But you're gonna pay for your sins, too." I was panting but I had to keep going and I started the monster sounds again, kinda growling like a wild animal. I made mad animal faces as I did it. I wanted to look towards Irene to see where she was but I knew I couldn't do it since the Brother might look there, too.

I was gonna swear at him again, but I knew the swear words wouldn't mask Irene's walking noises nearly as good as the monster sounds. So I kept growling and watched the Brother.

"You're a friend of Satan," he yelled up at me. "You'd better git ready for the fires of hell cuz you're headed straight there."

I took a big gulp of air to continue with the monster sounds, and then I saw Irene right behind him ready to hit him with the hoe, so I made the loudest most terrifying sound I could make. Irene was right behind him swinging the hoe. When the hoe hit his head, I jumped down from the tree and started following Irene, running as fast as I could. I didn't even look back to see if he was coming after us.

"Faster, faster," I yelled to Irene so she knew that I was right behind her. "Fast as you can, Irene."

We ran down the lane through the second meadow to the first meadow, through it and up to the barnyard and into the backyard. Irene was screaming and hollering but I jist sped up to the dinner bell and started ringing it. I was panting so hard I couldn't talk.

Ma and Flora came outa the house and Pa came running from the barn. I wanted Unc Elmer to call Sheriff Devlon so I kept ringing it while Irene explained to Ma and Pa what had happened.

Unc Elmer soon pulled into the driveway in his Model A with my oldest cousin Dan in the passenger seat. "I already called the Sheriff to come," he yelled out. "Is Hendrick in your barn?"

"No, worse," Pa said, and explained the situation.

"We gotta get him before he gets away," Dan said, shouldering his shotgun.

"No, wait for the Sheriff," Ma yelled out. She was in tears. "The man is crazy. He might kill you all before the Sheriff gets here."

"It's a chance we gotta take," Pa said, slowly and deliberately. "It'll be three of us, armed. As far as we know he only has that garden hoe."

So Pa, Unc Elmer, and Dan took off down the lane. The rest of us sat by the milk house and waited. Ma kept crying. It reminded me of the dead baby day, waiting, not knowing what was happening. Only worse. Soon Aunt Hazel and my other three cousins, Dalton and the twins, Jake and Alvin, walked up the drive at the same time that Sheriff Devlon drove in.

Ma ran up to Sheriff Devlon's car and told him what was going on.

"Any shots fired?" the Sheriff asked as he walked with Ma toward the lane.

"No one's heard anything," she answered. Then we saw Dan running up the lane toward us. Everybody held their breath.

"He was already dead," Dan said panting between breaths. "It looked like Irene had knocked him out with the hoe, but the blood attracted some critters including a female bear. He was trying to fight her off when we got there. She finished the job, looked at us, and walked away. Just like she knew we were friends, but he wasn't."

"Okay," Sheriff Devlon, said. "Time for me to take over." He looked at Dan. "Call the game warden since there's an animal involved. "Don't wanna take any chances here."

Irene
Saturday, November 24, 1934
Afternoon

My head hurt so bad when Ma reached me and Nellie in the backyard by the dinner bell. "What did he do to you?" Ma asked sharply. "Did he take your clothes off? Did he pull down your drawers? Are you bleeding?"

I just groaned. I hate Ma's questions when she's scared. There are way too many and she sounds so strange. So I just shook my head. No."

When everybody came back to the yard and the Sheriff and Game Warden had done what they needed to do, I just put my head on Ma's lap. The bear was dead. She had ambled under the oak tree, fallen down and died. No visible wounds.

It had gotten late while we waited for the game warden, but truthfully I didn't wanna see a dead man or a dead bear. I just wanted to get in the house and put on my warm nightgown. So that's what we did. Ma drew a bath for Nellie and me and oh, did that feel good. Ma said that Doc Holzer was coming as soon as he finished stitching up a man who had cut himself chopping wood.

When the doctor came he asked me a whole bunch of questions and asked where it hurt the most. I told him about the preacher punching me in the head and kicking my stomach. "Might be a concussion and broken ribs," he told Ma. "We'll just have to wait and see what happens."

Nellie and I climbed up the stairs to bed. Ma pulled up a rocking chair and slept up by our bed all night long. A couple of times when I woke up, moaning, Ma hugged me until I felt better and went back to sleep.

Flora
Thursday, November 29, 1934
Nighttime

Today is Thanksgiving and I have much to be thankful for. My sisters are alive and safe and the evil preacher is dead. I don't know how Ma and Pa are handling it because they both quit talking about the Brother. Ma first tried to pretend it never happened, but everyone started asking about Irene and Nellie so she had to give up on that. Now she's saying she made a mistake by forcing us girls to silence.

My sisters have strict rules not to leave the house without telling Ma. No one knows for sure if it was Brother Johnson who murdered the Spring Lake girls so everyone's being extra cautious. I myself went down and talked to May Hendrick again. I described Brother Johnson to her and she confirmed that it was most likely him that took her and got her in a family way.

So today, I'm thankful that all that horrible stuff is behind us. In addition, I will be marrying the love of my life, Tom Sharp, in a few short weeks. Both Ma and Pa have told me over and over again what a good guy I'm getting. He's a handsome farm boy who's a hard worker and the most decent person alive. He's told me over and over again how much he loves me and that he will take care of me forever. What more could a girl want?

I'm going to have a plain gold ring just like Ma's. It was Tom's grandma's ring, and I'm happy to wear it and keep it in the family. Tom's mother said how pleased she is that I'm coming into the family. She wants me to call her Ma, just like Tom does. That'll take a little getting used to but I'll be seeing her every day because we'll be living in the little house right next door. She's been very sweet to me, and when I told her how I've been trying to learn everything about cooking from Aunt Hazel, she told me not to worry. When I have questions I can ask her. She said she always wanted a daughter and now here I am.

So last night after Nellie and Irene had gone to bed, Pa said to me, "I wish you and Tom didn't have to start out in such hard times. We barely made payments on the mortgage and taxes this year with not a cent left over. But don't you forget to come to Ma and me if you're facing difficulty. We'll help you out the best we can."

Gee, did that make me feel good. I know that our whole family has gone to bed hungry many nights, but thank goodness the debts are paid until next year. Tom's family just made it by a thread, too. So next year is no guarantee. Hopefully, President Roosevelt will come through. There are some programs to help the farmers, but we haven't seen any benefits yet. Tom says it'll be easier to get farm loans with Roosevelt's New Deal. That could help us buy our own farm in a few years, maybe one closer to Ma and Pa's place.

This afternoon when we have our Thanksgiving meal, we'll all be grateful that we survived one more year, but I wish the hard times would come to an end for everyone. People are still losing their farms. There are long food lines. There still are shanty towns. Mr. Goldberg isn't able to buy a store in Toledo. The prices of farm products are going lower and lower, and the train riders are still coming by for bean sandwiches.

Nellie
Saturday, December 8, 1934
Afternoon

Ma's been crying a lot lately. I think she feels bad for those girls in Spring Lake that the preacher killed and she understands that if it warn't for me and Irene sticking together we woulda been killed, too. Ma is always checking on us. Sometimes after we go to bed I hear her coming up the stairs. She opens the door from the landing and looks in. Sometimes she comes in and gives us each a kiss. She's apologized to us for telling us not to talk about the dead baby, but at this point there's nothing more to say.

After the horrible "incident" as Ma and Pa call it, Irene and I have to stay home every minute that we're not in school. I walk to school with Irene, Jake, and Alvin, but Ma comes to school every day to walk home with me, so I'm never alone. She says she won't let me or Irene go anywhere by ourselves. Guess the "incident" was awful for her, too.

The good news is that all Irene's injuries are healing up. Mine, too. Turns out I had huge bruises from the jump down to ground from the oak tree. The bruises are now a yellow-purple color and Ma says that's a good sign. So yesterday Ma took us back to the doctor at his office. Doc Holzer smiled and smiled when me and Irene told him we were both feelin' so much better. He poked us both in a few places and asked lots of question. He said he'd been so worried 'bout injuries that we couldn't see, like broken ribs, but we we're both doing jist fine.

Before we left his office, Ma went to the desk to pay the bill. Mrs. Spinatti was working and said there was no charge. Ma started crying again. Mrs. Spinatti pulled out a chair for Ma and handed her a handkerchief. Then she walked over to Ma and reached down and gave her a hug.

"You poor thing," she said. "You've done such a good job of raising your girls and you've had to endure such horrors." Then she got Ma a drink of water. "Why don't you girls tell me about Flora's upcoming wedding while your Ma finishes her cry?"

Irene told Mrs. Spinatti 'bout the wedding and that Jean and Patya were gonna be invited. Then we left. It was the middle of the afternoon by the time we got home and Ma said that Irene and I could stay home from school for the rest of the day. Ma made us each a sugar sandwich and told us to play inside.

Since the weather's gotten cold I'm fine staying in the house. Me and Irene both go up to Aunt Hazel's and help her with her housework a lot these days. Then there's all the extra canning with Ma making soups and stews to sell this winter. So we help her with that, too.

I've also been helping Flora git ready for her wedding. She's been making pillows and sewing a quilt for their bed. Jist yesterday she started making a rag rug. All the ladies at church have been pitching in with any extra cloth, goose feathers, and rags for Flora.

I feel bad 'bout not gittin' to see ZeeZee anymore, but I think I've grown up too much to see my 'maginary friends. As usual, Pa tells me to write down all my stories so I won't forget. He hugs me a lot more these days, too.

Irene
Saturday, December 22, 1934
Forenoon

My sister is getting married today. I can't imagine life without Flora being here at home. No one can play the piano like Flora, and any time I need help with the Treadle she can fix it. Everyone is so excited, but I feel bad about losing my sister. She will be living so far away, about twenty miles from us.

Aunt Hazel is fixing my hair in a new way. She washed it and put it into pin curls with rags to make nice loose curls. Aunt Hazel also made new dresses for me and Nellie. They're pink with frilly lace on the front. She said she had been saving the pink fabric for years, expecting that they would have at least one little girl. However, that didn't happen. Lucky for me and Nellie, though.

Flora has been in such a good mood. She's helped me with my chores and fixed new recipes for dinner and supper. Who can tell we're in such bad times when we get to eat all these new things? I love dried beef gravy on toast, creamed peas, and toasted cheese sandwiches. Even Ma has been excited about Flora's cooking.

The one thing I can't stand about this wedding is that everyone goes up to Flora and talks to her. They walk right past me, like I'm not there, invisible. This happens at church, downtown, anywhere we go. No one asks me how I'm doing. They just flock to Flora and make a big deal that she's getting married. The exceptions are Mrs. Geist, Mrs. Vandenberg, and Aunt Hazel They always stop and talk to me and Nellie.

Ma says that someday I'll be the bride and get all the attention. But I'd just as soon have it right now, thank you very much.

Without Flora I'll have so much more work. Work in the garden and work in the house. Helping Pa outside. No fun at all. But maybe I'll get some attention.

I'm ready to have this wedding over and done. I just wish Flora and Tom would live at our house. She's become so much nicer since she met Tom, even letting me try on the wedding dress. It's pretty, but way too long for me. I'd better grow a lot taller before I get married.

Afternoon

The wedding was over so quickly. The best part was all the cake afterwards. We all went into the church parlor and ate cake, talked with everyone, and ate more cake. There were lots of giggles and hushed whispers around Flora and Tom, but I could tell Flora was having a wonderful time. She is so much in love with her new husband.

The worst part was that Mr. Vandenberg spilled coffee on the front of my new pink dress. He apologized, but he could see how upset I got. I almost cried; I know I had tears in my eyes. Mrs. Vandenberg soon came over with a wet rag and wiped and wiped the stain. She got most of it out.

"As soon as you get home, take off the dress and wash the stain with lots of soap," she said. "And if that don't do it, pour a tablespoon of vinegar on it and rinse it off again. Don't let it dry until the stain is gone. As a last resort put an egg yolk on it. That should take the coffee right out. But, sweetie, I know that eggs are dear these days, so try vinegar first."

By then Ma had come over and she musta seen the tears in my eyes.

"Irene, I'll do it for you when we get home," Ma said. "I've taken out many stains in my day."

I rubbed my eyes and smiled at both of them. I've been feeling so left out of this whole wedding business, but here was both Ma and Mrs. Vandenberg looking out for me. I couldn't think of anything to say, but "Thank you." Then, soon enough Flora and Tom were leaving for their little house on the other side of the county.

Nellie
Saturday, December 22, 1934
Afternoon

Flora's wedding today was so much fun. Me and Irene wore new pink dresses and stood at the front of the church with Flora and Tom. I have never been to a wedding so I didn't know what to expect. Turns out all I had to do was stand there. Reverend Blackman seemed to know how to do everything. He had Flora and Tom repeat his words, and soon enough he pronounced them man and wife. Flora was so happy. She and Tom even kissed right there in front of everyone. I've never seen them kiss before, but Flora had told me that their first kiss was back in August.

Mrs. Geist was 'specially nice to me.

"Nellie, you look so nice in your pink dress," she said. "And how do you like your new teacher, Miss Swanson?"

"She's the best teacher in the world, and she takes books out of the library for me and Irene. I'm learning all 'bout the sun and moon and stars."

"Oh, that's so interesting. I remember the colored shooting stars at the Fourth of July picnic," she answered.

"Yes, no one can explain that. They said it warn't Northern Lights or reglar shooting stars. Me, I used to think maybe some visitors from outer space were making fireworks for us. But now I think maybe science jist hasn't explained it yet. Lots of science warn't explained until lately."

"I think you're right," Mrs. Geist answered. "There have been so many wonderful discoveries and inventions. Think about the telephone, the radio, electric lights, and cars. Cameras, too. So many modern inventions." Mrs. Geist sighed and went over to talk to Ma.

Jist then Mrs. Vandenberg came up and started talking to me, asking me which cake I liked best. A bunch of the neighbor ladies had gotten together and made six different cakes for Flora, a very special gift, cakes not being plentiful these days. There was yellow cake, sponge cake, apple cake, pear cake, spice cake, and punkin cake. They were all cut into tiny little pieces so you could have more than one piece.

"Apple," I answered Mrs. Vandenberg. "But the pear cake is a close second."

"Oh, you chose my apple cake," Mrs. Vandenberg exclaimed, clearly pleased.

"And I didn't even know you made it," I answered her. "Ma says you're a very good cook."

"Well, maybe. Don't tell anyone, but I think you're right 'bout Mrs. Geist's pear cake; it's right up there at the top with my apple cake." She winked at me.

"Do you like to look at the stars at night?" I asked Mrs. Vandenberg, totally changing the subject since there warn't nuthin' else to say 'bout the cakes and I was still thinking 'bout those colored lights.

"Yes, dear, I do," she answered. "When I was about your age, I would go up on our roof in the summer and lie on a blanket and watch them for hours. Often my pa would have to come out and wake me up because I would fall asleep out there watching the sky. I always wanted to know the names of the stars, but I only knew the North Star, which is near the Big Dipper."

"Well, if you were a slave trying to run away, that's the best one to know."

Mrs. Vandenberg smiled and said, "You're right about that. If you're interested in runaway slaves, the next time you're over to my house, I'll show you our secret room. There's a trap door from the kitchen floor to a room below. The room's not connected to our cellar at all. We've never talked about it because we thought we might need it someday if we had to hide. But we've always felt safe here in Parson Creek, so it seems meaningless to continue to keep it secret when it has so much history.

"Why wouldn't people feel safe here?" I asked.

"My people came from the Ukraine," she answered. "They saw horrible things done to their friends and neighbors, particularly Jews. That's why we came to America. Now we treasure our freedom."

"I didn't know," I responded to her. "I jist found out recently that Jews have a different religion from us Christians. Our new teacher Miss Swanson taught the whole school 'bout religions around the world. But where is Ukraine? I don't remember seeing it on the map."

"It's in Eastern Europe, now part of the Soviet Union," she answered in a normal tone of voice. "My parents were so happy to leave that place."

Then Mrs. Vandenberg started whispering to me, "I'm fat because my family never had enough to eat in their town of Kiev. My parents snuck aboard a ship before I was born. I was born here in America after my father started working in a shoe factory. After I was born they had enough money to buy food so they kept feeding me all the time. They never wanted me to be hungry so I never knew when to stop eating. I got bigger and bigger."

I looked at Mrs. Vandenberg and saw that she had tears in her eyes. "So when you see a fat person," she went on, "it isn't necessarily because they're greedy. It may be because their family wanted to do the best for them. I don't want to be fat, but that's the way they raised me. Mr. Vandenberg, coming from both Ukrainian and Dutch people, understands, and I'm so very grateful he does."

I nodded sympathetically. Now that Flora will be gone from our house, I'm not gonna be a baby anymore and I understand grownups a lot more than I ever did. Mrs. Vandenberg taught me a lot today, not jist that I have good taste in cake, but more important grown-up things. I think that gittin' older has helped me figure out that when you look at people, maybe you don't really see or understand them at all. You think you do at the time but later on you realize how much more you need to learn.

Nighttime

"I wanna listen to Ma and Pa," I said to Irene right after we both got in bed.

"Me too," she answered.

"Maybe we can hear them through the heat register," I said.

So we both crept down my side of the bed. I was surprised at how quiet Irene could be. Neither of us made a sound. I could smell Pa's pipe smoke and hear Ma's rocking chair. Both Ma and Pa were silent for a long, long time. Finally Ma broke the ice.

"I got the stain out of Irene's dress with vinegar," Ma said. "Olga Vandenberg was so concerned about it."

"Yup," Pa answered.

Then we could hear Ma crying.

"Tears of joy or sadness?" Pa asked her in the gentlest voice I'd ever heard.

"Both," she answered. "Today our lives changed. I'm so happy for Flora, but I'll be so lonely without her."

Ma continued to cry.

"I wish they didn't have to start married life in such hard times," Pa said when Ma quit crying.

"I was thinking that, too," Ma replied. "We've talked about this all before. Tom will be a good husband, and they'll be right there with his folks when there's hardship."

Another long pause.

Pa cleared his throat. "Well, we have two remarkable

daughters still with us. Both Irene and Nellie are smart as whips and good workers. We'll all be able to make it through anything that lies ahead. This summer required us all to pitch in. We did, and the taxes and mortgage are paid until next year. Then, we lived through some mighty dark hours with Irene and Nellie. Both of them seem to be weathering that horrible ordeal and are back to their normal lives. The Lord has been good to us."

Another long pause.

"Let's go to bed."

"Yes, let's go to bed and enjoy the long winter night."

Irene and I silently crawled back up into bed. We both ducked under the covers.

"I miss Flora already," I whispered.

"Me too," she said.

Flora
Saturday, December 22, 1934
Forenoon

Today is the happiest day of my life. I am marrying Tom Sharp, the love of my life. The wedding is going to be at church with me walking down the aisle on Pa's arm and coming back on Tom's arm. We aren't going on a wedding trip because of money being tight. Last week Tom quit his job with the CCC in order to work with his father on their farm. I was lucky. You have to be single to work in the CCC and Tom's father needed him back on the farm. I was surprised that Tom didn't want to wait until next spring when farm work gets really busy, but I think Ma is secretly relieved. After those rumors she just wanted me married.

So this afternoon I'm putting on the family wedding dress, worn by at least three brides, maybe more. It's yellowed, but Ma says these days most brides can't afford a wedding dress, and just wear their best Sunday go-to-meeting dresses. The wedding dress is okay, but I'd prefer a fancy white one like in *McCalls* magazine. My gown is a linen fabric with a high neckline and buttons in the back. The front has little pleats with lace down them. Some of the lace is missing, so I added some that didn't really match, but it looks better than nothing at all. I hope Tom won't notice. I want him to be looking into my eyes.

Ma and Pa's gift to Tom and me is a shelf full of canned fruits and vegetables. Since we'll be living in the little house right next to Tom's parents, I imagine that we'll have a lot of meals with them, so we're not too worried about food. The little house has been empty for four years since Tom's grandma died. Tom's father and grandfather built it for his grandparents about twenty years ago. It's a cute little house with its own outhouse on the path to the barn. The bed is old and lumpy, but we'll make do for now. Same with the rest of the furniture.

So I was up in my bedroom getting ready with only about one hour left before becoming Mrs. Thomas Sharp when Pa called up to me to come down to the parlor. I sailed down the stairs in my housecoat expecting to find Aunt Hazel with some pre-wedding treat. That would be just like her to make my day magic. But instead I encountered a situation I'd never anticipated.

Miss Flatshaw was sitting on the davenport with a rumpled-up handkerchief in her hand. She dabbed at her eyes. I couldn't understand why she was sitting in the parlor on my wedding day. Pa motioned for me to sit down, so I did, feeling confused. Had something awful happened to Tom that Miss Flatshaw knew about?

Pa cleared his throat. "Miss Flatshaw has something to say to you," he said, and paused. There was such a long silence in the room that I was sure something awful had happened. Maybe it was about Ma or my sisters. They had all left for the church early to get things ready. Pa was gonna take me after I'd gotten dressed, and then we'd both be ready to walk down the aisle together.

Finally, Miss Flatshaw looked up at both Pa and me. "My life is in ruins. I thought God had shown me a way to avoid the consequences of my sins, but instead my life is gone. I have no job and I've lost the love of my life."

I looked at Pa confused. What was my former teacher doing here sitting on our davenport, ruining my wedding day? Pa just looked at Miss Flatshaw and said, "Please go on. We need to leave for the church."

To my surprise Miss Flatshaw lunged down on the floor. She was on her knees in front of me. "I'm begging for your forgiveness," she whimpered. "I won't leave until you forgive me."

"Forgive you for what?" I asked. I was getting annoyed. I didn't want to be late to my wedding because of my former teacher had lost her job. As if sputtering in front of me was going to change anything for her. Also, Pa wasn't on the school board, Unc Elmer was.

We all sat frozen for the longest time. I was gonna get up and leave. I'd had enough of her upset. But when I said I needed to leave, Miss Flatshaw opened her mouth, caught her breath, and began to speak.

"It was my baby. My baby with Brother Johnson. We were going to get married and move away. But after I had the baby, home alone and scared to death, he said no. He said he had his own life to live as a man of God." She scoffed. "A life without me. Both he and the baby rejected me. The baby died lying on his stomach a day later. He took it and buried it. I didn't know where at the time but I soon figured it out.

"I thought God was giving me another chance. But now I know better." She sniffled. "At the time I thought Brother Johnson was under God's grace. That he knew best. But now that all the facts have come out about your sisters and those Spring Lake girls, I know that he was evil. Pure and simple. So I beg for your forgiveness."

There was such a long pause as if I was expected to do something. I looked at Pa for guidance.

"I beg you for your forgiveness," she again implored. She was still down on her knees looking up at me, this haggard fat woman with jowls. Now I understood. She had started the rumors about me. Deliberately. Maliciously. It was her baby buried back in the woods.

I had lived through all the rumors that she, Miss Flatshaw, had started. She had made my life a living hell. She had made it appear that I was the loose woman when she herself actually had been the sinner. This behavior was beyond the pale. Why was she coming to me on my wedding day? Couldn't she behave like an adult? Instead she was here in our parlor robbing me of happiness on what should be the happiest day of my life.

"Your forgiveness," she persisted, moving around as if her large body couldn't handle being on her knees any longer.

"You need to ask God for forgiveness, not me," I answered. That was all I was going to say. There was another uncomfortably long pause.

Pa then cleared his throat. "We have a wedding to get to. You have to leave now and Flora has suffered enough. She don't need to have you on her mind today."

"Very well," Miss Flatshaw answered. She frowned and tried to pick up her heavy body with a long sigh, but she fell back on her knees to the floor. She struggled again to get up and this time fell back on her very large bottom. Finally Pa braced himself, reached for her hands and pulled her up, in a long painful struggle. When she steadied herself they both were panting.

Miss Flatshaw left without another word. No comments like "Best wishes on your wedding," or "May God smile on your marriage."

I ran upstairs, got dressed, fixed my hair and added a little extra rouge on my cheeks. Finally, I sat down and took some deep breaths. I wasn't going to let this incident ruin my day.

When I got downstairs again, Pa shook his head. "I think we need to put this whole thing aside and enjoy your happy day." Then he did something quite unexpected. He gave me a hug and told me that he loved me. I melted in his arms, once again the happiest girl in the world. We proceeded to the Model A and drove to the church.

Afternoon

My wedding was indeed magical. Aunt Flora had put together a nosegay of pine needles and red berries as a surprise for me.

The church was beautiful and my little sisters were so sweet in their pink dresses, with little sprigs of pine needles and red berries that Aunt Hazel had pinned in their hair. But most of all Tom was standing beside me vowing to love me for the rest of my life. It couldn't have been any nicer than if I was a princess getting married in a castle.

After just about everyone had left the reception, I told Tom I wanted a couple of minutes with my sisters. He smiled and told me he'd go spend some time with his mother.

So the three of us went back into the empty church sanctuary.

"We're going to have one more meeting of the Sisters' Club," I said, hugging both of them. "This morning Miss Flatshaw came to our house and admitted to Pa and me that it was her baby. The baby died when he was only two days old and Brother Johnson buried it in the woods. I guess all the rumors about Miss Flatshaw were true after all."

"It was like a weird dream," I explained. "I never considered Miss Flatshaw. Probably because you were so close, Irene."

Irene was looking puzzled and asked a couple of questions about Miss Flatshaw. Had she told the Sheriff? Where was she living and did she have a phone? I didn't know but I told Irene not to contact Miss Flatshaw, but instead to use her time and energy in doing well in school and helping out the new teacher. Pa would be contacting the Sheriff, but not today.

So we officially ended Sisters' Club for the second time.

I told my sisters, "We worked hard to find out the truth but we didn't find it until it came knocking at the door. I for one have learned a lot. Rumors can get way out of hand. May was a victim, not a bad girl. Gypsies are nice people, just living a different kind of life. There are all kinds of lessons here."

Nellie seemed a little upset. "But can we still meet and have you hug us when you come home for a visit even without the Sisters' Club?" she asked.

"Of course. I'll always be your big sister."

Nighttime

On the long drive back to Tom's farm from the church I told Tom the story of Miss Flatshaw and her begging for forgiveness on our parlor floor. I suspect that Pa was telling Ma the same story right about then. It felt good sharing stories like married couples do.

But I have to admit I was a bit scared about our wedding night. Ma was too embarrassed to say anything to me. Funny thing, Ma could talk to me for a long, long time about not getting in a family way, but wouldn't say a word about the opposite. Fortunately, Aunt Hazel took me aside one day during a cooking lesson and told me not to worry, that everything would be all right. She said she was scared to death on her wedding night so she wanted me to be prepared. She whispered some things to me that I thought I heard correctly. So that's all the information I got.

Anyway Tom and I got back to the little house just after dark, both of us stuffed full of cake. Tom said his father and brother were doing all the chores so we could have our first night together. When I asked him if he wanted me to make some supper, he said no. He grinned and led me into the bedroom. I have to say that all that necking had done some good over the past few months. I guess I was ready for the next step.

Aunt Hazel had warned me that I should put some towels and rags on the bed and told me the reason why. She said not to worry, there wouldn't be any more blood than my monthlies. So it all happened. Then Tom and I were lying together cuddling in the dark when all the noise started. Outside our window people were yelling and banging pots and pans.

"Chivaree," Tom said. "They won't stop until we go to the

window and wave at them." He seemed very pleased with the noise outside.

"Let's make them go at it a little longer," I said snuggling up to Tom. I was so glad the merrymakers hadn't interrupted us a half hour earlier. Probably because everyone outside our window had cows to milk and other evening chores.

Finally, after about ten more minutes of whooping and hollering, Tom and I got up and opened the window and waved to everyone. I recognized several of Tom's friends as well as some of his neighbors. Tom and I just stood and watched as they sang some songs.

"Irish beer-drinking songs," Tom said to me. We waited until there was a pause in the singing.

"We thank you for everything, now go home," Tom hollered out the window.

"One last song," someone hollered back. Then, in unison they all started singing "Goodnight Ladies." Even Tom and I joined the singing before we closed the window and crawled back in bed together. All in all, not a bad ending to our wedding day.

Nellie
Tuesday, December 25, 1934
Forenoon

Ma and Pa know that I don't believe in Santa Claus no more,
thanks to tattletale Irene. So I've been worried there'd be no
more Christmas stockings this year. After all, we both got new
dresses for Flora's wedding. That's a huge present, as Ma has
pointed out many times.

So this morning as soon as I woke up I shook Irene awake
and we ran downstairs to look. First I looked in the parlor at the
usual place where the stockings hang near the potbelly stove. No,
there warn't any stockings with a bulging orange in the toe. I had
this let-down feeling in my head, kinda sad and angry all at the
same time.

But soon I could hear Ma and Pa coming in from the kitchen
and I looked up and they were each carrying a wrapped-up present. Pa handed his to Irene and Ma handed hers to me. Me and
Irene both settled down to the floor and started unwrapping,
carefully saving both the butcher paper and the purty ribbons
around them.

Mine was a book, *Peter Pan*, and Irene's was *Anne of Green
Gables*. Irene opened hers and started reading. I did too. I kept
asking Ma to help me with the words. I didn't wanna stop reading 'bout Wendy and her family and Peter Pan, the strange boy
who flew into the nursery window.

When Ma went to the kitchen to make some breakfast, I snuggled up close to Pa and he helped me with the words.

Later at the breakfast table Pa said to Irene and me, "It was
a long, hard year, but we all survived. Always remember that

it's okay to believe in miracles. God has given our family some difficult trials this year, but He has also given us our share of miracles. When Flora and Tom come over this afternoon, let's not dwell on the hard times, but the magic of having our whole family with us for this one beautiful afternoon."

Pa's right. I wanna remember this day forever.

EPILOGUE

Forty Years Later

1974

Flora
Wednesday, February 6, 1974
Evening

Today counts as one of the worst days of my life, even though I've seen it coming for a couple of years. Ma died on Sunday and the funeral was today. I had prayed for Ma to be free of pain for a long time and people keep telling me this is a blessing. But Ma was never their mother. Irene and Nellie understand. They're just as raw as me.

Ma's funeral was nice enough. It was down at Parson Creek Church. Lots of people came and we had a lunch that was brought in by the church women. I felt fine about that. I've taken dozens, maybe hundreds, of dishes to church funeral lunches. My layered salad is now called the "Funeral Salad" because people like it so much and often ask for the recipe. It was one of Aunt Hazel's recipes that I changed up, adding bacon bits and taking out most of the onions.

Ma was buried right next to Pa at the church cemetery. She shared a gravestone with Pa that already had her name and birthdate on it. We only needed the death date, February 3, 1974. My daughter Lotta said she thought it was creepy to have a gravestone with your name on it before you died. But Ma was always a practical person. She counted pennies right to the end. So do I.

Somehow I don't remember much of Pa's funeral. That was back in 1958 and it was all so sudden that I think we were all in shock. I certainly was. I just remember so many people coming with food and all we could do was go through the motions. Pa had come up the lane from doing some plowing and fell over on the ground while walking to the house. Ma was watching from the window, surprised he had come up so soon. After Pa bought a tractor, she knew Pa's whereabouts most of the time because it was one noisy John Deere. So Ma saw Pa fall and she ran out to see what was wrong, but he never said a word. Must have been instantaneous.

After Pa died Ma was distraught, and I know time is supposed to heal all wounds, but I could tell how much she missed him, even years later. Every single day she talked about him. She took up reading the *Bible* for hours. By then all three of us sisters had chosen our own paths, so we all had the distractions of daily life to keep us going.

Ma and Pa had only a few golden years together when they weren't struggling. I guess it wasn't until the Eisenhower years when they quit worrying about money. By then they had paid off the farm and Nellie got married in a beautiful church wedding with a new long white gown and veil, not Ma's old yellowed linen dress that I had worn. It was a beautiful affair, and Irene and I were a little jealous, but we both agreed that it wasn't Nellie's fault she was born last.

After Nellie got married in 1952, Pa was still keeping long hours farming, and Ma was still gardening and peddling eggs. After Pa died, Ma worked out a deal with Henry and me that we would pay her rent and Henry would farm her land. Yes, that's right, Henry. Tom was killed in the Normandy invasion: June 6, 1944. I was inconsolable. There I was with two little boys and my twenty-seven-year-old husband gone. For the first year I stayed with Tom's parents, living in the little house, helping Ma Sharp out the best I could. The Sharps couldn't have been nicer, but they saw how much I was hurting and said if I needed to go home and stay with Ma and Pa they would understand.

So I took Paul and Walter and went to live with Ma and Pa. Finally the war ended and the soldiers started coming home, but not Tom. Taking care of our two boys took up so much of my time.

I did most of Ma's laundry and cleaning to help earn my keep. Also, I worked in the garden and helped Aunt Hazel with lots of her chores.

I didn't go to church for a while, thinking God had let me down. But soon enough we heard the awful stories about what happened in Germany and Japan, and I knew that Tom had served his country well. He was not alone. So many young men like Tom didn't come back, and I decided it was time to go to church again.

That's when Henry started courting me. I think this time it was "courting" not "dating," mainly Sundays after church. We'd go to his parents or stay with Ma and Pa for Sunday dinner, all very grown-up. No dances and movies like with Tom. If it was a nice summer day, Henry and I would take the boys on a picnic.

Funny thing, my main objection to Henry when we were in high school was that he had nothing to talk about. That was no longer the case. He'd be chatting away with the boys talking about his childhood or telling them about deer hunting or the latest farming advances.

Then, to my surprise one Sunday afternoon when the boys were off playing in the haymow, he asked for my hand. I hadn't seen that one coming. Henry wanted to marry me and raise the boys. He had made plans to buy his parents' farm, and they were going to buy a house in town. I was dumbfounded. Henry said he didn't want to lose me a second time.

We got married a couple weeks later and never looked back. Lotta was born the following year and then Carrie two years later. Four kids; that's a lot. I never expected that. Ma and Pa were so happy for Henry and me. They loved our kids so much. We continued spending most Sunday afternoons with our parents. Sometimes Nellie would come join us with her family, sometimes not. Now and then we'd take all the kids and visit the Sharps. They said over and over what a good guy Henry was and how happy they were that Paul and Walter had a new father. Irene visited when she could. Often she was living far away.

Those Sunday afternoons were some of the happiest days of my life. After cleaning up from dinner we would all go in the parlor, I would play the piano, and we all would sing along. If it was nice weather we'd have a picnic out by the windmill. The maple tree grew big and provided lots of shade for us.

Times change. I was happy as a farm wife doing all those things I learned from Ma and Aunt Hazel. But I saw my sisters going off in different directions and wondered what my life would have been like if I hadn't gotten married so young and had the boys right away. Maybe I could have figured out how to go to nursing school. Nowadays you don't have to decide right out of high school what you're gonna do for the rest of your life. You can go to community college any time, whether you're eighteen or eighty.

Women's lib is a big deal these days, too. I even know who Gloria Steinem is, and to tell you the truth, most of it makes sense. But I'm not sure if it's for me at my age—fifty-six. I'm happy being Henry's wife and taking care of the grandchildren three days a week. Still I wonder.

With Ma's death I have been thinking about my own mortality. Have I done enough to make my mark on the world? Why didn't I do anything with my musical talent? Or my sewing abilities? Nellie always said I should make dresses for wealthy women. I'm a good seamstress and I still could do that. However sewing was never a passion, like music. I'd rather just make doll clothes for my granddaughters.

Maybe I will learn to read music. No reason I can't learn as an adult. At the very least I could learn well enough to sub at church when our pianist is on vacation. Or I could get more ambitious and play at weddings and funerals. I might be able to make a little extra money. Wouldn't it be fun to save up so Henry and I could go to Hawaii?

Still, I wonder if I've done enough with my life. Nellie is writing more and more and now has a big contract. Irene has saved lots of lives as a nurse and is not shy about talking about it. But what have I done? After my grandchildren pass, there won't be anyone to remember me. There'll only be a stone in the cemetery with my name next to Henry's.

But I've lived a good, quiet life. I've loved and lost and loved again. That in itself is nothing short of a miracle.

Irene
Thursday, February 7, 1974
Morning

Ma's funeral was yesterday and I'm so glad to have it behind us. That Pastor Carol is something else. I always knew a female preacher would mess things up, including funerals. Pastor Carol had everyone holding hands and "passing peace." As if peace could be handed to someone like a salt and pepper shaker. Believe me, I know. I saw the Second World War up close and personal.

Just when I thought the funeral was going to end, Pastor Carol asked the people attending to give testimonials about Ma. I just about got up and left. How are bereaved people supposed to talk about someone they just lost? Certainly not me.

When Mr. Archway, one of Ma's egg customers, got up with tears in his eyes, I knew it was time for Ma's funeral to end. So many more people knew Ma so much better than Greg Archway, the owner of the local Rexall Drug Store. But Pastor Carol let him drone on, as well as Janelle Sallin, the owner of the dry goods store, who talked about selling Ma patterns, cloth, and thread back in the day. She said Ma always knew exactly how much material to buy and would look at a pattern to see if it could be cut differently so as to buy three yards instead of three and a half. Was she trying to say that Ma was cheap? It was the Depression, after all.

The only thing I enjoyed about the funeral was its ending. I'd had to pee from drinking all that coffee while visitors came up to see Flora, Nellie, and me. Thank goodness the church now has bathrooms in the hallway by the new community room. Flora said that for years there was only one tiny restroom in the basement for both sexes to use. Mostly people waited until they got home to go. Today I made a beeline for the women's restroom. It has four stalls and I got there when two were still available. Finally, relief.

Ma would have laughed at me. She always said she never fully appreciated me until the night I ran away to the Camp Meeting. That same summer I caught that miserable food thief, Mr. Hendrick. Later in the fall Nellie and I experienced the horrible ordeal with the crazy preacher. Ma and Pa never praised us girls. It just wasn't done. Children were to be seen and not heard, and, me, I've always had lots of opinions. I definitely wanted to be both seen and heard, then and now. I guess that's why I was always seeking attention from Miss Flatshaw, the country schoolteacher. But in the end, it was Miss Swanson who taught me so much more: the love of history, math, and, especially, science.

During these past two years as Ma's health has been declining I've been thinking about my own life and how things have unfolded. I never knew when I went to nursing school that I would end up on a hospital ship with the Army Nurse Corps. We were in uncertain waters somewhere between England and Germany during all of 1944 and 1945.

I know I saved hundreds of lives but I'm still haunted by those I didn't. Those two years gave me the skills and the courage to live my life the way I wanted. I have no husband and no children, but I could have had them. In spades. Dozens of those young men on the hospital ship would have married me, but by then I wanted a lot more than childrearing and housekeeping.

It was Flora who encouraged me to go to Kalamazoo to nursing school, her own unfulfilled dream. I think she secretly has been a little jealous of me over the years, but she has never said so. By the time I graduated from high school times were better, and Ma and Pa had the money to send me to nursing school. Flora was already married to Tom and had her two little boys. War was smoldering all over the world. I was only four months into my studies when the U.S. declared war on Japan and a few days later on Germany.

Nursing was a good choice for me. I like knowing how to do things the right way and nursing is an exacting science. You treat a patient differently if their temperature is 101.4 degrees than if it is 104.1 degrees. You always continue to learn. The advances in medicine over the years have been so astonishing that even I find certain drugs miraculous. And I do love being in charge. There are doctors, of course, but over the years many doctors have asked my opinion on special cases. They've also asked to watch me dress wounds and perform certain procedures like taking out stitches from sensitive areas, like near the eyes and nose. I have a good rapport with most patients. I'm kind, but authoritative. Most patients appreciate that.

After the war there were so many job possibilities. I could have worked just about anywhere in the world, but I wanted to see my own country. I worked in eight different Veteran Administration hospitals from border to border, before I finally decided to take an early retirement and come back here and help Flora and Nellie take care of Ma. Cancer is a horrible disease and even with my nursing background I had trouble watching Ma waste away.

Over the years I saved up, so now I have many choices. I need to decide where I want to go next. Somewhere warm sounds good; maybe Florida or southern California where it's always sunny. Or Hawaii. I have friends and acquaintances all over the country and a few around the world. But none are so intimate that I need to make my home near them. Wouldn't Pa have been absolutely dumbfounded at all the choices in front of me? He was proud that I served my country, but he never saw how far I went with my nursing career. Even as a kid I never expected to be more than a farm wife, cooking, gardening, and sewing.

My sisters and I have decided to spend today and tomorrow sorting out Ma's stuff. There's not many of Ma's possessions I want. I do get nostalgic looking at the iron frying pans, the huge yellow bread-making bowl, the various crocks for pickles. None of it is valuable except for the sentiment. The old Treadle is now in Flora's attic with cobwebs all over it, along with Aunt Hazel's washboard. I hope Flora will give those things to her grandkids.

So we are sorting into piles and chatting all the time. Wouldn't you know that Nellie is still making up stories and getting things wrong? This morning she told Flora and me an outrageous story about her own children talking to the animals that we had as kids—Rover and Three Foots, long gone. That girl has always had an active imagination. She still talks fondly about her imaginary friend ZeeZee who came from outer space. She said she flew with him up into the oak tree. I think she got that all straight from her Peter Pan story book. She couldn't be separated from that book after she received it as a Christmas gift right after Flora's wedding to Tom.

However, Nellie claims that her times with ZeeZee occurred before she had ever read Peter *Pan*, when Flora was still living at home. It's all a blur in my mind. But Nellie, herself, admits that she loved her imaginary friends and hated to let go. Even more than Santa Claus.

No wonder Nellie can write storybooks. Nothing has to be truthful in fiction. Fiction is just made up fluff. That's why I only read non-fiction. I do make exceptions, however, and read Nellie's books. She is my sister, after all, and her books reflect how she misunderstood so many things as a child. I find it absolutely amusing.

I did find a couple of things that brought me to tears. In a box way up in the attic were my *Bible Story Book* and Nellie's *Pirate Book*. I pulled them out, remembering all those evenings Nellie and I spent with them, both reading and pretending to read. Then I remembered the mystery chapters and verses.

"Nellie, you did this, didn't you?" I said pointing to the Biblical reference to Adam and Eve.

A huge grin erupted on Nellie's face. We both started laughing hysterically.

"Are you both crazy?" Flora interjected.

"No, just a little trick," Nellie answered still chuckling.

Then I pulled out the *Pirate Book* and fingered the last few pages. Sure enough my ZeeZee story was still there. "Did you ever find this?"

Nellie took the story and began to read. "No, no, I don't think so. Did you write it?"

I started laughing again. "Just to trick you, like you tricked me with the *Bible* story references," I answered.

Nellie took the papers and read the story. "How did you know about ZeeZee speaking both Animal and English?" she asked me.

I shrugged. "I don't even remember the story."

Nellie kept reading. "Or the Pottawatomi Indians back there?"

Once again I shook my head. "Maybe you told me or maybe it was in one of your own stories. Keep it," I said. "You can go back to your old stories and look up the references."

After Flora got married, Nellie and I settled into a friendly sister relationship, sometimes playing tricks on one another, often playing cards together, and sometimes listening in on Ma and Pa's evening conversations together through the heat register. We decided to continue sharing the same bedroom even though Flora's old one was up for grabs. Ma and Pa left Flora's room empty for a while, but then rented it to Mrs. Hendrick's sister Rose who moved here from Detroit. It worked out well as she kept to herself and paid the rent on time.

It wasn't like me to feel emotional about my childhood. I always viewed it as all of us pulling together to make ends meet. My childhood, I reminisced, was too much gardening, too much canning, and too much sewing, with too few leftovers. Many nights we went to bed hungry.

So as a way to put my nostalgic feelings aside and to bring closure to this process of moving on, I decided to walk down to the creek one last time. Neither Flora nor Nellie were willing to go. Flora said she was too dog-tired to walk anywhere, let alone all the way down to the creek. Nellie said she had gone down there a few times over the years and each time had relived the awful experiences.

I hadn't been back there since I was a kid. I don't even remember the last time I went. My childhood was like that; a web of incomplete memories. When was the last time Nellie and I played in the haymow? When was the last time I hoed onions? When was the last time I went with Ma to peddle eggs? Maybe it's better that you never know these last events of childhood when they're happening. Otherwise it would be so hard to let go.

I set out in mid-afternoon. Being a cold, muddy February day I had to be careful walking along the path. Henry had removed all the fences since he wasn't keeping any animals on Ma's farm. He was just planting corn and soybeans. Soybeans. That crop was unheard of in my childhood. Pa grew corn, wheat, oats, rye, and alfalfa, but never soybeans.

The bluebird houses along the lane were gone and a lot of brush had grown up in their place. The meadow was brown and muddy, but I still could picture the cows and the pink blossoms of the cherry trees in springtime. Most of the cherry trees were still standing as well as some of the lilac bushes.

But nothing remained at the end of the second meadow. Pa had wisely gotten rid of the old rusty bus and cleared out the old cabin foundation. Even the poison ivy tree and gate to Keller's lane were gone. No sign of the daffodils that Nellie and I had planted so long ago. The oak tree was gone. Just an ordinary corner of an ordinary field.

I climbed over the half-broken stile and when I reached the path through the woods I hesitated a bit. Nellie's bad experience finding the buried baby had taken place here, but that was forty years earlier. So I forged ahead. The path had become overgrown without any kids running back and forth over it. The hollowed-out ash tree was long gone, but still there was a familiarity about the wooded path. I kept looking around to see Nellie's phantoms. Then, I made my way around the bend in the path and something caught my eye several yards to the right of the path.

A little wooden cross, no more than a foot high jutted up from the mud. It was brown, unpainted with nothing written on it. Just a cross planted in the forest floor. I made my way over to it and looked for other things. I was expecting to find a little shrine like you find along the road where someone has been killed in a car accident. Flowers, photos, little mementos like necklaces, stuffed animals, or scraps of paper with poems. Nothing. Just the cross.

As I touched the cross I wondered how long it had been there. I had no idea if it was at the place where Nellie found the baby. Nellie and Flora certainly hadn't seen it, or they would have mentioned it. The cross looked weathered. It had been there at least a few years. Miss Flatshaw must have put it there, I thought. Maybe she didn't know the baby had been moved to the cemetery in town.

Finally, in anger, I pulled up the cross and threw it as far as I could into the forest. I decided I wouldn't tell Flora or Nellie about it. What good would that do? Nellie is already creeped out by the woods. And Flora and Henry don't even own the land. It had always belonged to Old Man Keller. It's changed hands a few times over the years and now it belongs to some new people Flora doesn't even know.

I turned around, no longer desiring to see the creek. Perhaps, I decided, it's better to keep the warm memories of pollywogs, water striders, and guppies rather than those of a cold, dark stream in February. Even fleeing from a rattlesnake is a nicer memory than whatever the creek might offer on this cold, damp day.

So as I made my way back up the path to the meadow I thought about my life ahead. I'll rent a little place in south Florida and see if I like it there. If not, I'll pull up and move on to the next place. My needs are few. Just a cozy place where I can enjoy the sunshine and maybe work as a nurse a few hours a week. I think I'll try woodworking, too; it's an exacting field that I could master. Of course, I'll work on my memoir a little bit each day.

I think Ma and Pa would be proud of me. I served my country in a time that few women were able to. Now as I face retirement I can enjoy the fruits of my labor. My government pension is more than adequate and my health is good. I'll live out my days as I always have, choosing a road that leads to proper behavior and good deeds. Fortunately, I have always had an uncanny ability to choose the right path. I'll continue down that road and enjoy the rewards of a life well-lived.

Nellie
Friday, February 8, 1974
Evening

Well, I believe the only dry eyes at the funeral Wednesday were Flora's, Irene's, and mine. We three already have shed tears for two years now as Ma's cancer worsened and worsened. No one should have to suffer what Ma has gone through. The cancer was eating her up, along with the nightmare effects of chemo and radiation. And we three stood by helplessly with nothing to reduce her misery. The few drugs that were available made her tired and woozy.

Ma would have loved seeing all the people who turned out for the funeral. Of course, many of her beloved family had gone before her. Pa, Aunt Hazel, and Unc Elmer being the closest. But with Flora's four children and my two children, plus all our cousins' families, we had a sizable representation today, including many friends and neighbors. Even my cousin Dan and his wife Patya flew all the way from California.

So after Flora, Irene, and I finish cleaning out Ma's house, I'll go back to my "normal" routine of housewife and author. Actually, since Amber and Jason are now both in high school, my author role will get top billing. John and I will become empty nesters in two years and he's been very happy with my writing—and the extra income. John's a history teacher at the high school, so we struggled with finances until I got some things published. Then I made a little pin money, and later started receiving sizable royalties.

I've had three children's books published, *The Bizarre Bazaar, Raining Pitchforks and Hammer Handles,* and *The Need to Knead*. After I wrote a few articles for some women's magazines, one of my editors got me in touch with an agent who said she would like me to write a detective series for teenage girls. It would be much like the old Nancy Drew favorites, only with an adult female protagonist. I've agreed to write the first book on spec. I'm calling it *The High-Heeled Gumshoe*.

Amazingly, I've finished a first draft. My writing has kept me sane. When I couldn't sleep worrying about Ma or our teenagers, I'd go into my office, the former den, and sit at the typewriter and write. Actually I have a brand new self-correcting IBM Selectric typewriter that I love. It has decreased the time I need to revise and retype. I simply can't believe how much easier it is to write with this new machine. People ask me how I can write and raise a family at the same time. All the hard work and perseverance came from growing up on the farm. Writing is a lot more fun than farm chores, and I love to play with words. Pa gave me so much encouragement about my writing. I hope he's up in Heaven looking down.

So this afternoon Irene opened the last box from Ma's attic and pulled an envelope out. "So why do you think Ma kept this old thing?" Irene asked as she opened it.

"Let me look," Flora said. In the envelope was a yellowed paper with "Nellie" and "Flora" written on it along with the remnants of crushed leaves. She took the tiny shards of leaves and put them in her hand and tears came to her eyes. "These were from Tom," she replied. "One beautiful autumn Sunday when we were dating and didn't have any money, we decided to go on a walk. He picked three leaves to give to me. Later Nellie and I pasted them on this paper. Nellie, do you remember that?"

I shook my head. "No, no memory at all."

Flora picked them up, putting them back in the envelope, and stuffed it into her purse.

"I'll decide later," she answered, to my surprise.

"That day I thought I had all the answers to my future," Flora said. "I knew my life with Tom was going to be as beautiful and golden as these leaves. Little did I know the tragedy that lay ahead."

Next, Irene pulled out a *McCalls* magazine dated January, 1934. It was so familiar, a beautiful cover girl surrounded by the covers from the previous year. Flora thumbed through it recognizing individual pages with pictures of dresses from *McCalls* patterns. She decided to keep the magazine as well. I wondered what had happened to all the other magazines that we'd saved. They were already third- or fourth-hand and well-worn before we ever got them.

Then I pulled out a child's picture of a farm. I had written my name at the bottom. This time tears welled up in my eyes. "From second grade," I told my sisters. "Miss Swanson picked it out as one of the best. I remember it as if it were yesterday. It's a picture of our farm. See the buildings, the lane, the cherry trees, the two meadows, the woods, and the creek? Maybe I'll frame it and put it in the kitchen."

Irene and Flora looked at me as if I were nuts. To each his own. But really, this was no weirder than saving crushed, broken leaves or a well-read magazine.

"I'm keeping nothing," Irene pronounced. "My basic philosophy has been to travel light through this lifetime. Take a few snapshots, perhaps, but that's it."

I realized right then that all this sharing memories with my sisters was a healing process for me. I don't know how we got on the topic, but someone mentioned the mystery baby, Miss Flatshaw, and the terrifying incidents when the cruel revivalist preacher so violently assaulted Irene and me. It all was woven together in ways we didn't know.

"Do you still have nightmares?" I asked Irene. I didn't even have to mention the day. She knew and so did Flora.

"No, the war replaced those nightmares with new ones," Irene answered. "But I'm still so angry at Miss Flatshaw. She and the evil preacher had taken up with each other and she was so fat nobody noticed she was pregnant. Totally disgusting. Once she told me she thought God was punishing her. Well, she deserved it. To think I had looked up to her and considered her a role model. I should have figured out the clues. Always going to the privy with May Hendrick. Moving so slowly. Wearing those loose dresses." Irene shook her head in disbelief.

"Every now and then I have a nightmare," I added. "Sometimes it just comes as a flashback when I'm wide awake. Those other girls who had been murdered. It was beyond cruel. We were just minutes away from the same fate."

"Pa told me to write the stories down," I continued. "But my childhood ended that day. I could never write about that horrible situation. Instead, I continued to write about my imaginary friends. But after that day they were just memories: ZeeZee, the Indians, and pirates. That preacher stole the remainder of my childhood."

"Mine, too," Irene added. We continued the conversation for a while and then I asked Flora, "What impact did that day have on you?"

"It ended my childhood, too," Flora responded. "I was so in love with Tom, but I lost my rose-colored glasses that day. I understood that evil could be real. I was so incredibly tough on my own kids because I worried too much. I was seventeen that year. It happened just a few weeks before I married Tom."

There was a pause during her reflection on Tom. But I know how much she loves Henry and in many ways I envy her marriage. Henry raised Flora's two boys as his own and they also had two girls together. No regrets from either of them. John and I, in contrast, have had some rocky times. But Flora and Henry have always been totally devoted to one another. A storybook marriage.

"I kept up with Sheriff Devlon all through his career," Flora went on. "He was so worried about the child abductions and murders. I never met a man so happy about that preacher's death. He would stop by the farm every now and then just to say hi to Ma and Pa. I know it made him feel good that you girls were spared.

"Miss Flatshaw was back," Flora added, looking at Irene who frowned. "About ten years ago. She had lost a lot of weight and looked tired. She had all that loose skin hanging down her arms where all the fat was gone. I didn't recognize her at first. I have no idea why she returned. She was on Main Street and I turned and walked in the other direction when I saw her. I'd never done that with anyone before or since. Of course, I've regretted doing such an un-Christian act, and I actually tried to find her a few days later, without luck."

All three of us remained quiet, somber really.

"Let's hear about your best memories," I suggested, trying to change the mood. I'd relived enough bad memories.

"The night I met Tom," Flora answered without hesitation. "He was so handsome and we talked all evening long. Love at first sight." Flora turned to Irene and asked, "Your best memories?"

"Learning science from Miss Swanson and finally accepting her as a teacher. I hated her for such a long time but she never gave up on me. That was a life lesson. It helped me with some of my most difficult patients. I told myself I wouldn't give up on them, no matter what. I know that saved some lives."

"How about you, Nellie?" Flora asked. What are your best memories?"

"Lots of fragments," I answered. "Talking to the animals. Seeing those people dance in the sky amidst the colors on the Fourth of July. Christmas day, 1934. Eating ice cream for the first time. Licking warm butter off a knife."

"You certainly had a different childhood from me," Irene responded. "Except the day the train riders helped me catch Mr. Hendrick. I loved that day."

"One of them came back and visited Ma a few years after Pa died," I said. "The tall one. He'd become a dentist on the GI Bill.

He was married with a couple of kids and lived somewhere near Chicago. He told Ma that the afternoon he spent with us was his fondest memory of train riding. He drove all the way here that weekend to see if Ma and Pa were still on the farm and thank them for their kindness."

I smiled. "He brought Ma a whole lot of gifts, including several rags and three Ball jars as a joke. And he was quite taken up with the fact you'd become a nurse, Irene. He said the nursing training must have taught you the difference between appendicitis and poison ivy." We all laughed.

"You know, May Hendrick's still in town and working at the drycleaners," Flora added. "One day she called me and invited me to her house to meet her biological daughter. So I went. It was rather strange, both May and her daughter being middle aged, and three grandchildren as well. May seemed so happy that day. I'm glad I went and shared that experience with her. Henry didn't understand, but I'm sure you both do."

Irene and I both nodded.

Flora continued. "My memories are so ordinary. Clothespin dolls, helping Pa milk the cows, making bread. Each of us had such different childhoods, even though we had the same parents and we lived in the same house, on the same farm."

"Our memories are different," I said, shaking my head. "And who knows how real? Are we all walking around believing our childhoods are different from what they actually were? And if so, isn't the part that we believe more important than what may actually be the so-called truth? I've been thinking about this ever since I started writing. Are my characters all part of me, my fears, my desires, my struggles?" I paused waiting for my sisters to respond.

"Well, I, for one, remember my childhood truthfully," Irene piped up. "I was smart, got straight A's and there were lots of kids at school who bullied me. That's it."

"Me, I'm not so sure," Flora said pensively. "Ma once told me that she was glad she grew up in the days of horse and buggies, not cars. She thought it was much more pleasant. But she never talked about those stinky outhouses, the blistering cold winters and hot humid summers, and shoes that never fit. She had blisters and bunions all her life."

"Yes," I chimed in. "Thankfully, it may be a lot like childbirth. Your happy memories cover up a lot of the pain. But it's no longer fresh and raw. Neutral memories become happy. And happy memories stay with us a long, long time."

We took the last few boxes out of the house and loaded them into the car. We had already taken dozens of boxes to the Goodwill store, antique shops, and the dump. What was left went into Flora's attic.

Back in my bed, lying beside John, I thought about the revelations of the day. Why are my memories so different from my sisters? Are any memories real?

John listened to me for a long while but this week was my milestone, not his. I said goodnight and he quickly fell asleep.

As I lay in bed wide awake, I started thinking about ZeeZee. He was so real to me and yet nothing about my experience with him suggests the kind of reality that is considered normal. Like Wendy in *Peter Pan*, I talked to him, flew up the oak tree with him, and cherished our conversations. Then, one day in a flash, I was grown up, and ZeeZee was gone, never again to appear in my metaphorical window. Tears dropped down my cheeks. Loss is difficult under any circumstance, even when it's something as ephemeral as childhood fantasies.

Peter Pan is as real to my children as ZeeZee was to me. In a strange way, children want more than simple day-to-day rational occurrences. A grown actress named Mary Martin played the boy Peter Pan and she twisted reality in a way that my children simply accepted. The takeaway for them was many special magical moments that transcended the routine of their day-to-day lives. Whether we watch the magical boy fly into a window of a

Victorian house via a television screen, or whether we see ZeeZee come for a visit in the back meadow, the vision becomes a part of our lives. Magic and wonder and poetry await us in so many ways. We simply need to be open to its beauty.

What I discovered from ZeeZee, the Pottawatomi Indians, and all those other terrifying and magical moments of childhood—is that life has fewer limitations than you ever could imagine. We marvel at the sunshine and the rain that create our food. We soak up the beauty of a blue sky at midday and the shooting stars at midnight. We find peace and comfort in little things, like a single spoonful of ice cream or warm butter on a knife.

Our lives are inextricably bound together by our shared experiences. We three sisters remember the train riders and their stories, and where we each were on the day we fought the fire in Old Part. We fondly remember Flora's wedding as if it were the greatest spectacle of the century.

We reminisce about the adults who so greatly impacted our childhood. Aunt Hazel, Mrs. Vandenberg, Mrs. Geist, Reverend Blackman, and so many more. Their stories become our common threads. Each had their impact on all three of us and we still benefit from their insights and generosity.

We also recall the little things that informed our childhoods. Playing in the haymow, picking strawberries, hoeing onions, gathering eggs, and bringing the cows up from the meadow. We listen back and hear our laughter, tears, and exclamations of wonderment.

Our voices blend together as we look back on those wealthy days of poverty and want. And finally we hear our parents' voices over and over again, as we listened to them day after day, night after night. Ma and Pa in quiet conversation. We understand that what remains after all those days, weeks, months, years, comes from them: their patience, their resolve, their love.

ABOUT THE AUTHOR

Charlotte Whitney grew up on a Michigan farm and often heard stories from her mother, aunts, and grandmother of the troubling years during the Great Depression. She has long been fascinated with childhood cognitive development, "magical thinking," and the gray line between fantasy and reality. She started her writing career with nonfiction, then moved over to romance with *I DREAM IN WHITE*. This is her debut historical novel. She lives in Arizona with her husband and Labrador Retriever, Athena.

DISCUSSION QUESTIONS

1. Why do you think the author titled the book *Threads*? What kinds of threads are represented in the book? What threads bind the three sisters? What isolates them?

2. The book is set in 1934. How important is that year to the characters and the social context? How are the characters both insulated from and exposed to the vagaries of the Great Depression?

3. How do you react to hearing the same story from one, two, or three points of view? Does the tedium of farm life portrayed in the book differ with each of the three sisters?

4. Describe the personalities of the three sisters. Would you be able to discern which character is speaking if she weren't named in the chapter heading? Is any one of the three sisters portrayed as more likable? More intelligent? More mature? More likely to gain material success?

5. How do you react to Ma and Pa? What are their strengths and flaws? How representative are they of Midwest farmers of the 1930s?

6. What is your reaction to Flora's goal of becoming a farm wife at age seventeen? Discuss the concept of teenagers then and now.

7. Nellie observes that you need to have good neighbors in order to be successful farmers. How is this portrayed?

8. Do you believe that the author revealed too much or too little regarding some of the characters, e.g., Mrs. Vandenberg, Mr. Hendrik, Mr. Goldberg?

9. What aspects of life in rural America changed from 1934 to 1974, e.g, finding arrowheads, living entirely off the land, reusing everything including rags.

10. What aspects of the sisters' childhood personalities do we continue to see reflected as adults in 1974. How do you react to their life stories? Why do you think the author chose 1974 as the year to end the book?

ACKNOWLEDGMENTS

I am grateful to a number of people who have encouraged me throughout this labor of love. This book has seen several revisions, some painful, some not, but all necessary. Keen editors and readers kept me focused and helped me back on track. In particular, I am grateful to my developmental editor, Ana Howard; general editor Jan Shubitowski; and beta readers Patsy Policar, Mark Nielsen, Vicki Smith, and Kayley Burnham. Special thanks to my son Steve for his excellent suggestions and to my husband Bill for his reading of various revisions and his patience throughout the entire process.

CPSIA information can be obtained
at www.ICGtesting.com
Printed in the USA
BVHW032007020521
606296BV00015B/173